PRAISE FOR CALDER SZEWCZAK

"The Offset's *searing critique* _____ *fascism what* Ninety Eighty-F_____ _____.....m and* Brave New World *did for eugenics."*
– Ken MacLeod, Prometheus and BSFA Award-winning author of *The Corporation Wars* series

"The Offset *crushed me. This is an expertly – and starkly – written, well-drawn eco-dystopian novel about the ultimate measure of austerity taken in order to save the planet. There's so much that was done well here: the world, the science, the societal conflict – but to get into the (possibly carnivorous) weeds would distract from soul of this book. It is a bare-knuckle punch to the heart. Calder Szewczak made me suffer – brilliantly."*
– Chris Panatier, author of *The Phlebotomist*

"The Offset *is a prophetic, urgent, gripping read that throws into question what saving the world really means. A tender warning of a book, lest our efforts become as futile as our tragedies."*
– Natalia Theodoridou, World Fantasy Award Winner and Nebula Finalist

"*Calder Szewczak's* The Offset *may be a literary first in giving central place to anti-natalism – the view that one ought not to create new people. Other novels, like this one, have depicted a dystopian future in the wake of environmental catastrophe. In Margaret Attwood's* The Handmaid's Tale, *the dystopia is pro-natalist.* The Offset *shows how anti-natalism could also take a dystopian turn. In showing this, it provides a cautionary tale – which, if read correctly, is not that anti-natalism itself is in error, but rather that even views aimed at reducing suffering can increase it if fanatics seize control."*
– David Benatar, world-leading anti-natalist and author of *Better Never to Have Been*

Calder Szewczak

THE OFFSET

**ANGRY
ROBOT**

ANGRY ROBOT
An imprint of Watkins Media Ltd

Unit 11, Shepperton House
89-93 Shepperton Road
London N1 3DF
UK

angryrobotbooks.com
twitter.com/angryrobotbooks
Family can't come first

An Angry Robot paperback original, 2021

Cover by Mark Ecob and Luise Roberts
Edited by Gemma Creffield and Andrew Hook
Set in Meridien

ISBN 978 0 85766 918 6
Ebook ISBN 978 0 85766 919 3

Printed and bound in the United Kingdom by TJ International.

9 8 7 6 5 4 3 2 1

MIX
Paper from
responsible sources
FSC FSC® C013056
www.fsc.org

"*I will revenge my injuries; if I cannot inspire love, I will cause fear, and chiefly towards you my arch-enemy, because my creator, do I swear inextinguishable hatred. Have a care; I will work at your destruction, nor finish until I desolate your heart, so that you shall curse the hour of your birth.*"

– Mary Shelley, *Frankenstein*

01

A hand over hers, the chafe of skin on skin. The first touch in months. Miri lashes out, thrusting an elbow hard into the stomach of the person who has come to stand too close; a tall figure who neatly side-steps the blow and, undeterred, presses forward. A dazzle-patterned scarf is bound over their mouth and nose, and above it are two black eyes that gleam like oil on water. Miri tries to draw away but is not quick enough to escape the strong fingers that circle her wrist and restrain her. A rough slip of paper is pressed into her open palm. Then the fingers loosen their grip, releasing her, and the masked figure disappears into the crowd.

Alone again at the edge of the square, Miri takes several steps back to shore up the distance between herself and the mass of people gathered there. Then she examines the paper. A flyer, bearing the usual line – *Say no to life* – above a short quotation. She balls it up in her palm and shoves it into her pocket.

She is only here to see the Offset. She wants – needs – to see the execution, but the longer she waits the harder it is to stay. The unexpected physical encounter has set her on edge. Without noticing, she starts pressing finger to thumb in a repetitive gesture she half-recalls learning in childhood. There is, she thinks, a rhyme that should accompany the motion but she cannot remember what it is. Something about an inchworm. No. A spider. A spider and a flood borne of a cleansing rain that hammered the Earth for forty days and forty nights. Or is that something else? Her brow creases into a frown as she tries to remember, but it's no good. All she has left is the mime. Finger, thumb, finger, thumb. There's something about it that makes her feel still. Calm. As though that one repetitive movement is enough to slow her racing heart: her nerves transformed into kinetic energy and heat. For as long as she can keep it up, she is safe. Or should be. Right now, it isn't working too well.

The square is packed. Miri struggles with crowds at the best of times and it's been a long time since she's seen so many people in one place. It's too much to contemplate, all those lives compacted together into one vast, sprawling beast. Even standing apart from the worst of it, the stench is inescapable; a pervasive musk of stale sweat beneath the occasional tang of urine and sulphur that wafts through in the heat.

For one fleeting moment, Miri imagines herself standing atop the empty capital of the blackened pillar at the square's centre. From that giant height, the crowd becomes no more than squirming ants. In her mind's eye, she lifts a heavy bucket aloft and tips it until water comes pouring out, crashing down onto the masses below, flooding the square until it becomes a sea, a watery grave thick with the bodies of the drowned ants. Then, just as suddenly as it came, the image is gone. Now, when she glances at the crowd swarming around the base of the column, the vacant plinths, she sees herself as part of it; another cell of the fetid mass that grows like a blight in the earth. Her heart spasms with revulsion and she stares down at her hands, focusing on the movement until the sense of stillness returns. Finger, thumb, finger, thumb.

Slowly, she turns her attention to the feel of the November heat on her hands and face, the scratch of her threadbare shirt against her arms and back, willing her consciousness out into her skin to acknowledge the barrier that holds her together and keeps her separate from the world. It helps. When she next looks up, she observes the crowd with newly impassive eyes. Even so, she is neither quite brave nor foolish enough to relinquish the protection of the childish ritual. Finger, thumb, finger, thumb. Like a talisman to ward off evil.

Now she's regained her composure, a wary voice in her head tells her to go, to leave now rather than risk suffering again the sensation of being subsumed into the heaving crowd. Or worse still, *touched*. But she can no more bring herself to turn away than she can learn to breathe underwater. Her place is in the square. She must stay and watch. She must give witness to the execution.

She's not sure how long it's been since the last Offset – she doesn't venture often into this part of the city. But, from the excited activity of the ageing crowd, she figures that it must have been quite some time. The mass of bodies swirls with eddies and currents as people make their way through to meet old friends, to get a better spot, to get closer to the action. But there's no mistaking where the focus lies: the steps that ascend from the square to the Gallery, an ancient building with a monolithic edifice of cracked white stone.

For now, the Gallery steps are empty save for a glass-fronted booth that stands between two of the crumbling pillars. It's a broad, squat structure, purely functional in design and comprised of little more than painted timber frame and glass. What lies within the booth changes from Offset to Offset. Sometimes it contains gallows and sometimes a guillotine. Today it holds a wooden chair, tall and narrow, with a number of broad leather straps hanging from it, rusted buckles trailing to the floor. A metal rod runs up the back of the chair like the frame of a medical drip and a round, metal bowl hangs from it at approximately head-height. A thick wire leads from the metal rod to a generator at the back of the booth.

Miri doesn't know anything about the person who is due to die in that chair, but she knows everything she needs to about the crime they have committed. It is the only crime still punishable by death the world over: the mortal sin of procreation.

Historically, the transgression was voiced by one of suitable authority – a mayor, a judge, a religious leader – who stood before the crowd and explained that the Offset was perfect retribution, exacting and brutal. How every birth, every act of creation, every new life threatened the fragile equilibrium of all things. That the imbalance had to be righted, and that the wages of sin was death. "For every birth, a death," they would say, in recitation of the law.

There is no such pronouncement anymore, though. There is no need.

The part of the crowd nearest the steps is thick with Activists, including anti-natalists baying for breeder blood. They are all dressed like the one who gave her the flyer, dazzle-patterned scarves bound about their faces. The banners they wave are daubed in red and depict graphic scenes of environmental destruction. Several bear the image of a bloodied ouroboros. Miri can't hear the slogans they chant but she can guess their meaning: save the planet, the Earth is suffocating, no mercy for breeders. In their midst, Miri spots one or two people who don't look like anti-natalists. They are white-haired and bear green spirals painted on their faces, and they are trying to tear down the banners. Miri thinks she could almost admire their courage if she didn't find their views so abhorrent. One of them has a crudely made megaphone and attempts to drown out the anti-natalists' shouts, but only serves to silence the voices of their own group. Others in the crowd – those marked by neither ouroboros nor green spiral – roll their eyes or laugh. Every Offset is the same; the Activists come in their droves to shout and mock, some in favour of the ritual and others against it. No one else pays them much heed. May as well protest the heat of the sun, for all the difference it will make.

Miri turns her eyes skywards. The sun is distant and remote, obscured behind the thick haze that permeates the city. Far off, a solitary tree rises up amongst the buildings, listing at a precarious angle, its charred branches stripped bare. Miri's eyes snag on its grim silhouette. For as long as the dead tree stands, it serves as a monument to the wildfires that coursed through the heart of London the summer before. Soon, though, it will fall and the fires will recede in public memory until they are as hazy as the smog that even now chokes the streets.

Even though Miri knows how easy it is to not see, and how much easier it is to forget, it still seems unbelievable to her that anyone could be quite as blind to their surroundings as those wearing the green spirals. They protest against the Offset even as they stand within sight of the most recent natural devastation. It's as impossible to understand as the selfishness of those who, like the person due to be executed, wilfully continue to add to the world's burden by creating more parasitic mouths to feed on the lifeblood of the Earth.

Parasites like you, says the voice in her head.

She quickly pushes the thought away. Finger, thumb, finger, thumb.

Silence falls on the square like an axe. At once, her attention snaps back from the sky and down to the booth, where two pigsuits have appeared. Their terrible forms cast dark silhouettes against the glass. They are vacant shells, dreadful chimeras of dented aluminium and transparent acrylic, each one encasing a fleshy hollow moulded into the shape of a body. The pigsuits have been empty for years; have long since outgrown the human officers who once wore them. Now they are driven by the frenetic command of their programming, of the sensors and circuitry that laces their articulated exoskeletons.

There's a sharp intake of breath somewhere nearby as fear pulses through the crowd. Heads jerk upwards. It reminds Miri of old footage of herds on the African savannah, before severe droughts turned the grassland to desert. An antelope catches the scent of a prowling lion and, one by one, the rest of the herd raise their heads in search of the coming danger. Unlike the herd, the crowd in the square doesn't turn tail and flee but merely cowers, trying to reassure themselves they have nothing to fear.

For now, at least, they do not. The pigsuits' interest is confined to the thin woman who stands between them, small and fragile. She is there of her own volition, honouring the choice that was made by her child, offering herself up in sacrifice. A mother.

Miri feels herself incline forward, rocking onto her toes, eager to drink in every detail of the woman. Next to the degenerating pigsuits – their fasciae blossoming with rust, their clear central casings so grease-smeared as to obscure the chasm within – her appearance is neat. Fastidious, even. She wears a plain brown skirt with a white shirt tucked into the waistband and her wiry ash-blonde hair, freshly dyed for the occasion, is drawn back into an elegant twist. She does not look up at the crowd but keeps her eyes downcast as she moves into the glass-fronted booth and drops herself heavily down into the wooden chair. Once she is seated, she waves a hand to indicate that she is ready. The closest pigsuit bends and reaches out a handless glove to fasten the straps, looping several around the woman's arms and legs and then another across her torso.

Miri wonders where the woman's partner and child are. Perhaps they are somewhere in the crowd, watching, revelling in this moment of glory, of righteous revenge and absolute power. If she were bolder, she would push through the crowd to get as close as possible, to be right up against the glass when the electric hits. But the very thought of stepping further into the mass makes her lungs tighten and constrict.

Finger, thumb, finger, thumb.

The woman is shaking with fear now, violently enough that Miri can see every quiver, even from her poor vantage point. The smaller of the two pigsuits is busy adjusting switches on the generator whilst the other straps a wet sponge to the woman's forehead. As it crushes the hanging metal bowl on top of the sponge, lines of water run down the woman's face, pooling in her eye sockets and making her blink hard. Miri can see her thin arms uselessly straining at the straps in an attempt to wipe the water away. The pigsuit, ignorant of her discomfort, sweeps a greasy brown blindfold over her face and pins it there. A small pool of damp spreads across the woman's skirt as she loses control of her bladder. The anti-natalists jeer.

Miri scans back past them, looking to see how the rest of the crowd are responding. They are quieter than the Activists, transfixed and silent. Insignificant details spring out at her; a man kneading a dry earlobe between his knuckles, a couple clasped together with circling arms, an old woman absently clutching a lumpen teddy, threadbare and grey, to her chest.

Miri turns back to the booth. It seems that the pigsuits are finally ready. The smaller of the two, the one that has been tending to the woman, straightens up and retreats into the shadows. As soon as it has, the other pigsuit raises an arm to the lever on the generator.

This is the woman's moment.

The crowd watches her intently. She wets her lips, tongue darting, and then nods. The pigsuit pulls the lever down.

Two thousand volts shoot down through the metal bowl and into the woman's body. She braces hard and then falls out of consciousness before beginning to thrash and jerk violently against the restraints. Blue lines of electricity crackle along her limbs and torso. The generator whirs loudly. Somebody in the crowd screams.

Without warning, the pigsuit throws up the lever. A sudden stillness. Ten seconds pass. Twenty. The woman's chest rises and falls with a weak, rattling breath.

Her respite is short-lived.

With another crank of the lever, the pigsuit sends out a second wave of voltage. This one ensures death. The frantic thrashing and jerking start up again but this time steam begins to emanate from the woman's body. Vast waves of it churn out from the glass front of the booth, drifting towards the crowd in the square.

The pigsuit raises the lever, allowing the woman's body to slump forward in the chair. The other steps forward and tugs at the bowl on her head. Once it comes free, Miri sees that the woman's hair is aflame, blazing so furiously that soon her entire head is consumed. It is no ordinary fire, but threaded through with electricity and unnaturally ferocious. The front rows of the crowd begin to retreat, even the Activists. Miri can see people turning away from the Gallery, gagging, hands pressed over their mouths and noses. The stench hits, dreadful in its familiarity. She thinks of the summer's wildfires; the blackened bodies laid out on the heath. Bile rises in her throat. Behind the glass, the pigsuits battle with the flames while the woman slowly burns.

Beyond the edge of the square there is a strip of wild grassland that once served as a road. Miri stumbles through it, beating aside the ragweed, thistles and yellow toadflax to scatter the air with clouds of dry, shrivelled seeds. Standing half-submerged in a dense thicket of blood-red filterweed is an old bus stop; a rusted metal frame is all that remains of the modest shelter. Miri lowers herself onto the rickety bench and takes a few deep breaths, stuffing her fists into her pockets. In one pocket is the crumpled flyer and in the other a folded postcard, a willing reply to Miri's request to meet at seven the following day, in the cool of the evening. It's from someone they call the Celt, a woman who she got to know in the volunteer-run ReproViolence Clinic out by the Soho tenements. Although she hasn't had cause to return there in the last few months – not since she recovered from that last bout of pneumonia – she finds her thoughts turn to the Celt with increasing regularity. Just thinking about her now, she can feel the blood begin to pound in her ears. Miri's not sure how she ever worked up the courage to ask the Celt to meet. She's glad she did, though. The chance of seeing the woman so soon is enlivening and fills her with anticipation.

Just then, a flash of movement catches her attention and snaps her out of her reverie. Leaning forward, she warily eyes the patch of filterweed. For a moment, everything is perfectly still. Then the weeds shiver in the windless air. There's another loud rustle and now she's sure that something is headed her way through the undergrowth. Tensing, she recalls the swarms that have plagued the city in years gone by – species of all kinds either fleeing fire, flood and famine, or simply surging unchecked with every new imbalance wrought in the food chain.

A rat darts out from the undergrowth and then sits back on its haunches, nose twitching. Miri notices at once the fleshy protuberance that stands proud of the creature's matted white fur, running like a ridge along its back: a human ear spliced into its spine. In all other regards, it is a perfectly ordinary white rat, with pink feet and a long scaly tail. Miri laughs, partly in relief. She's been half-braced for the harbingers of a carrion-beetle swarm, but after all that it's only a rat, no doubt escaped from some nearby laboratory.

"Hello," she says, stooping to lower her hand towards the creature. Tentatively, it noses at her fingers, its whiskers tickling her skin. Then it clambers up onto her palm, the ear on its back rigid like a sail. She lifts the thing up onto her lap and makes a maze of her hands for it to run through. It seems to know better than she does what her next move will be.

Although she guesses a laboratory rat would probably be used to humans, she is astonished by how much it appears to trust her. It makes no bid for freedom and seems quite content in her company.

Perhaps it thinks you're an escaped lab rat too, says the voice in her head, which she ignores. Probably the creature is from a long line of animals bred for the trait of docility. Yes, that vaguely chimes with what little she recalls of her half-forgotten genetics lessons. Assuming she's right, she doesn't see how a creature so tame could possibly have escaped of its own accord. The only other explanation is that the thing was set free. This is, she thinks, a cruel trick to play on such a beast. It won't survive the London wilds for long.

While she supposes that a docile lab rat would be more useful for experimental purposes than an aggressive one, she can come up with no good explanation for the human ear growing on its back. Try as she might, she cannot see the utility of it and suspects that it has been done for the oldest of reasons: simply because it is possible.

It's hardly the first time a genetic experiment has got out of hand. The crimson filterweed that surrounds the bus stop is a case in point. Although the intention was to create a super-strain of knotweed capable of filtering small amounts of carbon – and so improve the local air quality – the plant spread more aggressively than anticipated and spawned several new mutations, overwhelming other flora in the process. Worst of all, its effect on local air quality proved negligible. Several of its later variants seemed not to sequester carbon at all.

Idly stroking the rat, Miri stares out at the square. Now that the pigsuits have dealt with the fire, the crowd is beginning to disperse, surging down the arterial lanes that feed the square in clots of twos and threes.

Someone peels away from the crowd and heads towards her. It's a boy, a few years older than her, with a strong brown face and a crop of curly hair, an anti-natalist dazzle-pattern scarf pulled down beneath his chin. She recognises him at once as the figure who approached her before. Seeing him again, Miri notices that there's something in his bearing, in his artfully crumpled stretch suit, that reminds her of the kind of people she grew up with. As he draws near, her fingers twitch. It's all she can do to stop herself from slipping back into that repetitive gesture of finger over thumb. She knows instinctively that she must not, that it invites attention, that it makes her appear vulnerable; an easy target. To steady herself, she closes her hands tighter on the rat, taking comfort from the warmth of its fur and the strange feel of the ear's helix against the skin of her palm. Then the rat squirms and she becomes suddenly aware of how small and fragile its skeleton feels beneath her fingers. She loosens her grip.

"Alright?" says the boy, now a few feet away.

Miri tenses herself, ready to run. Seeing this, he stops, and raises his hands in the universal sign of peace. On his face is a blank expression that she can't read.

Miri switches to the defensive. "Your parents know you're an anti-natalist, do they?" she asks pointedly.

"*Parent*," he corrects her in a languid tone. "One of my dads died when I was a kid."

Miri chews on this, thinking, *no Offset – good for you*. All the while, the boy's eyes search her face. After a moment, his lips curve upwards with a triumphant smirk. "It *is* you!" he exclaims.

Miri's stomach drops. She isn't used to being recognised these days. There isn't much left of the girl who used to feature so frequently alongside the famous Professor Jac Boltanski in the news clips and promotional materials that document nearly every aspect of her mother's work.

Though Miri hasn't had much cause to look in a mirror since she left home, that doesn't mean she hasn't noticed how her body has changed. Two years of being constantly on the move and never knowing for sure where the next meal would come from makes a mark on a person. She is skinnier than she ought to be, ribs and collarbone pronounced and visible beneath her skin, which is so pale as to be almost translucent. Despite her gaunt frame, her stomach is constantly bloated, hanging low and distended, and her feet and ankles often swell dramatically, filling with fluid that puffs them to twice their usual size. She is always cold, even in the midday heat.

A few months back, she found a heavy cable-knit jumper in an abandoned tip and she has barely taken it off since, even though it is threadbare and smells faintly of urine. There are sores on her face, chest and back. Her hands, once soft and delicate as befitting her cloistered upbringing, are rough with callouses and her fingernails are torn to the quick. Her hair, which she wears short and streaked through with bright reds and oranges, hangs in greasy ropes about her face and is beginning to thin. She wonders what it would take to completely erase her genetic inheritance and every trace of her mothers: Jac's hard features and Alix's freckles.

"What are you doing here on your own?" asks the boy when she doesn't respond.

"None of your business."

"Your life is everyone's business."

Miri closes her eyes. He's right, in a way.

She gets up to leave but he grabs her thinning arm with enough force to bruise. She catches the smell of lemongrass, an expensively synthesised scent of the kind that often graced a home just like hers. The home that used to be hers.

"Hey – tell me who you're going to choose–"

Before he can continue, his words give way to a sudden howl of pain. He snatches his hand away as though it has been scalded and clutches it to his chest, peering down to examine where there are now two deep punctures in his skin, the red-wet marks of an animal bite.

Angry now, his dark eyes search out the cause of his pain and he finally sees the white rat, clambering down the leg of the bench. The boy lunges for it, set – Miri is certain – on grabbing the rat by the tail in order to smash its skull against the side of the shelter. Miri tries to block his path but the effort is needless, for no sooner has she scudded forward than the boy falls back, his face twisted in alarm and disgust. Miri follows his gaze and realises that he is seeing the ear half-sunk into the rat's back for the very first time. Judging from his expression, it's a sight he finds deeply abhorrent. It transfixes him for a moment and then he tears his eyes away, staggering back and shooting Miri a last, horrified look. Steadily, Miri releases a breath she didn't realise she'd been holding and then, for good measure, makes the sign again. Finger, thumb, finger, thumb. The rat on the ground at her feet now sits back on its haunches and begins to clean its long pink tail.

The boy is already out of sight, but his words ring in Miri's ears for a long time after.

Tell me who you're going to choose.

It's the question the whole world is waiting to be answered. They won't have long to wait. Miri's Offset is in two days' time.

02

Several hundred miles away, Professor Jac Boltanski is busy cross-checking a long list of figures. She is on a train to Inbhir Nis. A compact overnight bag sits at her feet, the top edge of a heavy, battered lab book poking out above the zip. Papers are strewn across the fold-down table in front of her, each one bearing a different graph or table of measurement. Her cat-like green eyes dart between them, lighting upon patterns of significance that would be invisible to anyone else.

After a moment, she gives a low snarl of frustration and leans back in her seat, letting her gaze fall to the window. As she does, the train hurtles into a tunnel and, for a moment, all she can see is herself in the fleeting black mirror. She catches an impression of dark hair cut short, of hard features and sharp cheekbones, and admires the elegant lines of the tailored white shirt she wears buttoned to the throat. Then the train exits the tunnel and she disappears, her reflection replaced by passing fields of stout pink banana trees.

In the last few years, the countryside north of London has become unrecognisable to her. New and unfamiliar industries have sprung up as the people of the Federated Counties have sought to adapt to the fast pace of change occasioned by climatic and political violence.

Some sights Jac can explain. The fields of bright orange corn, for instance, are the legacy of a genetic-engineering project which, as she recalls, was to develop crops that produce higher levels of beta-carotene, the intention of which was to combat vitamin A deficiencies in poorly nourished populations and reduce the risk of sunburn in pale-skinned northern Europeans. The project was not without success, but it transpired that high beta-carotene diets also had the alarming side effect of giving lighter skin tones an orange hue. This, at least, accounts for the startling appearance of some of the people she sees crowded on station platforms as the train hurtles past. What she can't explain is why so many of them wear purple face masks. They look like the kind designed to inhibit air-borne diseases, but she's not aware that any of the Counties are on high alert for infection. She supposes instead that the masks could be related to the outbreaks of gang warfare that so often plague the middle Counties, though what exact allegiances they signify she cannot say.

Her mind races ahead along the tracks. She is making for what most folk this side of the border still call Inverness, but which she – out of respect for her Alban colleagues – dutifully refers to in all official communications by the Gaelic name of Inbhir Nis. The Borlaug Institute, of which she is the Director, maintains a testing facility there and, although she is personally accountable for its operation, it has been many years since she visited. It's not that she intentionally avoids such visits, it is simply that the majority of her time is already spoken for. For the best part, she is bound to London, where she oversees the teams in the laboratory there. In truth, that is but a small portion of her work. In many respects, her job is as diplomatic as it is managerial. She liaises with governors and scientific organisations, and she courts those with the wealth and power that enables their vital work to continue. As much as she might wish it were otherwise, London is where that power lies, so that is where she focuses her efforts.

Although there have been the occasional cursory visits over the years whenever she could squeeze them in, the last time she really remembers being at the Inbhir Nis facility is when Project Salix began, more than eighteen years ago. It was from there that she remotely oversaw the first round of willow planting in the ARZ – the Arctic Remedial Zone – and, in the course of doing so, became the face of the project that would save the Earth. *Project Salix*, the op-ed headlines had run: *Making carbon neutrality a reality*. The articles were of a kind: all fawning, all spiked with the same jargon ("advanced phytogenetics" and "secure-system telerobotics"), all carrying Jac's picture.

The planting itself, hailed as a world-saving rescue mission on an unprecedented scale, was highly celebrated, beamed out to whoever could access it. All over the world, people crowded around what few televisions and computers remained – like pilgrims huddled in the night around the embers of a dying fire – to see Jac give a rousing speech from the testing facility while, out in Greenland, the first trees were planted. Robotically, of course, given that no human could set foot within the ARZ. Everyone who saw it still remembers the fire in Jac's voice, and how her loving wife Alix stood by her side, a small bundle cradled in her arms.

"This is for my daughter," Jac said, placing an arm around Alix's shoulder as, a thousand miles away, the saplings were set into the earth. "This is for us and all who come after: the children of the Arborocene." It was, several well-wishers assured her, an electric moment, bristling with hope and confidence.

In all the years since, Jac has dedicated her every waking moment to the project, never once doubting that it will be successful. They have now planted every inch of Greenland with Project Salix trees, genetically engineered to be radiation-hard and thereby transforming the nuclear wasteland of the ARZ into a set of branching lungs that draw in carbon dioxide and emit oxygen at an accelerated rate, the world's first and only hypernovaforestation. By all accounts, it is a triumph: already the Borlaug taskforce has seen year-on-year decreases in global carbon emissions. Not that failure was an option. Of all the concerted efforts to prevent the heat death of the planet, only Project Salix ever had a hope of succeeding. Its effects, combined with those of the Offset, are set to restore the planet's atmosphere to good health. It is an almost unthinkable eventuality, but maybe – one day – they will no longer need the Offset.

No sooner has she voiced this to herself than she dutifully sets the thought aside. They will always need the Offset; they will always need a check on the human tendency for wanton procreation. There could be no return to the unbridled behaviour of the past, not when that was precisely what had landed them here in the first place and what could so easily overwhelm the planet once more. And, anyway, the Offset was about far more than protecting the environment. Even if her Offset were two years away instead of two days, Jac would still feel the same deep need to level things off with their daughter, to atone for what she and Alix had done.

With a slight shake of the head, she knocks the idea aside and, at last, turns her attention back to the sheaf of papers spread out across the table; the report is one that she has personally compiled out of data drawn from both the London laboratory and the Inbhir Nis facility. Her eyes fall on one figure she took down that morning. *Global Average: 500 ppm.* It's the latest CO_2 level and exactly on track according to the projections, which should provide some comfort. But Jac is uneasy. Elsewhere, the pages are littered with asterisks and question marks in neat green ink. Each one indicates a statistical variation that, while not beyond the range of the project's parameters, she cannot fully explain. And she needs an explanation. Now more than ever.

03

Calmer now the square has emptied, Miri reluctantly drops the rat back into the long grass and sets off for the shrine. Though she longs to escape the danger of the city centre, she's come this far; she's seen the Offset through to its end, she can't turn back now.

The shrine is a short walk away, not far beyond the north-east corner of the square. When she reaches it, she finds the place deserted, the only guard a weathered block of Portland stone. A sleeping infant has been carved into the surface, a thick cable of umbilical cord twisting around one ankle, chaining it to the rock. There is a weathered inscription on the sculpture's base: *To light a candle is to cast a shadow.*

The tall door beyond is unlocked and creaks noisily on its hinges as Miri enters. She doesn't bother to pull it closed. Stepping further into the stone mausoleum, she hugs her arms across her chest to still a shiver. Once a church, the entire shrine has a dusty, unused feel to it. There are no flowers or candles by any of the plaques. Little wonder. The shrine dates back from when most considered the Offset to be a noble sacrifice. The memorials were intended to stand as testament to the bravery of those who gave their lives for the good of all. Now they are nothing so much as a malediction on those selfish enough to breed.

No one visits the memorials anymore. No one comes to give thanks to the dead.

Not far from the entrance lies a flagstone bearing a fresh inscription and a name that Miri takes to be that of the newly dead woman. It must have been started as soon as she was nominated, hand-carved with chisel and mallet by one of the Guild of Illuminators. There was a time, Miri knows, when inscriptions were laser-hewn by automasons, but those machines have long since been plundered for parts. Now, standing in the shrine, she thinks she can almost see where the transition was made to human stonecutters. There is a point near towards the end of what was once the nave where the lettering on the flagstones becomes distinctly less regular in every respect: script, size, kerning. Despite these irregularities, every memorial bears precisely the same information. Each records the name of the Offset alongside the name of their surviving partner. Beneath those names is written that of their child and, in rare cases, that of any surviving sibling. Towards the back of the shrine there are even memorial plaques on the walls that list three or four names in that space. The very thought of this makes Miri shudder. *How far we've come as a society*, she thinks. *You would never see that now.* The crime of having one child is already hard enough to forgive.

For a moment, Miri struggles to focus on the dead woman's memorial flagstone, her eyes flicking to the other names carved into every inch of the pillars and walls. When she tips her head back far enough to feel the base of her skull between the tops of her shoulders, she sees that the ceiling is also covered with the names of the Offset and their successors. Some have grown worn and indistinct with age. Some have been all but obliterated by past infestations of the filterweed cracking through the stone with its powerful tendrils.

Soon, Miri will have a plaque of her own. There is an empty space next to the dead woman's memorial. She tells herself that is where her own plaque will be and squints, trying to imagine her and her mothers' names cut into the flagstone. For a moment, she can see just what it will look like: the name

"Jac Boltanski" in large letters at the top, her name and Alix's in smaller letters below. She's been waiting for it so long that she can hardly believe how close it is.

Considering this, she brings her thumb to her teeth and gnaws at a tab of dead skin. She rips it away, leaving a raw strip running down the side of the nail, past the cuticle. She dabs at the tender patch with her tongue, relishing the sting of her saliva in the open wound.

When she shuts her eyes, she sees the dead woman again, thrashing against the constraints of the electric chair, and superimposes Jac's face onto the image. She thinks of how crowded the square was today and how much busier it will be in two days' time when it's Jac's turn. There can't be a single person in London who would miss the chance to be present at the historic occasion of Professor Jac Boltanski's death.

Finger, thumb, finger, thumb.

For years after, people will come to see their memorial in the shrine. There seems to be no bounds to the affection the public holds for her mother. Of course, Miri thinks with a stab, they don't know Jac like she does. Jac might be idolised and admired for her work – they even say she's saved the world – but the truth is she's no better than any of the other thoughtless breeders whose names are recorded here; none of them caring one bit about what happens to the children they created, the children they left behind.

Miri feels a sudden pressure in her bladder. She pulls down her jeans and squats low over the blank stone. In the next moment, a yellow stream of urine – steaming in the chill air of the shrine – hits the floor and pools between her feet, seeping into the porous surface. A healthy quantity splatters onto the dead woman's memorial as well. Miri straightens. She's just zipping her jeans when there's a mechanical hiss and clunk from beyond the shrine door.

Startled, Miri turns to see a pigsuit stalk in, its pressure-sensitive footpads unexpectedly silent on the stone floor. The machine is in a poor state of repair; the empty gauntlet of one arm tapers to nothing but the frayed ends of loose wires, and the metal carapace is edged with rust and deep grooves where it has been scratched or scuffed in the course of executing its commands. The clear central casing is compromised by a long, jagged crack. In the murky gloom beyond, Miri can just see the pale spots where spores have begun to bloom across the worn foam fittings; the hollow become a rotting cavity.

Pausing in the doorway, the pigsuit turns, panning its body camera from Miri to the dark puddle at her feet. Seeing the desecrated shrine, the pigsuit's apprehend-and-arrest programming kicks into gear. Before she can think of fleeing, it crosses the stone floor and grabs her by the arm, its articulated digits vice-like across the bruise left from where the boy sought to delay her escape. Even in its dilapidated state, the pigsuit is much stronger than he was and certainly stronger than Miri.

The pigsuit drags Miri around on the spot, holding her in place with one hand and then pushing the end of its amputated limb to tilt her head upwards, forcing her to look directly into the flat black eye of its camera. Something clicks. The pigsuit chokes out her name.

– Miriam Ford-Boltanski

Miri stiffens at the mention. For two years, she has gone by simply Miri Ford. She has wanted nothing more than to remove all association between herself and Jac.

As much prompted by the insult of this as anything else, Miri draws mucus into the back of her throat with a snort and then spits, propelling a stringy glob of saliva directly at the camera where it splatters against the lens. Then she feels something sharp jab into her arm and everything goes black.

Miri's head is spinning. She tries to open her eyes but that only makes it worse, white noise humming at a deafening volume in her ears. She waits for it to subside, lying very still.

When she next tries to look around, it's a little easier – now at least she can squint at her surroundings without the threat of passing out.

The room where she lies is narrow, barely larger than a cupboard. There are no windows, no kind of ventilation, only a locked door in the opposite wall with a thin band of white light that seeps in around the edges. The air is close and warm. Even though she cannot see out, she has no doubt about where she is, roughly speaking anyway. All the pigsuits come from a south-side hub, a squat depot attached to the city's only working prison: the Eye. Its cantilevered wheel overlooks the river and, given its enormous size, can be seen from almost anywhere within the city limits, particularly since the skyscrapers were razed. Its stern look can only be avoided by hiding away inside or underground.

Miri is too dazed to panic. As dire as the situation is, she is dimly aware that it could be worse. At least she's not in the Eye itself, not in one of the glass pods where the prisoners are usually kept. She must be in some sort of holding cell in the depot, safely stowed away while they work out what to do with her. Sitting up, she feels her head swim again and remembers what happened in the shrine. With slow, sluggish movements, she seeks out the tender spot on her bony arm where the needle punctured her skin and massages it with her hand.

There's a muffled squeak and then she feels the scratch of claws against her bare arm. In the next moment, the white rat emerges from her sleeve, the ear on its back marked with ridges from where it has been pressed against the weave of Miri's jumper. She frowns, wondering if she's imagining things, but there's no mistaking it. The rat is definitely there. She supposes vaguely it must have followed her into the shrine and burrowed into her clothes when the pigsuit sedated her. The rat snaps reproachfully at her fingers and then sits back on its haunches to cuff the dirt from its two ears, apparently unharmed by what can only have been a most uncomfortable journey.

Staring half-dazed about the cell, she notices a few shoots of filterweed rising up through a crack in the floor. The thick crimson stems divide and split into nodes from which sprout broad oval leaves, truncated at the base and with a serrated edge. The leaves are darker than the stalks, a deep bluish-red that makes Miri think of dried blood.

There's a flicker of movement. An aphid flits through the air and settles on one of the leaves, palely green against the deep red of the plant. As she watches, the filterweed does something she's never seen before: the edges of the leaf shiver and begin to curl up. At first, she thinks that what she's seeing must be on account of a draught or a trick of the light, or even some side-effect of the tranquiliser that is still making her dizzy and lightheaded. But soon there's no mistaking it. The leaf is definitely moving, flexing and contracting of its own accord. The aphid senses it too and it startles away from the leaf only to find itself unable to move, caught in a thick, glistening mucus. In the next moment, it disappears from view as the leaf wraps around it to form a narrow, upright pitcher, tightly constricting about the struggling fly. It is some time before the leaf unfurls again. When it does, the aphid is gone. Absorbed. There's nothing to show what happened but a bright sheen across the leaf.

Before Miri can investigate further, the cell door swings open. Fearing the rat will starve if she leaves it behind in the cell, she tries to lunge forward and scoop it up, but it's as though her hands belong to someone else and they fall inches short. The rat, seeming to sense her intentions, burrows into her jumper and nestles there against her skin. Holding the warm lump to her chest, Miri pushes herself to her feet with an enormous effort. The room lurches dangerously around her so she steadies herself against the wall. Lightheaded, she squints dazedly towards the open door and sees the bulky silhouette of a pigsuit. Beside it stands a familiar figure, one she hasn't seen in almost two years.

"Mum?" she says – or tries to say. Her lips slide numbly over the word and make no sound.

For a moment, Alix hovers uncertainly by the pigsuit and then, in two quick strides, she crosses the cell and folds Miri into a fierce hug. Miri hangs limply in her arms, unable to respond. Perhaps it's better that way, better that she doesn't have to decide whether to return the embrace or push her mother aside.

"You're being let off with a warning," Alix murmurs into her hair. "I'll explain later."

Miri allows one of her arms to be pulled across her mother's shoulders and then, when she feels Alix's arm snake about her waist, she leans heavily onto her. In this position, she is half-supported, half-carried from the holding cell.

Beyond it is a room lit by harsh strip bulbs and bare of all furnishing save for a single row of chairs lined against one wall. They serve as the sole concession to the idea that the occasional human visitor might need to be accommodated. That and a lone, faded poster bearing the lines of the Global Constitution, its long list of amendments dwarfing the brief bill itself that gives only the universal tenet: for every birth, a death. Otherwise, the only distinguishing features are the pigsuits themselves. Most stand arrayed together in neat rows as though waiting to be switched on, only the occasional flashing light or mechanical whirr betraying the fact that they are already powered up. Many of these, Miri notices as the room swims around her, bear deep gashes that have been hastily soldered over or covered with strips of scrap metal. A short way off, two pigsuits are busy cannibalising a third with violent precision, stripping the vacant exoskeleton for working parts.

The pigsuits ignore Miri and her mother as they make their halting way across the floor. After several minutes of panting and heaving, they stumble together through a set of double doors and out into the cool of what is now night. Together, they continue in silence for a few more feet and then Alix stops and turns her face upwards.

Head spinning, Miri follows her gaze. She sees the squat prefabricated depot they have just left. It is completely windowless, so neither the pigsuits nor the holding cells therein can be seen from the outside. Above it rises the Eye. She's never been this close to it before, close enough to see into the glass pods that are riveted to the edge of the rusting white wheel at regular intervals. Not all of the pods are occupied, but those that are have been filled to two or three times above capacity. There is so little space that the prisoners within can neither sit nor lie down, their bodies pressed tight against one another between the curving walls of the pod. Miri wonders how they sleep. How they breathe. She feels a tightness in her chest and tries to jerk her hands closer to press together finger and thumb but her arms barely move.

In one pod, glass speckled with condensation, there are no discernible shapes of people or their distinct parts at all, but only a thick fluid putrefaction. As the wheel sways gently in the wind, a shuddering ripple passes across the surface of the viscous matter and a few blunt knuckles of bone emerge. Miri turns away. The Eye is a prison, its inmates either eventually released or taken away to be executed and buried. At least, that's what's supposed to happen. Perhaps the pigsuits' deterioration is even worse than she guessed.

"That could have been you." Alix's voice trembles as she speaks, her gaze still trained on the Eye. Not knowing what to say, Miri inclines her neck so that her head rests briefly against Alix's. As she does, she catches the scent of Alix's perfume, which jolts her. She hasn't thought of it in two years, but it's just like she remembers: wild rose and poppy.

"Come on," Alix says at last. "It's time we got you home."

04

It's late when the train pulls into Inbhir Nis, too late to go directly to the testing facility. Jac has a room booked in one of the boarding houses by the station. It's run-down and spartan, but perfectly clean. She goes to check in, greeting the sullen, doe-eyed girl behind the desk with a terse smile.

"The kitchen is closed," says the girl. "Though we can probably find something if you're hungry. It'll cost extra, mind."

This last is said with a deep reluctance that, Jac suspects, is restrained only by the respect due to her being a customer of standing.

"I don't want anything to eat," she replies. "But I could use a drink."

After a brief negotiation, Jac slips a few notes across the desk and retires to her room – a shabby affair with the only notable feature being the heavy, cloying scent of cheap disinfectant – and is rewarded half an hour later by a light knock on the door.

It's the same girl as before, carrying a green bottle the length of her forearm. The glass is poor in quality, the walls of the bottle thick and uneven, and dotted with bubbles of trapped air. Jac is used to finer things, but no matter; it's only the bottle's contents that concern her. In the dim light of the hall she can see that it is half full of a fizzing golden liquor. Local homebrew.

"It's all there is," says the girl.

Taking the bottle, Jac hands her another note and dismisses her with a curt nod.

The girl, however, lingers. She has bunched up her lank hair into an untidy knot on the top of her head and is wearing a fresh layer of heavy makeup.

"Maybe you'd like some company for the night?" she asks in a tone more optimistic than alluring.

Jac groans inwardly. Despite the girl's crude attempt to hide it, she is plainly too young to have even made her Offset. Jac wants to ask: *Where are your parents?* But she knows better than to pry into the lives of Albans, and instead shakes her head.

"No, thank you."

It comes out rather more curtly than intended and the girl looks hurt by the cold dismissal. As she begins to turn away, Jac is gripped with the sudden desire to give her something.

"Hang on a second…"

Jac disappears back into her room, carefully placing the bottle on the nightstand before rummaging through her bag. The girl shifts into the doorway and watches Jac with curiosity, unsure whether or not she should come in any further. Jac takes out an old, dog-eared photo. It is a commemorative shot of her shaking hands with the Chief Scientific Officer of Éire – taken long before the hostilities, of course. Taking a pen, she signs the bottom of the photo. *Warmest wishes, Jac Boltanski.*

Gesturing for the girl to come and take it from her, Jac says, "Please, I want you to have this."

The girl crosses the room and takes the photo from Jac's hand. Her eyes rake the image – uncomprehending of its political content, perhaps even unable to read the writing, but certainly recognising a much younger-looking Jac. Even *she* knows the value of a signed photo of Professor Jac Boltanski. With a keen smirk, she leaves the room.

Jac passes into the girl's wake and pulls the door closed behind her, making sure to double-bolt it. Then, returning to the nightstand, she yanks the rubber stopper from the bottle and takes a generous swig. And another. The liquor is unexpectedly strong and burns the back of her throat when she swallows. After a moment, she feels a slow warmth spread across her face and shoulders. With a deep exhalation, she sets the bottle down and reclines on the hard, narrow bed.

No sooner has she done so than her phone begins to vibrate. She takes it out from her pocket. It is small and compact, fitting neatly into the palm of her hand. The phone she normally uses for work is twice the size of this one and capable of doing a great deal more than simply receiving calls and text messages, but she knows she's taking a risk carrying around even this pared-back version. Phones are rare enough in London. Out here, just having such a device on her person makes her a target.

She sees her wife's number on the screen and answers in a low murmur. "Alix?"

At first, Alix says nothing. Jac can hear only her breath, distant and faint on the crackling line. Then, eventually, a sigh. "Miri's back."

For a moment, it is as though everything has stopped: her heart lies still in her chest, her lungs freeze and become two scrunched-up plastic bags. Even the synapses in her brain seem to come to a halt. There is no thought in her head, not one, just Alix's words ringing in her ears over and over.

Finally, the lights crackle back on and she returns to herself. Jac clenches and unclenches her jaw. "What happened?" she asks.

She listens attentively while Alix explains about being summoned to the Eye to find their daughter in a holding cell after having apparently desecrated a shrine. "She's been let off with a warning, though," says Alix, who then tells her about the tranquilisers. "The dose was too high – a malfunction, is my guess. You know what the pigsuits are like these days. That's probably why she's been let off so lightly. But she's in a bad way. I had to bring her back here. She's sleeping it off now."

Jac pinches the bridge of her nose, trying to keep up. "I thought–"

"She looks like she hasn't been eating properly either," Alix says quickly. "Or taking care of herself at all."

"Should I – can I speak to her?"

A pause. "I already told you, she's asleep."

"Yes, you did. Sorry. Probably just as well. She wouldn't want to speak to me anyway."

"That's not true–"

"Does she sound as though she's had a change of heart over the last two years?"

Another pause. "We haven't really had a chance to talk yet."

"But she didn't ask after me?"

"She was still half-sedated when I got to her. She didn't say much at all. I'm glad you didn't have to see her that way; it clean broke my heart. She could barely tell up from down." Alix takes a breath. "I know she loves you, Jac. I know she does. She's just still working through her problems, that's all. You're too hard on her."

"I *know*," says Jac, a little testily. "It's my fault."

"That's not what I said."

"It's true, Alix. You're a brilliant mother. If it had been just you and Miri, maybe everything would have turned out differently."

"So you've said. And you know what I think of that. Miri needed you to be around more, not less, whatever you tell yourself."

Echoes of the old debates ring in Jac's ears. Though she can't deny Alix has a point, it's still a hard one to accept when everything she tried to do only ever seemed to make things worse. Increasingly in the months before Miri left home, her every interaction with the girl had ended in tears and red-faced declarations of hatred.

"I really did try to be there as much as possible," Jac says at last. "We both did. But work–"

Alix softens. "I know. Miri might not understand it now, but she will one day. She'll know that everything you did, every decision you made, was for her benefit."

Jac chews her lip. The girl she remembers had always been resolutely unimpressed by her work, to the point where Jac sometimes thought Miri would prefer it if Project Salix failed and the world burned – to prove Jac wrong, if nothing else. "I didn't think anti-natalists set much store by their parent's wishes, however well-intentioned."

"Jac–"

"It doesn't matter, Alix. She can hate me forever, so long as she's safe. I'm glad she's with you. I know you'll look after her." Then, after a thought, she adds, "Don't try to change her mind, Alix. She made her decision a long time ago. We should respect that."

Alix remains silent.

"I never thought she'd come back," continues Jac, "not after the way we left things… Maybe I should come home." She sits up a little straighter. "What am I saying? Of course I should come home. I'm not sure when the next train is, but–"

"*Jac!* Slow down for just a minute, would you? Let's not be hasty here."

"What do you mean?"

"What I *mean* is that not so long ago you were busy telling me that you had to go away for work, that you knew how awful the timing was but that it was still too important, that it couldn't be avoided, that there was no one who could go in your place."

"Point being?"

"I don't see how Miri coming home changes any of that, much as I wish it would. Unless you were exaggerating about how serious things were?"

"Of course not."

"Well, then…"

Jac hesitates for a moment, and then something settles in her mind. "You're right. I'm needed here. I have to set things straight. But I'll be home tomorrow night, OK? Or sooner, if I can." Then she adds, with urgency, "I love you."

"I love you too," replies Alix, her voice thick with emotion, before hanging up the phone.

Jac stares at the blank screen for several long minutes. *Miri.* For a moment, the girl's face swims before her eyes, angry and tear-stained like on the day she left home. Miri's back. She lets herself linger on the thought for a moment, feeling anew the ache of distance that lies between her and home, the long miles that stretch between Inbhir Nis and London.

Pocketing the phone, she firmly redirects her mind to the matter in hand. She settles back against the headboard and, for what must be the hundredth time, she submerges herself in the document she brought from work, propping it up against her knees on the heavy lab book from her bag. Taking up the bottle of homebrew, she sips at it until it is empty and then cradles it in the crook of her arm.

She reads through the report over and over, looping back through it until the early hours of the morning when, at long last, the numbers begin to blur and lace together so that she can no longer make head nor tail of them. When, finally, she sets the report and empty bottle aside and sinks down into her pillow, the warping figures are the only thing she sees against the black of her eyelids.

She dreams of a rising tide of numbers. They mean to drown her; any minute now.

05

As soon as Alix puts down the phone, it takes hold: a spark that catches and spreads through her body like wildfire consuming dead bracken. *Not now,* she thinks. *I can't deal with this now.* But she's already burning like a furnace. Peeling away the thin cardigan she wears over her nightdress, she stumbles to the nearest window and hauls it open, even though she knows the humid night air will offer no relief. Gripping the sill with sweat-slicked palms, Alix breathes deep and tells herself that it will pass in a few minutes and that at least she is alone. She need not fret about the unsightly redness of her face nor the sweat pouring from her brow, she need not explain herself to some politely bewildered onlooker as she has on previous occasions. Small mercies.

A few breaths more and it passes. As the heat subsides, Alix checks her watch and grunts. It's the same time as always, the first episode of the night. They happen with an unerring regularity, as though her reproductive system is running its programme of self-destruction to a strict timetable. She should have been better prepared. Usually she would have thought to throw some gel packs in the fridge but tonight she clean forgot. *Hardly surprising,* she thinks.

Miri lies asleep in the room directly above. Granted, the girl's been knocked about, but now, at least, she is safe. Alix's thoughts wander back down the same path they have been treading all night, circling the same question: *Will she stay?*

As if in response, an uneasy vision crosses Alix's mind of the day her daughter left: Miri alternately tearful and coldly distant, driven by some righteous anger that Alix could not grasp beyond registering – deep down – that this was their fault somehow, hers and Jac's, that they had driven Miri away–

Alix's cheeks burn anew. It is as though a last, dying ember has been rekindled and the heat of shame is every bit as agonising as the hot flush. It's still hard for Alix to think about those first days after she and Jac lost their daughter. She stored the memories away; nuclear waste in a shielded cylinder that must never be breached. It hadn't occurred to her that she might need to confront them, least of all now with their Offset so close at hand. But with only days to spare, here Miri is, her reappearance the last thing either she or Jac was expecting, and disruption enough to bring those memories flooding back.

Caught by a sudden irritation, Alix swipes at the back of her neck with a hand and her fingers come away shining with sweat. She leaves the drawing room and, painfully aware of her daughter's sleeping presence, climbs the stairs on careful tiptoe, not trusting the thickly piled carpet or solidly built walls to muffle the noise of her passing. Once she reaches the safety of her room, she dries off with a clean towel from the *en suite* and then changes her nightdress. Bundling the drenched garment into the laundry basket, she wonders whether this is going to be one of the hell nights when she soaks the bedding through every couple of hours. If only Jac were home. When the night sweats hit hard, she fans Alix down and helps her change the sheets, countering Alix's mortification with easy humour. Sometimes they will stay up and brace themselves through it, stick a film on the overhead and chat until sunrise, Alix wrapped up in cold flannels like a living mummy.

In truth, though, she only half-wishes that Jac were home tonight. Her absence gives Alix the chance she needs to make sure Miri knows what her nomination means, to make sure she understands the consequences her choice will have both for herself and for the planet. Alix saw the opportunity the moment the call came through from the Eye. And, to her relief, it hadn't been hard to convince Jac to stay where she was in Inbhir Nis.

It's Miri's decision, that's what Jac always says. Alix doesn't disagree with this. But she also knows their daughter. Miri has always been stubbornly short-sighted, prone to the most self-destructive of passions. She has already proved herself capable of tearing apart their world. Alix cannot let it happen again. She won't. Whatever Jac may think of it, Alix knows she *needs* to make Miri see sense, to help the girl shore up her resolve. There isn't much time left.

Opening the drawer of her bedside table, Alix withdraws a small, battered piece of paper, the words "Say no to life" emblazoned across the top. It is a flyer she found buried in Miri's jeans when she helped the drugged girl into bed. Now, holding the flyer almost at arm's length, Alix reads it again, as aghast as before.

> *I saw the tears of the oppressed –*
> *and they have no comforter;*
> *power was on the side of their oppressors –*
> *and they have no comforter.*
> *And I declared that the dead,*
> *who had already died,*
> *are happier than the living,*
> *who are still alive.*
> *But better than both*
> *is the one who has never been born,*
> *who has not seen the evil*
> *that is done under the sun.*

Her face still as stone, Alix tucks the flyer back into the drawer. She wishes she knew where it came from; Miri's hatred, Miri's anger. Hadn't she and Jac done everything they could for her? Given her every advantage? Sinking down to sit at the edge of the mattress, Alix reaches a hand across to the shallow imprint that marks where Jac's body has lain beside hers for more than twenty years. She wonders if they will ever be forgiven.

06

It is morning before the tranquiliser completely wears off. Miri wakes early in her old bedroom and can't help but wince at the sight of the brightly patterned bedsheets, the clutter of nail varnishes and rings littered on the dresser, the row of soft toys staring button-eyed across at her from a low shelf; the paraphernalia of her childhood and teenage years, all of which she was too dazed to take in properly the night before. There's her guitar, leaning against the bookshelves in its scuffed case. Her old football jersey is slung over the desk chair; she can see where her name is embroidered on the back and the crude scribble where she tried to cross out the "Boltanski" part with marker pen. She rolls over and sees all her posters are still plastered around the bed. Peeling and faded now, most of them bear the faces of Octavia and the Butlers, her favourite band.

Everything, she realises, is just as she left it two years ago. It feels alien to her now, as if the room belonged to someone else entirely. The only difference she can see is the patch of wall by the door where she once sketched a massive ouroboros in provocation of her mothers. It is blank now, painted over in block magnolia. She can just make out the faint lines of her drawing beneath the emulsion.

With a rush of gladness, she sees that the white rat is curled in a neat ball on her bedside table, the ear on its back twisted in such a way that the sunken lobe nearly touches the top edge of the helix. Although the position looks deeply uncomfortable to her, she figures that it can't be troubling the rat, for it remains fast asleep.

Sitting up on the bed, she swings her feet down to the floor. As she catches sight of herself in the mirror on the dresser, she instinctively recoils. She doesn't recognise herself in the thin, hard face that stares back from her reflection any more than she does in her memories of the girl that once inhabited this room. It is the first time she's truly been able to see the change that the last two years have wrought on her; the effect is worse than she thought. Even she can see that she looks half dead. It's a wonder that Alix knew her at all in the holding cell. How that boy managed to recognise her at the square, she cannot fathom.

Reasoning that there isn't much she can do about her looks now, she climbs out of bed with a sigh and peers around for her clothes. To her surprise, she finds the cable-knit jumper where she left it on the floor, still stiff with dirt and reeking of urine. Once, Alix would have almost certainly taken it away to wash or – more likely – bin, causing an almighty scene. Perhaps, Miri thinks, her mother has changed in the years she's been gone. That, or maybe Alix is just more scared of her now she's proven she won't stick around and put up with being treated like a child.

Leaving her room, she finds that her mothers' home looks just as it ever did – at least at first glance. The décor is sophisticated, all muted tones with the occasional flash of colour: royal blue lampshades, modern stained-glass windows in one of the many bathrooms, bright flowers peering in from the balcony. On closer inspection, however, Miri sees the same tell-tale signs of decay that blight much of the city. The overhead lights in the hallway flicker intermittently, the paint is peeling away from the walls in several places and there are cracks in the ceiling. Miri even thinks she sees the first shoots of filterweed sprouting up from between the floorboards in the hall. She pauses, the sight of the red stalks inspiring a sudden dread that wells up beneath her breastbone. She vaguely recalls seeing a patch of filterweed in the holding cell but cannot say why the hazy image of it troubles her so. Then all at once she remembers. The struggling aphid. The leaf curled like an upright pitcher. With a shudder, she tries to shake the sensation away and presses on through the house.

Miri finds her mother in the kitchen. Alix is sitting hunched over a counter, her flyaway hair wild about her face. Where it was once a vibrant strawberry-blonde, it is now streaked with grey and shorter than Miri remembers, cut level with her round shoulders. There are deep lines around her mouth and eyes, and there seem to be more freckles than ever scattered across her cheeks and the bridge of her nose, and these have darkened with age and exposure to the sun. She wears a pair of square glasses – the lenses bound with a rim of gold and a thick top bar of glossy tortoiseshell – that are held on a fine chain which loops down around the back of her neck.

As soon as she sees Miri, Alix drops what she's doing, pushes her glasses up into her hair and hurries over to fold her into a warm hug. This time, Miri gives into it. She sinks gratefully into her mother's arms and takes deep lungfuls of her wild rose and poppy scent. For all she might have told herself otherwise, there is no denying how much she's missed her mother in the last two years.

When they pull apart, Alix's eyes are glistening. For a moment she looks broken, defeated; her brow is furrowed and her lips press together into a tight line that turns down at the corners. Then she recovers herself, snatching a quick breath and fixing her face into a smile. "You must be hungry," she says.

Miri doesn't respond right away. She merely stands where she is, jaw slack, finger and thumb of her right hand circled around her bony left wrist. Then she gives a slow shake of her head. Alix frowns, but Miri ignores her. She doesn't want to be forced to acknowledge aloud how thin she has become, even if she can see how much it's frightening her mother. Right now, the thought of eating is too much.

"There's chopped fruit in the fridge," says Alix, trying again.

Once more, Miri shakes her head. Fighting the urge to lace finger over thumb, she stuffs her hands into her armpits. Her right leg begins to shake uncontrollably, her heel bouncing against the tiles.

Seeing this, Alix throws up a conciliatory hand. "Alright," she says. "We can come back to that later. For now, why don't you just sit down and make yourself comfortable?"

That, at least, Miri thinks she can manage.

There is a breakfast island in the middle of the kitchen with four tall stools around the edge. She draws one back, scraping the chrome feet across the tiles, and then heaves herself laboriously up onto the seat. With her toes, she finds the footrest and presses the balls of her feet onto the bar, which makes her right leg bounce more than ever.

Alix regards her for a moment but says nothing. Then she pulls her glasses back down and turns her attention to what she was doing when Miri came in; darning a net that lies sprawled across the kitchen counter.

"To keep the dragonflies off my sagittaria," she says, apparently sensing the direction of Miri's glance, even though her back is turned as she hunches over the counter to work. "This is the third one they've eaten through."

The net is gossamer-fine. There are large, ragged-edged holes in the mesh from where the dragonflies have laid their eggs and the hatching larvae have eaten away at the fibres. Like the filterweed, the neon hawker dragonflies are the legacy of yet another failed genetic-engineering project. Reconstructed from an extinct genus of *Meganeura* – an ancestor of the dragonfly from the Carboniferous era – the neon hawkers are instantly recognisable by their distinctive pink markings and their incredible size, some of the larger specimens having wingspans of up to seventy centimetres. Unlike the common dragonfly, the neon hawker is not quite so reliant on wetland environments and is a more effective predator, developed specifically to keep London's swelling mosquito population in check. While they proved an effective measure against the mosquito, the neon hawkers bred rapidly and, having no natural predators of their own, quickly reached vast numbers. They are particularly attracted to the sagittaria and lilies that, Miri now recalls, grow in the water garden on her mother's patio.

The silver needle flashes in and out of the net. For a long while, Alix says nothing, keeping her eyes firmly on her work, but then tries a new tack: "How about if I put some fruit out for you? You don't have to eat it if you don't want to, but at least then it'll be there and ready if you decide that you *do*."

Miri can't find the words to argue with this, so she watches in helpless silence while Alix crosses to the fridge to retrieve two tubs, one white plastic, the other glasslock. She snaps off the lid of the glasslock and then, taking a small ceramic bowl from one of the cupboards, doles out a few spoonfuls of chopped fruit. Then she adds a dollop of strained natural yoghurt from the plastic tub. As Alix returns to the fridge and opens the door, from her position, Miri catches sight of a single magnet on its surface. It is a souvenir from the Borlaug, an image of the Pancras building towering over the Institute's slogan: *Breed fewer. Breed better.*

The door closes and the magnet disappears from view. Alix sets the bowl out on the breakfast counter in front of Miri and then hastily turns back to her darning, as though trying to demonstrate indifference to whether Miri eats or not.

Yeah, right, says the voice in Miri's head.

She stares at the bowl. Beyond the occasional mealy apple, fruit is hard to come by for most Londoners. The pineberries, pluots and blood limes that furnish the bowl in front of her all come from the complex of greenhouses at St Pancras. Only certain lab members have access to the in-house market stall where the fruit is sold, and Jac is one such person. Miri pushes the bowl away.

At the sound of ceramic sliding across the surface of the breakfast bar, Alix hopefully glances around and then her face falls. She sighs, then stops what she's doing to mop away the sweat from her brow with a nearby tea towel.

"Mind if I turn the ceiling fan on?"

Miri shrugs, leg still bouncing. "It's your house."

Alix pulls the cord and then stands beneath the fan with her arms stretched wide as the blades begin to spin. "This is the only one in the house that works now," she says. "The pigsuits took the motors out of the rest."

When she has cooled down a little, she takes up her needle once more and returns to the net. "That's better," she says, weaving the thread deftly in and out of the delicate mesh. "These hot flushes are driving me mad. Half the time I can't tell if it's me or the room that's too hot. Are you alright?"

Miri is clutching her arms to her chest, huddling against the sudden chill of the fan. "Fine," she lies, tucking her fingers into her armpits once more and staring about the kitchen. Now Alix has mentioned the pigsuits taking the fan motors, she notices that other things are missing, too. The front of the oven has been ripped away and the grills and heating element have been removed from its blackened interior. The metal handles have been taken from some of the cupboard doors, half of the shelves are bare and, where once there stood a dishwasher, there is nothing but a gaping hole.

Perhaps this should be no surprise. London has been gripped by a shortage of supplies and skills for years now, ever since the fall of the final trading bloc. Miri has come up against the hard end of it often enough in her time since leaving home and the evidence of it is everywhere, from the decaying appearance of the pigsuits to the automasons being decommissioned. But Miri wasn't aware before now that materials were being seized from citizens and it's strange to think that even her mothers are affected. If anyone is too important to be made to wash dishes by hand, it's Jac. In the past, when droughts or blight or infestations drove parts of the city into famine, they'd always been able to carry on as if nothing had happened. They would perhaps wear grim expressions and speak in hushed tones of the terrible circumstances, but they always had plenty to spare. If the shortages were finally having an impact on them, things must be far worse than she thought.

"Is Jac here?"

Hearing Miri refer to her mother by her first name, Alix stiffens but does not reprimand her. "Away on work," she says, making a final stitch that she ties off with a knot before cutting the trailing thread with her teeth. She holds up the net to inspect her handiwork in the light. Satisfied, she places the net back on the counter, rethreads her needle and starts on the next hole.

For a moment, Miri's leg stops bouncing. She sits perfectly still, her spine arched against the back of the stool, her eyes fixed on Alix; a cat intent on its prey. Under the intensity of her gaze, Alix shifts uncomfortably.

"I know what you're thinking, but it's not like that. Your mother would be here if she could."

Miri laughs softly, thinking of the great many things Jac missed "because of work". The school recitals, the birthday parties, the Sunday afternoons that should have been theirs. A flash of annoyance crosses Alix's face. "Your mother works very hard. She always has. You know how important it is. And with so little time left…"

Silence lapses between them. They have lasted this long without talking about the Offset, but she supposes they have to deal with it sooner or later. Miri's birthday is tomorrow, after all. They are running out of time. Not that she ever imagined she would have to confront either of her mothers again before making her nomination.

"Have you decided?" Alix asks quietly.

An image springs into Miri's head of the dead woman from the day before, thrashing and convulsing against the constraints of the electric chair.

"You know I have."

Alix turns away from the net and leans back against the counter to face Miri, her arms folded across her chest and her eyes narrowed behind the thick lenses of her glasses. "I wish you would speak to me first."

Miri's leg starts to bounce again, heel pumping up and down against the footrest of the stool. "I don't need your advice."

"But you don't understand–"

Before Alix can finish, Miri snatches up the bowl and hurls it at her.

Alix manages to duck just in time. The bowl smashes into the cupboard at head height right behind her. There's a loud crash as the bowl shatters, covering the countertop in jagged shards of ceramic. Smears of white yoghurt and fruit pulp spatter the walls and bleed dark juice into Alix's carefully darned net, now ruined.

Miri's conscious mind is two beats behind her instinct. As soon as it catches up, a horrified gasp tears itself from her lips. She begins to shake violently and her hands jerk in her lap, automatically lacing together. Finger, thumb, finger, thumb.

Alix straightens, her face completely drained of colour. She looks over the tops of her glasses at the destruction that litters the countertop and then across to where her daughter sits trembling and twitching. Then, taking out a new bowl, she goes to the fridge and doles out a second serving of fruit and yoghurt. She places it down firmly in front of Miri.

"Eat," she says, face set, jaw jutting forward.

This time Miri does as she is told, the spoon in her hand clattering noisily against the bowl as she scoops food into her mouth. She whimpers as she does, hating the way the wet flesh of the fruit turns to pulp on her tongue, struggling to choke it down, every mouthful a painful atonement.

Alix watches sternly over her while she eats, not moving

until Miri has emptied the bowl. Then, at last, she goes to clear up the mess on the countertop, folding the broken bowl and fruit up into the net and then sweeping the whole lot into the bin. When she is done, she goes to the sink to wash the sticky residue from her hands and wrings them dry with a tea towel.

"There," she says, returning to take Miri's empty bowl. "That wasn't so hard, was it?"

Still trembling on her stool, Miri says nothing. In her lap, her hands move frantically like a dynamo: finger, thumb, finger, thumb. It isn't helping.

07

That morning, Jac dresses with care, packs her bag and checks out of the boarding house beside the station while the sun has barely crested the horizon. There is a different girl behind the reception desk, much to Jac's relief.

"Where can I hire a rickshaw?"

"There's a rank by the old cemetery. It's a few minutes' walk from here. Just follow the road north. You can't miss it."

Stepping out into the cool of the morning, it strikes Jac for the first time since arriving how much cleaner the air is in Inbhir Nis compared to London. The thick smog that hangs over so much of the city is entirely absent here. Far off, she sees a white mist settling on the hills but the sky is otherwise clear. When she inhales she can nearly taste the salt-tang of the nearby sea.

The buildings she passes as she leaves the vicinity of the station are in much better condition than she would have expected, based on the strength of evidence provided by the shabby boarding house in which she spent the night. They stand tall and majestic, imposing facades of pale stone that look barely weathered at all despite their age. Further along, though, these give way to squat buildings of crumbling brick, plasterboard and pebbledash, all in varying states of disrepair. Most of the windows she passes are boarded up. A legacy, she guesses, of the violent storms that are said to roll in from the sea. As if confirming her suspicions, she comes to a stretch of pavement littered with broken glass. The splintered fragments catch the weak light of the rising sun and scatter it out in a bright array of rainbow colours, making the pavement glitter like crystal. The window of the nearest house is empty, nothing but a few jagged shards clinging to the frame: an eerie smile of broken teeth. The room beyond is pitch black. Were it not for the Alban flag hanging above the door – its white saltire and blue field are faded and look a little worse for wear – Jac would think the place deserted. The streets are quiet, too – since leaving the boarding house, she hasn't so much as glimpsed another living soul.

When she has walked just long enough to start thinking that she must have come in the wrong direction, she finally reaches the old cemetery that the girl mentioned. Beyond a low wall stand rows and rows of grey tombstones, many of which are partially hidden behind tall growths of nettles, the occasional crimson-red fronds of filterweed instantly recognisable within the thickets. Here, at least, the evident neglect is familiar from the London cemeteries; these days, most corpses are sent to a composting facility within a few days of death. The old religious traditions of burial and cremation are now only practised in a handful of places. Though, on closer inspection, she thinks that Inbhir Nis may be one such. Not all of the graves, she notices, have been given over to ruin. There are several that appear well maintained – the weeds cut back and the headstones scrubbed clean of lichen.

Not far from the cemetery's boundary wall she spies a freshly dug grave, the turned earth starkly brown against the surrounding green of the nettles. Atop the mound lies a simple doll made from a scrap of grey cloth. It has black buttons for eyes and they glare reproachfully at Jac as she passes. She doesn't need to read the headstone to know that it is the grave of a child. She finds herself wondering where the parents are and if, somewhere in the depths of their grief, they aren't secretly relieved. So went the logic: *no child, no Offset*. It was something Miri had accused her of; wishing that Miri had never been born, of wishing that she and Alix would not have to face the Offset. Jac had treated it like a joke, arguing that it was a bit rich coming from a girl who spent the rest of her time railing against her misfortune for existing at all. Now she wonders if Miri had a point, if she had perhaps picked up on some primordial fear of mortality that Jac herself had not been able to acknowledge. Not that she has ever regretted Miri's birth; not once, not even on the worst days, not even on the day Miri left home. But, certainly, she has wished the world were different from what it is. Who's to say that the girl had not observed that resentment and assimilated it, assuming herself to be the cause?

Before she can consider the matter further, she reaches the rickshaw rank, marked by a wooden sign with a crude image of one of the three-wheeled vehicles daubed onto it with a thick, tar-like paint. At this early hour there is only a single rickshaw parked beside the pavement; a simple cart attached to a rusting bicycle. The rider looks half-starved and she can't help but notice the bruises on his arms and the long, red scratches on his face. They might have been caused by anything – or anyone – but from the way he eyes Jac warily as she approaches the rickshaw, she feels sure that the injuries have been inflicted by some of his customers.

"You want to go to the Borlaug?" he asks, before she has even had the chance to say anything.

"Yes," she replies, her sense of unease increasing. Jac supposes it must be evident enough from her face and clothes that she isn't from around here; in her experience, County dwellers and Albans alike can spot a Londoner from several paces. And in a small township such as this, it would be reasonable to assume that the testing facility is the main draw for foreigners. What she cannot square away so easily, though, is how the rider flinches away from her as she climbs into the cart. All at once, she is convinced she knows exactly the kind of customer responsible for his dark bruises, and the realisation makes her stomach turn.

As soon as she's in the cart, the rider sets off, pedalling at a furious pace that seems quite at odds with his emaciated figure. He follows the old tarmac road north. Before long, the dilapidated houses fall away. The grey expanse of the River Nis stretches out to the left, swollen to the highest part of its banks, and the road becomes uneven, pitted and cracked. When the sky blackens and fat raindrops begin to drum thunderously down on the roof of the cart, the rider merely whips out an umbrella that was strapped to the bicycle frame, opens it single-handed and keeps going at breakneck speed, swerving dangerously around the large potholes that appear here and there in the tarmac. Whenever he does, the cart rocks dangerously on its chassis, threatening to send Jac flying. Groaning, she closes her eyes and pinches the bridge of her nose. The sway of the cart is making her lightheaded and she can feel the bile rising at the back of her throat. Suddenly, she is uncomfortably warm despite the rain, and she's not sure if she should attribute it to the motion sickness or if she is experiencing another hot flush. Alix started getting them a couple of years back, but they are still relatively new to Jac. Whatever the cause, there's little she can do but wait it out.

Jac only opens her eyes again when the rickshaw finally comes to an abrupt halt.

"We're here."

She peers around. They seem to have reached the very edge of the land. A vast body of water stretches out before them, dark and turbulent in the rain. This inlet is the start of the North Sea. For a moment she struggles to dredge up the name and then she has it: An Cuan Moireach. This close, the strong smell of brine is undercut with something danker – the rotting stench of decomposing marine life: seaweed, molluscs, fish bloated with plastic. Peering back around the headland, she sees the ruin of a collapsed bridge half-submerged in the middle where the road has buckled. A few limp suspension cables hang from a listing tower. It is in the process of being reclaimed by the sea, its rusting metal skeleton furred over with algae and red dulse, both strains well-adapted to the acidity of the water.

She snatches her attention back inland to where a tall chain-link fence lines the road; coils of barbed wire run along the top. Laminated signs rendered in bold colours and stark fonts have been attached to the fence at regular intervals. Jac casts her eyes across them. *Danger: Unauthorised personnel keep out. Caution: Radiation controlled area.* The same signs are displayed in Gaelic nearby. They all bear an identical symbol, a black trefoil with a single circle in the middle and three thick blades radiating out from it.

A broad-shouldered guard stands sentry by the gate and eyes the rickshaw with undisguised suspicion from beneath his red beret. Across his body, he holds an automatic rifle, the muzzle pointed down at the ground, a few clips of ammo visible at his belt. There is no sign to say that this is the Borlaug Testing Facility, but there can be no doubt that they have arrived.

A little shaky after the rough ride, Jac leans forward to pay the rider.

"Thank you," she says, giving him a generous tip as though that will in some way compensate him for the suffering she suspects he has endured at the hands of the testing facility workers. *Her* staff.

The rider takes the money with a dull grunt. Then Jac steps down from the cart and into the rain, setting her face into a determined frown as she approaches the armed guard.

08

The fruit sits heavy in Miri's stomach. As a wave of nausea crashes over her, she runs to the bathroom, where she falls to her knees on the tiled floor. Reaching up to the sink, she turns the tap in the hope that the running water will conceal the tell-tale sounds of dry-heaving if Alix comes to listen at the door. Then she leans over the toilet bowl. It smells faintly of bleach. Her mouth slickens at once with saliva, and the vomit comes in the next moment; two mouthfuls of curdled yoghurt spatter against the white porcelain. But though the nausea does not abate, that is all she can manage. She retches heartily and digs her fists into her stomach, desperate to get every last morsel out of her system. Nothing more comes. Stopping just short of sticking her fingers into her throat, she lies on her side, curled on the hard tiles around the base of the toilet, and waits for the sensation to pass. She ignores Alix when she comes knocking on the door, glad that she had the foresight to turn the lock.

At last, the intense discomfort begins to subside. When it does, she slowly pushes herself to her feet and then peels the clothes away from her body before going to stand in the shower. She jabs the on button with her thumb and gasps when the hot water crashes down over her head and shoulders. She notes with detached interest how the water trickling from her and into the shower tray is black and scummy with dirt; she grabs a bar of soap from the hanging wire rack and works it into a foam, lathering it methodically over her body. Then she massages the soap into her scalp, working her fingers through her wet, knotted hair. Some of the red dye bleeds out onto her skin and into the shower, but it quickly rinses away. She turns the dials to increase the water pressure and temperature as high as they will go. Soon the entire bathroom is clouded with steam. It is the first time in months that she has felt truly warm.

When she finally shuts off the water, the pads of her fingers are puckered and the callouses on her palms have softened and turned white. The dead skin is beginning to peel away, exposing pink tissue beneath.

It occurs to her then that she doesn't have anything to dry herself with, but there is a small hand-towel by the sink. She takes it from its hook and pats away the droplets of water from her skin. Once she has pulled her greying underwear back on, ignoring the crust of dirt across the gusset, she does what she can to towel her hair dry, teasing out the tangles as best she can with her fingers. She wipes the mirror above the sink and frowns at her reflection. Her hair is still too wet to tell exactly how much of the dye washed out, but she thinks she looks a fraction better than before – distinctly cleaner if not entirely presentable.

As soon as she has said this to herself, she gives an involuntary grimace. *Presentable.* Appearing presentable was always something Jac cared about. Miri can't think how many times she must have heard the same old lecture; *we all have to put our best foot forward if we want to give a good impression of our family for the Borlaug donors.*

Not presentable, then, she thinks. *Just more myself.*

She frowns again. That's not right either. She's still not sure what that would look like. But even if she can't find the words to explain the alteration, there's an undeniable comfort to being clean and warm. Once she took both those things for granted, but that feels like a long time ago now.

As she stares into the mirror, her mouth gapes into a wide yawn, revealing yellowed teeth and pale gums. The effort of her ablutions has sapped her energy. Bare skin prickling as she steps out of the steam and into the sudden cold of the corridor, she shuffles automatically back towards her old bedroom, carrying her clothes in her arms. The white rat, she sees, is still curled up asleep on the bedside table, the fleshy ear arching along its back rising and falling with each breath. Hugging her bundled clothes to her chest, she sits on the mattress and stares at the rat for a long minute before finally dropping the clothes to the floor in a careless heap and climbing beneath the bed covers. She has her appointment with the Celt to keep, but given that it is scheduled for the evening, there's time enough yet. She can afford to rest for an hour or two.

The last thing she's aware of as her eyes close is Alix, staring in at her from the door, brows knitted together in concern. Miri tries to protest as her mother slips onto the end of her bed and presses a warm hand along her face, but it's no good. Before she can say anything, she slides uneasily into sleep.

09

A flash of her Borlaug ID and a stern expression is enough to get by the armed guard at the facility gate. It's a long walk from the perimeter, but when the guard offers to call up to the main office and have a solar buggy sent down for her, she refuses. Fortunately, the rain is easing off, and a strong wind is gusting the clouds away across the grey sky as abruptly as it brought them in from the sea. The wide stretch of land that circles the facility has been seeded with a short, thick grass that Jac does not immediately recognise. Seeing how quickly the earth dries out, she figures that it is some hybrid she hasn't come across before, no doubt specifically designed to draw up standing water and protect against flooding.

At one time, she remembers, several laboratories competed to produce a variety of plant strains with such abilities, but after the Wash in East Anglia finally broke and the fens were lost, their funding was cut. Perhaps, she thinks, one of the labs found an alternative backer and managed to release a successful strain after all. Or perhaps the local grass has naturally evolved to be flood-hardy. Without closer examination, it's impossible to tell.

The facility itself is a massive complex of concrete and reinforced glass. The levels of the building are set back from one another, layered like the steps of a Mayan pyramid. Although broad glass panels run along the front of every tier, the complex looms so large and dark against the landscape that it gives the impression of there being no way for natural light to enter the building. The design was inspired by the Hanging Gardens of Babylon: "An old, ecological vision for a new, greener future", that was the line in the architectural pitch. There were plans to plant the outer walls with ivy and clematis but no one realised until too late that the concrete had been treated in such a way that rendered the stone impermeable to plant life. Knowing this makes the complex look strangely bare, like a cable stripped of its insulation or a skull with the scalp ripped back.

When, at last, she reaches the entrance, Jac is shown into a private office by an apologetic secretary and told that the Facility Manager will be with her shortly.

The office is half the size of Jac's own in London and it has no windows. But it is a neat and tidy space, one wall lined with shelves of lever-arch files, each one pristine and carefully labelled. As she waits for the Facility Manager, Jac's eye is caught by a flash of movement. There is a monitor on the far wall, showing a live drone feed from the hypernovaforest in Greenland. Even from the distant aerial view shown on the screen, the trees appear healthy, their gracefully drooping branches thick with bristling silver leaves.

As if in accordance with some unheard command, the drone descends for a closer look. It swoops down into the canopy and hovers at branch level to focus on a flash of movement in the undergrowth. A wide-hipped bipedal robot with no head and spring-coil feet bounds through the detritus of fallen leaves up to the base of the nearest willow. Extending two claw-like hands, it steadies itself against the tree trunk. The front of its carbon-fibre carapace hinges open, revealing a narrow metal shaft that abruptly fires into the bark of the tree like a cap from a pop-gun. Almost immediately, the robot yanks the shaft out from where it is buried and stows it away. As its carapace hinges shut, the camera catches a flash of the brand emblazoned across the front: BORLAUG. The drone, seemingly satisfied with what it has observed, drifts back up through the foliage. Then the feed cuts. It is a moment before Jac realises that the Facility Manager – an Alban woman in her seventies – has finally arrived. She's holding a remote control in one hand, thumb pressed over the off button.

"Good morning, Director," she says, with a curt nod that makes her short silver hair fall across her face. She is chalk white, her expression severe. Although Jac has only met her in person a handful of times, they have been in constant communication for so long that she feels she knows the woman well. And she can tell at once that something is troubling her.

"What is it?" Jac asks. "What's happened?"

The Facility Manager takes a deep breath and runs a hand through her silver hair. "There's been an incident," she says, not quite meeting Jac's gaze. "One of the staff broke into the nuclear annexe. He... he wasn't wearing a hazmat suit."

Jac stiffens. "Hadn't he been vetted?"

"What? Yes, of course. His record was clean."

"You're sure about that, are you?" Jac crosses her arms over her chest. "He didn't show any tendencies towards anti-nuclear principles or have any connections with rival labs?"

"No. As I say, his record was clean. I don't see–"

"And yet he intentionally exposed himself to fatal levels of radiation?" Jac leans forward, placing her hands on the Facility Manager's desk. "Something quite in keeping, I think, with the general manner of anti-nuclear protests."

A sudden look of comprehension crosses the Facility Manager's face. "Oh, it wasn't anything like that. To tell you the truth, I don't think he had any idea what he was doing. The man was blind drunk. Grieving, apparently. Word amongst the staff is that his parent died recently, and that he took the loss harder than expected. He seemed alright in the immediate aftermath, but then his behaviour became increasingly erratic, culminating in a few days ago when he turned up barely able to walk straight."

Jac raises an eyebrow.

"Or so I'm told," the Facility Manager adds quickly. "I wasn't there myself. The clean-up team certainly found crates of empties in his flat afterwards."

Jac thinks fleetingly of the bottle she left in her room at the boarding house. "Why didn't you send him home?"

"We were going to. At least, that was the plan. Only it didn't seem safe to send him back alone. We put him in one of the offices to sober up a bit while we found someone to accompany him. According to the reports, he can't have been unattended for more than three minutes. But... it was enough. Perhaps he drunkenly decided it was time to get to work, I don't know. He was assigned to work in the nuclear annexe that day, and he headed right to it. We sent people after him, of course, but they couldn't get suited up quickly enough. By the time we did get to him... he had opened one of the test capsules with his bare hands."

Jac winces. The idea of walking into the nuclear annexe unprotected is bad enough, but physically handling one of the core samples? It would be suicide, or thereabouts.

"It was a mess," continues the Facility Manager. "Severe burns to the skin, acute vomiting, diarrhoea. He passed out with a fever shortly after. We're keeping him in isolation for the time being. His condition is stable for now, but the latent phase won't last long. Given his level of exposure, we think he'll be dead within a week."

Pinching the bridge of her nose, Jac wonders briefly if that was what the man wanted all along. If, driven mad with despair and drink, he had settled upon the one course of action that would set him free. The idea offers little comfort. Whether it had been the man's intent or not, his actions are as good as sabotage.

The decision to plant the hypernovaforest out in Greenland was always one of the most contentious aspects of Project Salix. But it was the only viable space left. If it couldn't happen in Greenland, it couldn't happen at all. Like many others in the scientific community, Jac privately thinks that a marginally increased risk of radiation poisoning is a small price to pay for the survival of the entire human race, but the tide of public opinion is against her. The Borlaug has worked overtime to provide assurance that the planting site would only ever be operated remotely and that anyone handling the radioactive samples would be adequately shielded. If word gets out that a worker has suffered a fatal exposure, the entire project could be at risk.

"Talk to me about containment," Jac says. "How many people know what happened?"

"Everyone on the staff, I should imagine."

"They're under NDA. Does anyone outside the facility know?"

"I don't *think* so."

Jac stifles a *tsk* of annoyance. If she were in the Facility Manager's position, she would have made it her business to answer such questions precisely. "Does he have any family?"

"No, none."

"Good. So the chances are that no one will come asking difficult questions or seeking compensation. But we'll have to be on high alert." Jac takes a breath. "I need to make a call."

The Facility Manager looks on bemused while Jac takes out her phone and calls the Head of PR in London. She relates the news of what has happened and is quickly assured that, at the first rumour of radiation sickness, her PR department will do everything in their not-inconsiderable power to quash it.

Jac hangs up the phone and turns back to the Facility Manager. "There will have to be a formal report to the Board of Oversight, of course."

The Facility Manager gravely inclines her head.

"You may be suspended," Jac adds in an even tone.

"Suspended? I was hoping–"

"You will count yourself lucky to escape this with so small a punishment," says Jac sternly. "An inebriated worker was permitted onto the premises, a man who will now likely die as a result. I don't care where you were when it happened; you run this facility, you're responsible for what happens here. Make no mistake, I would fire you if doing so wouldn't draw more attention to the incident."

The Facility Manager's eyes widen at that, but Jac ignores her. "Now, unless you have any other cases of gross negligence to share, I should like to press on with my inspection."

The Facility Manager shakes her head, struggling to recover herself. "Wh– What do you want to see first?"

"The nuclear annexe," Jac replies bluntly, aware that the Facility Manager will think she wants to check the scene of the incident. The woman blanches a little, but is in no position to protest, and so nods nervously. She presses a button on the intercom and speaks clearly into the speaker, summoning the staff member – a hazardous specimens archivist – who has been assigned to accompany Jac for the day. A few minutes later, he arrives at the office; a man about Jac's age. He is of ancient Alban-Pakistani stock, with dark brown skin, fine black hair, and a heavy scowl etched onto his face. Jac recognises him at once and suppresses a groan. She should have known.

"Jac, this is–"

"We've met," Jac quickly interjects.

"That we have," says the Archivist with a joyless smile. "You could say Professor Boltanski is the reason I'm here."

"Good to see you again," Jac lies. She extends her hand to the Archivist, who takes it reluctantly, his face contorted into an expression of barely concealed loathing. It is a look that reminds her uncannily of Miri.

10

It's gone ten by the time Miri wakes and, when she does, her head is strangely clear. The effects of the tranquiliser, she supposes, must have finally worn off. But it's more than that. Her thoughts, which for so long have been fractured and scattered, now seem to bear a calm order. They are precise. Focused. For a moment, she is aware of every muscle and sinew of her body beneath the sheets. It is damaged and thin, but it is hers; for once she is anchored in her own physicality rather than simply seeking to escape it. It gives her a sense of deep calm. She doesn't feel at all like the trembling girl who aimed a heavy ceramic dish at her mother's head.

On the bedside table, the white rat stirs, whiskers twitching. Then with a chirrup of greeting, it clutches its tail between its front claws and starts to lick away at the barely discernible patina of dirt.

"Hello to you, too," she says.

Getting up, she ignores her dirty clothes where they lie sprawled across the floor and goes to the cupboard. She digs out an old steel-blue jumper that once fit snugly and now hangs loose from her body and a pair of jeans that she has to cinch at the waist with a woven belt to stop them from sliding down over her bony hips. Picking up the rat and lifting it to sit on her shoulder, she goes to find her mother and apologise.

Leaning against the kitchen counter, Alix gives her a tight smile. "Let's say no more about it, shall we?" Then she casts an appraising eye over Miri's appearance, taking in the clean skin, the fresh clothes.

"You seem in better spirits."

Miri shrugs. "I guess. The sleep must have helped."

Silence falls. It should be uncomfortable, the feeling of not knowing what to say to her own mother, but with her newfound sense of calm Miri finds that it doesn't bother her.

"Sit down," says Alix. "Let me brush your hair."

It's a peace offering of sorts, a gesture towards moving past what happened that morning. Miri doesn't have it in her to refuse.

Soon they are in the living room, Alix on the sofa and Miri at her feet, her bony tailbone protected from the hard floorboards by a satin-covered cushion, her back pressed against her mother's shins. Alix, glasses perched on the end of her nose, is gently teasing a comb through Miri's hair. There's something about it that Miri finds intensely comforting, though she isn't sure whether it's due to the intimate touch of her mother's hands, or simply because it reminds her of the times when she was a little girl and they would sit like this for hours together: chatting, laughing. Happy.

"I can plait it for you if you like," says Alix, when she finishes combing.

Miri nods, reluctant to move away. She feels a soft tugging at the roots from where Alix is running her hands through her hair, deftly dividing it into sections to be laced and woven together.

For the first time, it occurs to her that Alix is home in the middle of a working day. She has been so out of it since she arrived that she hadn't considered it before now, but it is distinctly unusual. The Alix she remembers, the Chief Consultant Paediatrician at Great Ormond Street, had a zealous commitment to her patients and often worked long, irregular hours.

"How come you're not at the hospital?" Miri asks.

For a moment, Alix falls quiet. Then: "I retired."

"When?"

"About a year and a half ago, maybe a bit longer."

"Oh." Miri doesn't know what else to say. She had never thought of Alix as the type to retire early. As much as she wants to ask what happened, Alix's silence gives Miri the distinct impression that she doesn't want to talk about it.

The white rat is crawling over Miri's lap, occasionally racing down a leg of her jeans to make an exploratory circuit of the room but always returning, the ear quivering on its back as it runs. When the rat climbs up Miri's jumper to sit on her shoulder and nose at a loose strand of hair, she feels Alix shudder. Wordlessly, Miri takes the rat and keeps it secure in her hands, running a soothing palm along its back.

"I found it yesterday," she says, in a bid to shore up the shaky peace that lies between them. "Must be from a lab. Maybe there was a break-in? I mean… look at it. It hardly got free by itself. Someone must have decided to release it into the wild."

"It shouldn't be hard to work out which lab it's from," says Alix after a moment. "We could call your mother and ask. She'll know exactly where this kind of experiment is being run."

Miri considers this, repressing the urge to flatly refuse anything that requires Jac's assistance. "Then what?" she asks.

"You could return it."

"Why would I do that?"

"Well," says Alix, "for one thing, it's clearly a valuable piece of research. Just think of all the resources that went into making that rat, all of which will have been completely wasted if the thing is never returned and the experiment never completed. For another, you'll have a hard time finding somewhere safe to release it. The creature won't last long on its own."

"But it's not on its own. Not now, anyway."

Alix sighs. "What do you know about looking after a rat? And one like that probably requires special care. Honestly,

Miri, you might be doing more harm than good keeping hold of it."

This catches Miri short. She hadn't thought of that. The idea of being locked up and experimented on is so instinctively wrong that she didn't stop to question whether or not it might actually be better for the rat. Alix is right. Depending on what's been done to it, the creature might need specific food or medication to survive – though for now it seems healthy enough, except for the monstrous ear growing from its back.

All the same, the thought of giving up the rat makes her feel sick to her stomach. Its trust in her – however undeserved – seems so complete that she can't help but think returning it to a laboratory would be a savage betrayal, a gross misuse of the physical power she has over the small creature. She could be the first human – the first living thing – to ever touch it. Not prod at it with a syringe or rubber-gloved hand, but to actually touch it with care and affection. Maybe the rat thinks Miri is its mother. She doesn't voice any of this to Alix. Instead, she says only, "I'll think about it."

Suddenly, the rat squirms free of her hold and races along Miri's leg. She grabs it easily, circling her fingers around its body. The motion reminds her eerily of the curling filterweed in the cell and how effortlessly it trapped the aphid. Then an idea occurs to Miri and she twists round at the hips to address her mother directly. "You know, you could always plant some filterweed on the terrace."

Alix frowns as the strip of hair she'd been holding slips from her fingers. "Keep still, won't you?" She gently nudges Miri to turn back around and then resumes her work on the half-completed braid. "And why would I want to plant filterweed on my lovely terrace?"

"To help protect your plants from the dragonflies," Miri says, or is about to say, thinking to tell Alix about the filterweed she saw in the cell, how there must be a new carnivorous variant. But she catches herself just in time. Bringing up her arrest is the last thing either of them need right now, not if she doesn't want to threaten what little peace has started to grow between them. "Never mind," she mutters.

Alix is barely paying attention. With a few swift turns of her wrists, she announces that she is done. Shifting the rat so she can hold it in one hand, Miri raises the other to lightly pat the back of her head, tracing the tight plait with her fingers. She turns automatically where she sits so her mother can admire the effects of her handiwork from the front. With a soft smile, Alix reaches forward to tuck a loose strand of hair behind Miri's ear.

"I've been so worried about you," Alix says, her voice barely louder than a whisper.

"I know." There isn't anything else to say. Even now, seeing so clearly the anguish that it has caused her mother, Miri cannot regret leaving home.

Pulling away from Alix, she sets the rat down to run free across the floorboards. Then she pulls the cushion out from beneath her and places it on the sofa. Her legs and back ache after sitting still for so long, and she stands so that she can twist and turn on the spot, easing out the stiffness.

"What were you doing at the shrine yesterday?"

The question is sudden but not altogether unexpected. Up until now, Miri's hardly been in a state to talk about anything serious. While it's only natural that Alix wants to know, Miri's not sure she can explain it – not without hurting her.

"There was an Offset," she says simply. "I went to watch."

Hearing that, Alix falls still for a moment and Miri knows why. When she was growing up, her mothers refused to take her to a single Offset, not even to those of family friends. They argued that such occasions were not to be taken lightly nor to be enjoyed as a form of mass entertainment. While Miri doesn't disagree with this, the cruel vindictive voice in her head tells her another story: that her mothers didn't want her to watch an execution because it would mean ceding control. It would allow her to experience the Offset entirely for herself, without the filter of their own explanations and rationale.

Whatever the truth of the matter, Miri has seen enough executions by now to make up her own mind. Generally, she thinks, they are to be avoided – although this is more on account of her reluctance to find herself among a crowd rather than any particular squeamishness on her part. What drew her to the Offset yesterday wasn't a ghoulish desire for entertainment, but something deeper: an urgent need to test herself, now that her own Offset is looming. Yesterday she watched a woman die in great pain, all the while imagining Jac in her place. It dispelled any lingering doubts she might have about whether her decision is the right one.

"What happened?" asks Alix, pulling her glasses from her face and letting them hang on the chain, side-stepping the argument about whether Miri should have been there in the first place.

Miri thinks of the woman bursting into flames. "Something went wrong. I don't know what. A malfunction of some kind."

"I heard," says Alix.

"But otherwise it was pretty standard. A mother-father family. The mother was Offset."

"It's always the way. The mother takes the punishment, even though the crime is not of her making alone."

Miri's ears prick up at that. It's the first time that she's ever heard Alix refer to procreation as a crime. Although Alix has always claimed that she and Jac understood exactly the consequences of what they were doing when they had Miri, she's only ever spoken of the Offset as a necessary sacrifice made on behalf of the child rather than as a punishment for the sins of the parents.

Before Miri can say something to this effect, Alix interrupts her thoughts: "What have you been doing all this time, Miri? Where have you been?"

She looks at her mother: Alix's face is lined with worry and her eyes shine with tears. Miri feels something inside her cave. She doesn't want to add to Alix's pain. But the life she has forged for herself in the last two years is hers alone. She isn't ready to share it with anyone else. Not yet.

"I've... been a world away from here," she says eventually. "That's all."

"Hmm. Not so far away," says Alix.

Miri is about to ask what she means by that, but Alix gets up from the sofa and disappears into the hall. When she returns, she's clutching a handful of postcards. Miri recognises them immediately – they're hers. The pile contains every postcard she sent home in the last two years.

Alix peels the uppermost card off the stack. It bears an image of the sunken wharf at Lake Canary, photographed at dusk from the north of the city, looking out towards the dark of the Greenwich Enclave beyond. On the back, Miri knows, will be a brief message pointedly addressed to Alix alone that explains – in the vaguest terms possible – that she is safe and well.

"Why were you in hospital?" asks Alix, scanning the back of the card.

Miri groans silently. She should never have mentioned that when she wrote the postcard. "I had pneumonia," she admits. "It was nothing. I'm fine now."

"I knew you weren't looking after yourself," says Alix. "You're not eating properly, you're clearly anaemic... If you're going to live like this can't you at least think of your health? For *my* sake?"

"I'm sorry, Mum," says Miri weakly. "I'm sorry for everything."

They both know this isn't strictly true. But even so, a part of her can't help but think: *I could deal with this. I could deal with her. If it was only her. If it was just Alix at home, maybe I never would have left.*

"At least you're here now," says Alix, softening once more. "But we do need to talk."

Miri slumps back against the sofa cushion. She supposes it was a matter of time before Alix drew her into discussing the upcoming Offset again. It looms large between them, impossible to ignore.

"Please, Miri. Just hear me out, won't you? It can't hurt to listen." When Miri doesn't stop her, she takes her chance and presses on. "This is about more than just our family. Your mother, she… I know you've been told this before, but I'm not sure if you believe it. So please, Miri, if there's any doubt in your mind… Project Salix is the only thing standing between us and extinction. Without your mother, there *is* no Project Salix, whatever the Borlaug might like to think. It's as simple as that."

Miri shrugs like it doesn't matter in the slightest. She's heard this all before. "I don't care. This is my decision to make and no one else's. I'm not going to nominate you. *You* aren't the reason why I left. *She* is."

"You've really made up your mind, then?"

"Yes."

Alix opens her mouth and then closes it again. "Perhaps one day when you have your own child, you'll understand the sacrifices your mother has made for you. That we both have. What?" she adds. "Why are you looking at me like that?"

Miri shakes her head in quiet disbelief. She is never going to have a child; she is never going to do to another living being what her parents have done to her. They knowingly condemned her to life on a dying planet in full knowledge of what that would mean and the hardships she would have to face.

She wishes her mother could understand that, but it seems entirely beyond her. Sometimes the gap between them is so vast that Miri struggles to see how it will ever be bridged.

11

At first, Jac considers insisting some other staff member be found, but she is keenly aware of the seconds slipping by. Already an hour has passed since she arrived at the testing facility, and she doesn't have much time.

"Did you volunteer for this?" she asks quietly as she follows the Archivist from the Facility Manager's office.

"Think I was that desperate for a chance to see *the woman who saved the world*? Don't flatter yourself," he says with disdain. "I was the only one who could be spared."

Jac is not entirely sure she believes this. If she knows anything about the Archivist, it's that he enjoys holding a grudge and wouldn't miss the opportunity to make her life difficult. As far as she knows, he has never forgiven her for taking the directorship that should – in his mind anyway – irrefutably and undeniably have been his. Jac wonders how the Inbhir Nis team can bear to tolerate him; she had certainly detested every moment of working with him in London before she had him relocated.

As if to prove her point, he begins channelling his palpable resentment into sneering at his fellow members of staff who, as Jac passes them, stop what they're doing to nudge one another and point excitedly in her direction. Jac smiles and doles out a few cordial greetings.

"Fascinating paper on the abiotic stress adaptation of large-subunit ribosomal proteins," she says to one woman whom she recognises. "Well done indeed. Especially with the optimisation of the Yonath-Ramakrishnan protocol for crystallisation."

"Surprised it made it through peer review with those R-free factors," says the Archivist dismissively.

Jac ignores him, spotting another familiar face. "And you! Excellent work on the new electrospray nozzle," she says.

When the Archivist opens his mouth to voice another criticism, Jac shoots him a warning look and he thankfully keeps it to himself. Not for the first time does she regret that she cannot have the man fired. At least, not without major reprisals. While she would normally hate to lose so skilled a worker, in his case it would almost certainly be worth it. But the Archivist has powerful connections in this neck of the woods, and Alba's political class wouldn't take the dismissal of one of their more prominent scientists lightly.

Still, observing the dark glances that are cast in his direction, Jac wonders whether firing him wouldn't be worth the risk. Then again, after the mess with the liquid nitrogen supply contract...

Her expression sours. It's the last thing she wants to be thinking about. Awarding the contract to a supplier in the Amber Valley was a mistake, one that had gone down badly with the locals in Inbhir Nis. There were riots outside the facility for weeks. Jac held firm, but the Board forced her hand in the end. Reluctantly, she granted the contract to an Alban-based company instead – causing a headache and a small fortune in contractual breakage fees – but the damage was already done, and the Albans still regard her Institute with suspicion. The prospect of provoking further hostilities doesn't bear contemplating.

Crossing the secure computing terminal, Jac glimpses large windows that overlook an expanse of the steel-grey North Sea. The vastness of it captivates her and she stops briefly to peer out.

"Looking for the NAX?" asks the Archivist, his lip curling.

"Hardly," she says. The North Atlantic Xylem is a pneumatic cargo pipe that stretches from Alba to Greenland and lies many miles below the sea's surface. It is all that remains of a vast network that once carried passengers and freight across the world. That was before the Bogotá Accord, of course. Even after that, this one line of the NAX continued to operate for many years – bringing fuel from the oil fields of Greenland – until it was finally mothballed. Reinstating its use for Project Salix had been something of an early triumph for the Borlaug.

Once used to bring fuel from the oil fields of Greenland, its sole purpose now is to ferry samples between the Inbhir Nis facility and the final station in Greenland. The cargo pods travel at incredible speeds, turning a distance of nearly a thousand miles into a journey that takes no more than a few hours. It's a remarkable feat of old-world engineering, though one that is not, of course, visible from above the sea's surface. There is a command centre, she knows, buried somewhere deep below the facility at the bottom of an eighty-metre mineshaft. As much as she'd like to see it again, it will not feature in her inspection today.

Once they have crossed the length of the terminal, the Archivist leads her through a maze of corridors until they come to the airlock in the outer wall of the annexe. The door appears to be solid steel and is set into a concrete recess. Either side of it are signs not dissimilar to the ones Jac saw at the facility perimeter attached to the chain-link fence, the black-and-yellow trefoil glaring sternly at them from the grey wall. Above the door, a green light tells them it's safe to enter.

"Were you here the day of the incident?" she asks, her need for information outweighing her desire to remain silent.

The Archivist scans his ID card on the reader beside the door. "When that idiot got drunk and broke in? No."

"Do you know him?"

"A little."

There's a metallic clunk and then the door slides open, rising up into the wall like a shutter. The Archivist steps over the threshold and Jac follows suit. Now they are in a narrow chamber barely larger than a cupboard. There is a steel door ahead of them that, save for the warning red of the LEDs that run the length of its sides, is identical to the one behind.

"You don't seem very upset."

The Archivist shrugs. "Neither do you."

"He's not one of my colleagues."

"Like I say, I only knew him a little. He *is* one of your employees, though. Some might say you have a duty of care. Not that you seem remotely concerned by that. Then again, I suppose I shouldn't be surprised."

"If you've got something to say–"

"What, me? I wouldn't dream of criticising the great Jac Boltanski. Just look where it got me the last time." He presses a button and the door behind them slowly descends. Only when it is firmly shut do the LEDs blink and change to green. "I'm still waiting for an apology," he says.

"For *what*, exactly? I acted as I saw fit given the circumstances. Anyone would have done the same in my position, even you."

He snorts. "Forgive me, but I've never been so threatened by the competition that I felt the need to have them relegated to the back of beyond."

The idea that he counts himself as her competition is laughable, or would be if it was the first time she had heard this claim. He is not the only one who thinks he could do her job, despite being supremely unqualified to do so.

"That's not what happened and you know it. HR had more complaints about you than the rest of the staff put together. It was starting to cause serious problems. That's why I had you moved here," she says. It's not a lie, not exactly, but it's not the entire truth either. "Besides, I thought you'd be glad," she continues. "You always were going on about how much you missed life in Alba. And I can completely understand. It is beautiful up here. The air–"

"That's not going to work on me, Boltanski," he says, pressing a second button that makes the door ahead open, rising in just the same way as the first. "I know what you really think about us Albans. *We get in the way*. That's why you didn't want me down in London. Scared the powers-that-be would see my worth." He steps out of the airlock into the cleanroom beyond. A low bench runs along one wall and, above it, a row of empty hooks. There are more hooks on the opposite wall, and from these hang several hazmat suits, lurid and lime-coloured.

"Do I need to remind you I *am* the powers-that-be?" says Jac. "If you're not up to the job, I'll get the Facility Manager to assign me someone else."

"If you're too intimidated to deal with having me as your chaperone, that's your call."

"Don't be ridiculous."

"Well, then." The Archivist picks out two rolled-up coveralls from a tray and thrusts one at Jac. It is pastel green with elasticated wrists. "Put this on."

She takes the coverall and slings her bag onto the bench. Knowing he will expect her to turn around for modesty's sake, she does exactly the opposite. She kicks off her shoes, pulls off her jacket and starts unbuttoning her shirt, all the while holding his gaze levelly until he blushes and turns away, muttering something about putting on his own coveralls. It's a petty victory and one she cannot truly savour, not with the Archivist's accusation ringing in her ears.

He's wrong, she thinks. *I've always ensured my Alban staff are treated fairly, just like anyone else.* But she cannot ignore the nagging sense of doubt. Loath as she is to admit it, her Alban staff do get a raw deal. Despite relying so heavily upon the work done here in Inbhir Nis, the glory, celebrity and power of Project Salix sits firmly in London. And though she tries to reassure herself that the Alban team are well-compensated for the literally life-risking work they undertake handling the radioactive tree cores – their wages are certainly higher than the local average – she knows it's nothing compared with the perks of working in St Pancras.

With a rush of shame, she thinks of the various petitions her Alban team have presented her with over the years, demanding the Borlaug's headquarters be relocated to Inbhir Nis. She had turned them down every time, arguing that it wasn't possible, that it was too expensive. Now, she reluctantly acknowledges to herself that this was not entirely true. The patents revenue alone could have covered the cost of moving, and there are plenty of world-class researchers and potential collaborators in Alba to make such an action desirable. The fact of the matter was that she simply did not want to leave her comfortable life in London; she would never have traded it out for this, no matter how good the air was here. She really hadn't spared her Alban staff a second thought.

Jac turns to face the wall at last, pulling off her shirt and trousers, which she hangs from one of the empty hooks. Then she tugs the coveralls on over her black underwear, tucking the bottom of the legs into her woollen socks. As an afterthought, she takes off her gold wedding ring – the only item of jewellery she wears – and slips it into an inside pocket of her bag. Better to leave it here than have it confiscated for decontamination on the way out.

When she turns back, she catches the familiar look of loathing on the Archivist's face, the one that reminds her so much of Miri.

"What?"

"Nothing," he says quickly. Before she can challenge him further, he turns to the hazmat suits and picks one out. "This looks like the right size," he says. "Have you worn one of these before?"

"Not for a long time," she admits.

"You need to check all the components for tears and abrasions. Pay particular attention to the seams. Then I'll show you how to check the air level and the breathing apparatus."

The Archivist's assured, methodical approach is as familiar to Jac as his antagonism. For all his faults, he never was careless in his work. That is part of what made him so frustrating as a team member; knowing his potential and seeing it stifled time and again in the pursuit of his own personal vendettas. If he had kept his head down in London, he could have gone on to distinguish himself in his work. But he always was his own worst enemy.

"Alright," he says when they finish checking the suit. "Sit down and put your feet in."

She takes a seat on the bench and pulls her legs into the suit. When she stands, she lifts it up around her and holds it while he adjusts the internal belt that cinches in place around her waist to secure the suit.

"Let's set up your comms." He straps a throat mic around her neck and helps her secure the earpieces that are connected to the suit's radio. "The mic is voice-activated," he tells her. "Though if there's a failure and it stops working, you can hit the button on the front of your suit to activate the radio."

"Got it."

"Now take this." He hands her a facepiece, the clear lens cased in black plastic and foam with a bulky valve at the bottom that is attached to a rigid hose which loops around to the suit's air canister. "Slide it on... yes, just like that. Now, dip your head for me and I'll tighten the straps." She can feel the facepiece's harness against her skull, and the light pressure of it is strangely comforting.

"Look up," says the Archivist. He checks the fit of the nose cup around the lower half of her face. "And the air's coming through?"

She nods. Once he is satisfied that everything is working properly, he helps her with the top half of the suit. "Slide your arms into the sleeves. Good. Now I'm going to pull the zip up over your head." In the next moment, she is completely encased, her head and facepiece shielded by a capacious hood that has a wide, tinted visor set into its front. The silence is abrupt and all encompassing. She watches as the Archivist sets up his own throat mic and earpiece.

"Alright in there?" he asks, his voice tinny on her radio.

"All good."

He fiddles with the Velcro strip that covers the zip of her suit and runs Jac through a few more tests. Then he hands her a pair of heavy steel-capped boots and kneels to pull the cuff of the suit legs down over the boot shafts. Finally, he attaches a dosimeter badge to the front of the suit.

"If it beeps once, you have to leave immediately," he says over the radio. "You won't be allowed back into the annexe for somewhere between one week and two months, depending on post-incident analysis. Not that we'd expect another visit from you so soon, of course," he adds, lapsing back into his earlier tone of disdain. "I know how you like to leave these things for years at a time."

Jac's eyes narrow behind her visor. "What a shame," she says in mock pity. "You were doing so well there, for a moment. It was *almost* like talking to an adult."

"Look, this is no joking matter," he says, becoming solemn again. "If you're not going to take this seriously, I can refuse to accompany you into the annexe. Doesn't matter if you're the Director or not."

Furious with herself for rising to his bait, Jac resists the urge to snarl a retort. The Archivist – satisfied with her silence – continues.

"Now, if the dosimeter beeps twice, that means you'll have received your yearly dose of radiation."

Unbidden, an image flashes into her head of a white stone edifice and a set of cracked steps leading up to a glass-fronted booth. The Gallery. She blinks and the image disappears.

"And if it beeps three times?"

He looks stern. "There is no third beep."

They both know this is not quite true. Thinking of the worker who broke in and the amount of exposure he would have endured, Jac raises an eyebrow but says nothing.

Now it's the Archivist's turn to suit up, starting the laborious process again from the top. Following his instructions, Jac helps him run through the same set of tests and checks.

"I still don't understand why we need hazmat suits," he says. "We already use glove boxes and shielded containers in the annexe. Provided everyone followed protocol, we could use a much simpler scrub. It would be far cheaper."

The comment is meant as criticism, however obliquely. Jac seizes upon it, delighted to be able to prove there is at least one aspect of the hazmat suits she knows more about than the Archivist. "I'm afraid the project wouldn't have got off the ground without them. Given the Kvanefjeld disaster, we had to demonstrate that we would take every possible precaution when it came to handling radioactive material. In this case, it meant developing suits that could hypothetically protect you from even the radiation levels of the ARZ itself. For a short period, at least. Not that any human will ever get the chance to test it."

"Still seems like overkill to me. Here," he adds, handing a pair of heavy-duty silver gloves to Jac.

She pulls them on. "Is that everything?"

"That's everything. Come on. Let's get this over with."

She follows the Archivist into the airlock on the far side of the room and patiently watches the slow rise and fall of the shutter-like steel doors. At long last, they step out into a cavernous room, harshly lit by caged bulbs that glare white from the recessed ceiling far above. The concrete walls are lined with sturdy metal shelves, each one bearing a series of identical wooden crates. A row of long work benches runs down the centre of the room and Jac can see a door in the corner that she guesses leads through to the other chambers of the complex.

Once the door of the airlock has sealed shut behind them, the Archivist turns to her expectantly, with the unmistakable air of a scavenger trailing behind an injured beast. "What do you want to see first?"

Wishing that she were alone, or that anyone else had been selected as her escort, Jac thinks fleetingly of the minutes ticking by. The last train is in six hours. If she wants to get home as soon as possible – to see Miri again, to hold her wife in her arms and say goodbye – there's no time to lose. She'll just have to work with what she's got, even if the circumstances are less than ideal. She takes a deep breath that makes her microphone crackle. Then, in calm and level tones, she slowly explains to the Archivist what she needs him to do.

12

Miri stands in Jac's study, finger and thumb of her right hand braceleted around her left wrist. Hanging on one wall is the antique enamel sign that, long years hence, used to grace the front of the house: a red ring with a blue bar across its centre. Stamped upon it in thin white letters are the words "Warren Street Station", a name the house still bears although it is simply referred to as "the Warren".

Beneath the sign stands a glass case with a few books laid open at relevant pages, ones that chart the history of the house. Versions of her home stare back at Miri from beneath the glass – architectural plans, photographic plates, sketches – each one showing a different guise the house has worn throughout the ages: underground station, theatre, depot, overspill for the nearby hospital. That was long before it was turned into residential accommodation. From what Miri understands, it has been in her family ever since and, one day, it will be hers – a fact which Jac never missed an opportunity to remind her. "I inherited it from my parents, too. It's only fair," she would say, as though it were adequate compensation for Miri's existence, as though she had the right to hand down a piece of public history as easily as she might a set of cast-offs.

A colour photograph shows the Warren as it is now, a sprawling urban mansion well-deserving of its familiar name. Four floors of industrial brick jut up above an imperious stone front that curves outward like a great domed belly. Its oversized double front door opens directly onto the street and is painted a deep, forest green. There's no escaping its vast scale: the Warren is far larger than any of the squats she's stayed in, and bigger even than the clinic on Peter Street where she will later meet the Celt. When Miri was younger, she had often been embarrassed by living somewhere so ostentatious. Now, looking at the pristine photograph, she supposes for the first time that there's a sort of brutal honesty about the place. It's not like the expansive, richly decorated houses of family friends that feign modesty behind the uniformity of neat terraced facades. At least the Warren embraces its own excess.

Miri drops into the chair behind the desk where a few moments before she set down the empty plastic tub that now holds the rat, a few holes pierced in the lid. It seems unkind, keeping it cooped up like that, but at least this way it won't be able to cause any damage to the house or get lost. She rifles absently through the desk drawers but there's not much to find: old textbooks, a few stray paperclips, a neat line of velvet boxes holding the medals for the various prizes and honours that Jac has been awarded over the course of her *illustrious* career.

In the bottom drawer, however, is an enticingly fat manila envelope. Miri lifts the unstuck flap and tips out the contents, causing a startling array of letters, cards and notes to spill out across the desk. From what she can see, no two are written in the same hand and some don't even appear to be written in English. The postmarks, where still intact, seem to come from all over the Federated Counties and even beyond: Baile Átha Cliath, Versailles, Den Haag, The Maghreb, each one as improbable and far-fetched to her as Atlantis.

Before she can look more closely, Alix appears in the door of the study, glasses dangling about her neck. "There you are."

"Everything alright?"

"Yes. I wanted to ask – have you decided what you're going to do?"

Miri's eyes narrow. "I already told you."

Alix shakes her head. "No, I mean, are you going to stay here? Until the Offset, that is?"

The directness of this question takes Miri off guard. She isn't used to having to account for herself, or having to plan more than one step ahead at a time. It takes her immediately back to the uncomfortable dependency of her adolescence.

"I don't know."

"Would you come to the Borlaug with me?" asks Alix.

This is so unexpected a proposition that Miri does not know immediately how to respond, but the quiet desperation on her mother's face is more than she can bear. "Please," Alix continues. "I want you to see it one last time before you make your decision."

"I told you. I've already made my decision."

"Do it for my sake then. I wouldn't ask if it wasn't important."

Miri presses her lips together in a tight scowl. She has no desire to return to the laboratory where Jac works. Besides, she's meeting the Celt at seven.

"I have somewhere to be, actually."

Alix says nothing for a moment and then, seeming to notice the letters strewn across the desk for the first time, comes to stand at Miri's shoulder. She lifts her glasses to her nose then reaches out and begins to sift through the pile. "From your mother's admirers," she says by way of explanation. "Back before cross-border communications collapsed. Look, here's one that might interest you." She picks out a letter written on thick cream card and hands it over. Miri catches sight of her own name in amongst the ornate calligraphy.

"It's from the Director of the Global Monitoring Division," Alix explains. Then, reading aloud: "Congratulations on the birth of your daughter, Miriam. I trust she will be a light to you and your wife in the years ahead. There can be no doubt that she will be the best of breeds."

Flinching at the implicit reference to the slogan of the elite, Miri turns to Alix. "I don't think much of your friends."

"No," says Alix, blinking rapidly. "No, I see that. Sorry, I wasn't thinking. That wasn't why I wanted to show you. It's just... we got hundreds of these, Miri. More than we could possibly keep. Everyone was so excited to welcome you to the world. It was a very special time."

"Yeah, but even so..." Miri trails off.

Alix is staring into the distance, a fond smile playing across her lips. "You were such a beautiful baby," she murmurs.

Miri's anger drains away as suddenly as it arose. Deflated, she drops the letter back onto the pile and stands, knocking the chair away as she does. The action startles Alix back into the present.

"OK. I'll come," Miri says.

For a moment Alix looks as though she doesn't understand. Then she reaches out a hand to grasp hers. "Thank you, Miri."

Miri smiles weakly and squeezes her mother's hand in return but her heart flutters uneasily. Despite Alix's best efforts, Miri knows that seeing the Borlaug will not change her mind. But perhaps it will be enough, for now, to go along with it. To let Alix believe it is possible, to give her this small piece of happiness.

13

"You want me to walk you through the handling process," says the Archivist flatly. Even behind the visor, there's no mistaking the suspicion in his eyes.

"That's right."

"Why?"

"Because I'm asking you to. It's my prerogative to run a spot check of any procedure I so wish. Or perhaps you're not familiar with how an inspection works?"

"Come on, Boltanski, I think we both know you didn't come all this way to run a few little spot checks. Isn't your Offset in a few days?"

"It's tomorrow," she says, her voice tight.

"And yet here you are instead of at home with your wife and child. Your show of dedication is certainly impressive. It must be nice, knowing that you won't be the one nominated."

So that's what he thinks. Well, he clearly doesn't know the first thing about Miri, and she's not about to enlighten him. "Kindly keep your opinions about me and my family to yourself," she says. "Frankly, it's none of your business. Not only that, but you are wilfully obstructing the work of a superior. If you do not do as you are told, I shall report your conduct to HR and they'll take it from there."

The Archivist is unmoved. "Yeah, I don't doubt it."

Jac says nothing, pressing her lips together into a tight line, waiting for him to back down. It's not like he has a choice.

Whatever his feelings about Jac, he knows all too well that she can make life difficult for him, even if she can't dismiss him. He has already suffered the indignity of one pay cut, something about which his friends in the scientific community weren't hugely sympathetic, given their lower Alban wages. Jac's stern expression is all that is needed to remind the Archivist of this fact, her silence puncturing his ballooning ego. She can almost see him deflate. And when he next speaks, his tone is more guarded than before.

"Did it occur to you that if you just tell me what you're looking for, I might be able to help you find it?" Then, before Jac can laugh in his face, he adds, "The sooner you find it, the sooner you're out of my hair. And I know this place far better than you do. I'm pretty good at my job, too, you know, despite what you may think."

Loath as she is to admit it, Jac knows he has a point. The Archivist is far more familiar with the workings of the annexe than she is. "Fine," she says at last. "We've been seeing elevated levels of oxidised lipids in the test cores from the trees. That's what I'm here to investigate."

The Archivist's brow furrows. "Is that all? From the look on your face, I thought it was something serious."

"This *is* serious."

"I don't see how. It's not like oxidation affects the total carbohydrate storage capacity of the tree tissue. And I thought that was the only metric that mattered."

Jac blinks. Much as she'd like to dismiss his words as merely obstreperous, they have the ring of genuine curiosity. And given what he knows, the Archivist's point is not unreasonable – even if it is one she has already discounted in the course of her personal investigation. "Oxidation can affect the overall lipid readouts in the test cores," she says. "That's why I'm concerned. Not to mention that it will mask variations in extra-xylemic gains as well. We were expecting to see a twenty-three percent increase in total aliphatic biomass by this point, but we're only at twenty-one percent."

The Archivist considers this. "That's negligible. A meaningless fluctuation. That small difference must be well within the predicted variance for the model," he says, referring to the bioclimatic simulation run by the Borlaug's supercomputer that assimilates various factors – biological data from the trees, atmospheric readouts, and so on – to more accurately forecast future results. It takes into account the numerous variations inherent in *any* biological system, and Jac can see why the Archivist would assume this difference in levels of oxidised lipids is one such variation.

"The thing is, it wasn't the only fluctuation," Jac continues, counting off the rest on the gloved fingers of one hand. "The phytosterol content is lower than predicted. The cumulative wet biomass is higher, lipid or otherwise. And before you ask," she adds, "*yes*, the model does account for these kinds of fluctuations. But I've checked the biochemical output from the sample cores against that for the trees in the control group in the London greenhouse. It's not good. The control trees produce more long-chain lignin than the Greenland trees."

"How much more?"

"Not a great deal," she admits. "But *consistently* more."

"It's probably just a seasonal variation."

"Yes, perhaps. Or perhaps the sample cores are being oxidated."

"But *how* exactly? There's still a major gap in this theory of yours."

"There's only one explanation I can think of," she says quietly.

It's a moment before he catches her meaning. When he does, their brief détente dissolves into bad will. She sees the muscles of his jaw spasm angrily beneath his visor. "So *that's* why you want a walkthrough of the handling procedure. You think we aren't adequately flushing the capsules with neutral gases and they're getting exposed to oxygen. You're accusing us of incompetence."

"That's not what I said."

Unconvinced, he splutters into the mic. "You didn't need to. Well, damn your walkthrough and your ridiculous theories! Everything is done by the book here."

"Tell that to your colleague with the severe radiation burns."

"That was different," he says with a frown. "And anyway, he's a Borders man by blood. What do you expect?"

Finally, Jac snaps. "Just do it, will you? It's a working theory and I need to rule it out. Prove me wrong, by all means. But we need to get to the bottom of it. If oxidation isn't to blame for the difference in long-chain lignin, then there could be some other problem. And if that's the case, the repercussions are serious. The trees might be strong enough now, but in the next five to ten years that difference will mean weaker timber and trees that don't withstand the weather. The entire project could fail."

The Archivist throws up his hands. "Fine. But you're wasting my time. And yours."

She can see his lips moving through the visor, but his muttering is so low that the mic doesn't pick it up, which is probably just as well. She watches as he takes a capsule from one of the containers and carries it to a glove box, a transparent cabinet with two heavy mitts attached to the front that allow a technician to reach inside without disturbing the carefully controlled environment within. It reminds Jac irresistibly of the closed incubators Alix once showed her in the neonatal unit at Great Ormond Street; each infant a fragile specimen. *Focus*, she thinks. *This is no time to get distracted.*

Unlike the incubators at the hospital, the glove box is completely sealed, an airlock on one side the only point of access. It replicates in miniature the airlocks that protect the nuclear annexe, and the Archivist performs a variant of the same halting ritual: open the first hatch, place the capsule in the airlock, close the hatch. He slips his already protected hands into the heavy mitts and opens the second hatch, the one that can only be accessed from within the glove box. He retrieves the capsule, pulls it into the main handling chamber and closes the second hatch once more. Only then is he ready to begin.

Contained within the glove box is a purpose-made tool that resembles a stout, two-pronged fork. The Archivist takes it up and fits it into a pair of barely noticeable notches on the side of the otherwise high-sheen capsule. With a gentle but firm push of the tool, the capsule splits into perfectly symmetrical halves, revealing its cargo – a test core from a Project Salix tree – ready for sample-taking.

The procedure is a difficult one: the mitts allow little room for hand movement, and the closure of the capsule for transfer and storage requires another degree of patience and dexterity. Jac moves closer, crouching awkwardly in her hazmat suit to get a better look. The Archivist works quickly and deftly. Once the test core is slotted back in, he balances the two halves of the capsule on an outstretched hand, with just the thumb and slight curvature of the mitt preventing the capsule and its contents from tumbling down onto the work surface of the box. At the same time, he uses his free hand to operate a small pistol-like implement with a trigger button on the top and a narrow, brass nozzle connected to a line that feeds in high-purity nitrogen from a gas cylinder outside the glove box.

As soon as the capsule halves fill with gas they have to be quickly closed, an action that requires a swift motion to rotate the halves from the upright position towards each other and bring them together. The halves connect with a dull click and Jac lets go of a breath she didn't realise she'd been holding. The Archivist has performed the elaborate routine flawlessly. He has done everything just as he was supposed to.

"There," he says hotly. "Happy now?"

Jac straightens up, back cracking in protest, and gives a non-committal grunt into the mic. Just because the Archivist can perform the procedure adeptly, doesn't mean his colleagues can. But certainly the theory of systematic worker error seems far less likely than before. Her relief is limited: she is no closer to explaining the elevated levels. In an automatic gesture, she goes to pinch the bridge of her nose as she thinks, only realising the futility of this when her gloved hand knocks against the visor of her hood.

"Let me inspect the cores."

"You won't see anything," says the Archivist. All the same, he deposits a few sample cores in the glove box airlock and then stands back as she dons the heavy mitts herself to have a look at the samples.

He's right, there are no visible signs of oxidation: the tree tissue is not discoloured and the pattern of the xylem and cambium is still clearly discernible. Of course, that kind of damage is unlikely to be visible to the naked eye. What she really needs is to examine the samples on a chemical level. "I want to test these in the mass spectrometer."

"To what end?"

"If the samples are being oxidated by some other means, the mass spec will prove it beyond doubt."

"I can tell you right now what the mass spec will show: nothing. The cores are fine."

Jac ignores this. "Are you going to help me or not?"

"If it will get rid of you faster, gladly."

To be analysed in the mass spectrometer, samples from the cores have to first be dissolved in organic solvents. Jac instructs the Archivist to prepare a dozen test tubes and slide them into the glove box through the airlock. Then she uses a scalpel to scrape a small piece of plant tissue from the surface of each core and drops a clutch of shavings into each test tube. It is fiddly work, made no easier by the watchful presence of the Archivist. Doing her best to ignore his resentful glare, she finishes preparing the samples and removes them from the side port of the glove box. Then she falters. The Archivist spots her problem at once and laughs.

"Don't know where you're going, do you?" he says. "Jesus Christ. It's this way."

He leads her across the hall to the mass-spectrometry room, where three large, grey cabinet units sit in see-through cases designed to protect them from any overspill radiation. Jac opens up the side portal of the nearest mass-spectrometer and places the twelve test tubes into the standardised holder. A robotic arm slides the tubes from the airlock into the main chamber, where the contents are vapourised for analysis. Jac stares hard at the machine while it runs, her hopes torn between the two possible outcomes. If the results prove the cores *are* somehow being oxidated, then they definitely have a problem but at least she'll be one step closer to solving it. If, on the other hand, the results show nothing untoward, then she'll know for sure that oxidation is not to blame for the read-out difference in long-chain lignin. The thought offers little comfort: if oxidation isn't the reason for the discrepancy, then it can only mean the trees aren't gaining enough biomass. And that wouldn't make sense at all – carbon levels are down, global ppm just what it should be. In that regard, the trees are performing exactly as expected.

The results, when they finally come, are displayed as a spectrum on a small computer screen to the left of the window; the tall, sharp peaks corresponding with varying atomic masses. Each specific chemical molecule produces its own unique pattern. It's like a fingerprint; an image of the exact chemical makeup of each tree sample.

"Well?" asks the Archivist as Jac checks the spectra against that of a pure oxidised phospholipid. But the fingerprint pattern that would be the proof of oxidation Jac is looking for is not there. She clicks her tongue in disappointment.

"See," says the Archivist, gleeful in his vindication. "None of the cores have been oxidated. There's no sign of it at all. You're losing your touch, Boltanski."

Jac ignores his taunt, lost in her own concerns. She knows she should be glad that the sample cores show no sign of having been oxidated, that their chemical makeup is just as it should be. There's no evidence at all, in fact, to confirm her concerns about the health of the Greenland trees. But worry sits heavily as ever in her heart.

14

Alix trails behind Miri down the length of Euston Road. She's struggling in the midday heat, constantly pulling at the neck of her linen blouse and stopping every so often to mop the sweat from her brow with a white handkerchief she keeps in her sleeve. At least they don't have far to go – the Borlaug is in the heart of the St Pancras complex. Miri is carrying the white rat in its plastic tub, holding it loosely against her hip. She has a vague idea that she'll be able to ask someone in the Borlaug to take the rat, but the truth is she's reluctant to leave it behind at the Warren.

One of the benefits of coming outside at such an hour is that the streets are practically deserted. Everyone else is safely inside, either at home or at work, no doubt laid out beneath their fans – assuming that the pigsuits haven't stripped out all the motors.

Later, Euston Road will become a lively thoroughfare as the Borlaug employees and the staff from the surrounding complex of laboratories walk or cycle home in the relative cool of the evening. For now, though, the road is all but silent. Miri and Alix keep to the shade of the pavement. The road stretches out ahead of them, the white tarmac scuffed and dirty with the marks of a thousand tyres belonging to bicycles and tricycles, hand cycles, recumbents and all manner of custom tandems. The surface glistens in places where, despite the protection of its reflective covering, the tarmac is beginning to melt in the heat.

After a few minutes they come to the Guildhall of Illuminators, an imposing structure of marble and granite. It is raised above a sunken courtyard on four monolithic piers so that, at the right angle, it appears to be floating. Having grown up so close to it, Miri knows the story of the building well. It once housed the sprawling Copyright Library – the largest of its kind, it was claimed, anywhere within the city or the Federated Counties. Although no expense was spared to equip it with the latest environmental defences – pumps and flood barriers along with foam hydrants and flame-retardant cladding – it didn't survive for long. The Activists broke in during the riots that raged in the weeks that followed the signing of the Bogotá Accord. The treaty introduced a raft of punitive, global restrictions. It was meant to save the planet from burning. Some felt it asked the top too little and the bottom too much; others said what was the point when the horse had already bolted. The discourse grew muddied and irate. In the end, nobody really knew what to think anymore, and the only thing left was violence.

In the midst of one of the many brutal clashes that followed, the library was breached and a fire started. Some say the Activists overpowered one of the pigsuits and, in the course of destroying it, accidentally set off a stray spark that quickly turned into a roaring blaze. Others say that a pigsuit shot a taser at a man whose clothes had been smeared with gasoline and he spontaneously burst into flame. Either way, everything was destroyed. The wildfire defences, geared towards combatting the threat of external flame, proved useless against the blaze. No one knows exactly how many books were lost in the conflagration, but the figure was certainly in the millions. When the fire finally died down, all that was left within the charred bones of the building was ash and blackened fragments of paper.

Were it not for the resurrection of the Guilds following London's descent into ruin, it may have remained as a dark scar on the landscape for evermore. But when the trade routes in and out of London – both virtual and physical – became treacherous and the automasons started to fail, there was a sudden and urgent need to, amongst other things, recover the lost art of making paper and books by hand. Accordingly, the Guild of Illuminators was founded, and its Guildhall constructed on the very site where so many books were once read and enjoyed. Part of the old edifice, soot-black and brittle, has been cased in sheet glass and incorporated into the Guildhall's reading room, preserved as a cautionary tale on the fragility of recorded knowledge for all those who toil within.

Pausing to catch her breath, Alix glances across at the Guildhall, her gaze wistful. "I always thought you'd be an illuminator, you know."

"What?" asks Miri, taken aback. "Why?"

"You loved to draw when you were little."

Miri frowns. "I don't remember–"

"And you were good, too," insists Alix. "That *thing* you painted on your wall. I can't say I care for what it represents, of course, but it was well done. You clearly have an eye. You would have been a fantastic illuminator, I know it."

Miri doesn't know what to say. Alix seems so certain, so confident in her understanding of who her daughter is, and the difference between that and what Miri knows to be true is jarring. What bothers her is not so much Alix's insistence upon her supposed artistic talents as her belief that Miri would ever join a Guild. Miri thought she had made her aversion to that path quite clear when she was still at home. Despite there being a hundred or more Guilds in London, Miri cannot bring herself to be interested in any. They are all of a kind, based on routine or manual services that were once automated but are now increasingly conducted by human operatives using more primitive technologies. At the Guild of Agrarians, they till the parched soil with a wooden plough, rear livestock and milk cattle by hand. At the Guild of Weavers, they spin wool and turn it into long bolts of coarse fabric with looms and shuttles. There are many more guild crafts besides: lens grinders, coopers, blacksmiths, and cooks, as well as lawyers, accountants, engineers and teachers.

"I don't think it would have been for me, Mum," she says at last.

"Shame. It would have been the making of you. But there's still time if you change your mind. Nothing can compete with the Guilds for career stability. They're the future."

Miri turns away. She's heard this argument before, about how important the Guilds are. Their purpose, she knows, is to relieve the burden on the city's stuttering automated systems. The target is to have over half of all processes in London made fully manual within the next ten years – a target that is wildly optimistic and unlikely to be met. As far as Miri is concerned, there isn't much point retraining the human populace to take over the automated tasks. All that industry – it's what choked the Earth in the first place. And it's easy enough for anyone to see that the land is still suffocating.

"I don't think I'm going to change my mind," she says quietly.

"You never know," says Alix, undefeated. "Perhaps you haven't found the right thing to catch your interest yet." Then, a little uncertainly: "There was *something*, as I recall…"

Miri prickles uncomfortably, suddenly realising what Alix is grasping for. "I wanted to go out to the Kernowyon mires," she says.

"That's it. It was just after you found out about the Drownings."

"Yes," says Miri, a vivid image flashing into her mind of the perfectly preserved infant bodies that had been unearthed in the peat, the skin hardened into shining leather.

"You were far too young. When your mother found out you'd been shown the news footage at school, she was furious. You had nightmares for weeks after that."

Miri nods, though what she remembers more is pleading with her mothers to be allowed to go and help, to join the aid groups that were setting out to help the desperate, isolated communities of Kernow, only to be told she was too young, that she would get upset, that there was nothing she could do. *"This is for the adults to take care of,"* Jac had said, her refusal final.

"But if it's aid work you're interested in–"

"Please, Mum," says Miri, cutting her off. "Do we have to talk about this?"

Alix frowns at her daughter. "You have your whole life in front of you, Miri. Sooner or later, you're going to have to decide what to do with it."

The Borlaug lies a stretch away beyond the Guildhall. It is housed in the old gothic-style palace of St Pancras. Although Miri visited it often as a child, it has been many years and she looks at it now through fresh eyes.

The building dazzles in the hot November sun, the bright orange bricks clashing with the cool ashcrete and white timber buildings that surround it. Beyond the gothic palace stands the world's largest scientific greenhouse, a massive complex of glass erected on the site of the old train shed. The effect is one of grandeur and opulence, which, she supposes, is only fitting. The Borlaug's monopoly on resources exceeds even that of the pigsuits.

Within its walls, the institute holds all manner of materials, tools and priceless equipment. Miri has, of course, been there before. She knows that nearly every room in the Borlaug is kitted out with expensive hardware: slick devices made from silicon and ceramic, brushed metal and glass. Without even taking into consideration the specialised lab equipment, the cost of all that technology – computers, phones, intercoms – could easily be enough to feed everyone in London for... how long? A week? A month? A year? Thinking about it makes her feel faintly ill.

Alix cuts across the lobby and goes to speak to the security guard behind the counter. Miri stays frozen on the spot. On the walk over, it felt like all of London was empty but for them. Now she's suddenly in the midst of a busy hive of activity as lab workers, technicians and couriers hurry in and out of the lobby. Her eyes follow them as they hurry about like swarming insects and her skin begins to crawl. But before the panic can build, Alix calls over and Miri clings to the sound of her name, following it through the clamour to safety.

"Come on," says Alix. "Special dispensation for the director's wife. We're being allowed in." She nods at the security guard who hits a button on the counter, causing one of the barriers to zip open. Alix hustles Miri through, away from the busy lobby and into the Borlaug.

It's like crossing the threshold into another time. The effect is so powerful that for a moment Miri quite forgets her intense dislike of the place. For she is not merely entering a resplendent bygone era but, less distantly, her own past, a time when she used to visit the Borlaug as a child, brimming with pride at her clever, powerful mother. Within as without, the building has been expertly preserved and is unlike anything else in London. Pink and white stone columns run along wallpapered walls of royal blue, vermillion, gold and mustard yellow. Intricate carvings adorn every niche and alcove; lewd gargoyles leer down at them and sit incongruously alongside delicate flowers and overflowing bowls of fruit. The decadent spoils of the past.

Alix stands beside her on the fleur-de-lis patterned carpet and together they gaze up at the ornate granite window recesses and the loud empty spaces left by paintings long since sold off, like so much of the public art during the regeneration years, to a handful of private collectors. Miri understands the building's place as a piece of history and the well-rehearsed arguments for its preservation. All the same, it is hard to reconcile it with the run-down conditions she's become familiar with in the last two years.

Yet, even as she flinches away from the splendour of the place, she finds an old fondness catching at her heart. She ran down these hallways as a girl and now a hundred ghostlike child-selves dance around her. There's the pillar with the worn-out notches that make perfect handholds for climbing, and there is the gleaming bannister she had so longed to slide down if only her mother and her courage would allow her. And there is the very place where, unsupervised for ten glorious minutes, she had dragged a red crayon all over the eggshell wallpaper. She knows it is the same place because, instead of scolding her, Jac simply dragged over the marble bust of a crumbling Angela Saini to hide the incriminating scrawl. That is the exact same bust, she is sure of it; she remembers its soft smile and arched eyebrows – a promise to keep their secret.

Alix gently squeezes her shoulder. "If it wasn't for your mother, none of this would be here."

This brings Miri crashing back to the present. She wants to tell Alix that she is well aware of what Jac has done and how important she is, but that it doesn't change anything. Her mind is made up. Before she can say anything, however, Alix beckons over a slim man in a smart suit who looks somehow familiar.

"Hi Miri," he says, sticking out a hand. "You probably don't remember me–"

Suddenly, a memory springs into Miri's mind. She is four or five, lying stretched out on her stomach on a carpet so densely piled it feels like an iron brush against the skin of her arms, which extend bare from the short sleeves of her t-shirt. In front of her is a sheet of paper and a few crayons. She is trying to draw a picture of something mythical – an ice bear, perhaps – and it keeps coming out wrong because every time she presses the tip of the crayon to the page, the paper crumples into the carpet. When she finally does manage to straighten it out and draw a line across the page, it takes on the texture of the carpet's rough pile. Frustrated, she grabs the paper and gets up to run through to the next room where she can hear her mother talking loudly on the phone. Before she can open the door, however, a pair of strong hands wrap around her stomach and gently pull her back before lifting her up into the air. The hands belong to a man who has a friendly face and who carries Miri with ease. When he asks her what's wrong, she tells him about the stupid carpet and the stupid paper and the stupid crayon, and he laughs and hoists her up onto his own desk. From somewhere, he magics up a clean sheet of paper and scoops up her crayons from the floor. When she starts her drawing again, the crayon glides over the flat page just like it should.

"I remember," says Miri, shifting her hold on the tub to shake the man's offered hand. "You used to watch me when Jac was too busy to do it herself."

Alix clicks her tongue at that but the man laughs. "One of the many perks of being your mother's personal assistant. It was always a treat when you came into the office. You were such a cute kid." As his eyes travel across the sores on Miri's thin, pale face, she can almost see him thinking: *what happened?*

As much as the unvoiced reproach grates on her, she doesn't hold it against him. She knows what she looks like. But, for the first time, Miri wonders exactly what her mothers have been telling their friends and colleagues these past two years she has been gone and how much this man actually knows. In her mind's eye, she sees Jac confessing that her own child has run away from her and she feels a vindictive stab of pleasure at the humiliation she paints on to her mother's imagined face. Then she glances at Alix and her cheeks burn with shame.

15

"What's the next logical step in lipid oxidation analysis?"

The Archivist groans. "Surely you've seen enough now? There's nothing to find. And shouldn't you be getting home?"

"I'm not finished. So come on, what's next? What haven't we done?"

"We haven't normalised the mass-spec output with the total absorbed carbon data," he says, begrudgingly.

"Right. And to do that, we're going to need to get the statistical parameters of the biomass. Let's start with the seasonal growth rings. Where's the UVD?"

He sighs and gestures behind him. "Back through here."

The UVD, or ultraviolet dendrochronometer, sits white and square within a glove box, connected to an OLED display on the outside. It's a device that Jac invented herself, one that allows rapid monitoring of tree growth. When a core is loaded into the lidded rectangular slot on top of the UVD, a pattern of colourful rings appears on the display, annotated with numbers relating to the dimensions of the growth rings for the latest Greenland season and each of those preceding it.

"We'll have measured the growth rings for these cores already, you know," says the Archivist, looking at the unique seven-character code etched into the sample capsule. "I could just look it up in the digital record. Unless you think we've been misusing your precious UVD."

Jac grimaces. If there was any upside to Miri leaving home
– and she silently reprimands herself for even admitting as
much – it was not having to deal with this sort of adolescent
attitude. It was hard enough to take coming from Miri, but
from a grown man it is entirely unbearable.

"A *child* could take accurate measurements with the UVD,"
she says coolly and with more than a hint of pride. Her device
is elegant and simple, easy to use. "But it can't hurt to double
check. I'll measure the growth rings by hand and we can
compare them to the logged measurements." She says this
more to bait the Archivist than anything else and, judging
from his expression, it works.

"You want to do it?" he scoffs. "When was the last time you
did any manual lab work, *Professor*?"

"Less of the scepticism, thank you," she says, hoping
she sounds more confident than she feels. The Archivist's
suspicions are not far off the truth. Managerial responsibilities
occupy much of her time and what remains is spent courting
financiers and donors, lobbying bureaucrats for favourable
legislative treatment, running press to shore up the reputation
of the Borlaug. Jac has conducted less and less laboratory work
over the years, and this procedure is a deceptively tricky one.
It's a long time since she's needed microcalipers – they became
practically obsolete after the introduction of the UVD – and
using them to take the precise hundredth-of-a-millimetre
measurements requires a great deal of practice.

Fortunately, Jac had plenty of this when she was working
on the pilot project back before the UVD was invented, and she
is pleased to find that the old skill quickly returns to her. She
takes hold of the microcalipers and carefully rotates the thimble
at one end of the barrel so that the two jaws spread apart from
one another; a metal mouth opening in a slow yawn. When
the tips of the jaws are lined up with the growth lines, she
locks the device into place with the lever and then reads off the
measurement from the bevelled edge of the thimble. She calls

it out to the Archivist so he can check it against that which was originally taken using the UVD and digitally logged in the system.

"0.955 millimetres," he repeats. "Are you *sure* about that?"

"Quite sure."

"Really? Because it doesn't match what's in the log."

Jac takes up the microcalipers once more and remeasures the core. 0.955 millimetres. There's no doubt about it. She moves over from the glove box to check the records on the Archivist's screen and sees to her consternation that he, too, is right. The digitally recorded measurement doesn't match the one she's taken with the microcalipers.

"Let me try," says the Archivist. "You can't have done it right."

Jac steps aside to let him take the measurement. She can tell from the sudden drop in his shoulders that he has arrived at exactly the same result. He turns to her, open-mouthed.

"Just make a note of it," says Jac, her voice low. "We'll measure the rest of the samples and compare."

But already her mind leaps to a new theory, a new explanation: instrument error, a fault with the UVD that's rendered every core measurement to date inaccurate. It would certainly account for the difference in projected biomass... but if it's true, then the consequences are too wide-reaching, too terrible to contemplate.

They measure another core, and another, and another. Each one confirms her fear. After the sixth, the Archivist strikes triumphantly on the same theory, but Jac cuts his gloating short.

"I'm not jumping to any conclusions until we've measured the lot," she says flatly. "We need to chart this. We need to be sure."

"Alright then," he says, perhaps more out of deference to process than to her. Moving with a new urgency, they work through the remaining cores in the case, measuring the

samples by hand and then checking them against the UVD
measurements for the same cores in the digital records.

They are all wrong. Every single core.

Plotting out the differences in a graph, she sees how the
normal distributions for both sets of results are shifted apart.
The figures are two tenths of a millimetre off, every time.
Seeing the graph, the Archivist gives off a low whistle.

"You're really fucked now, Boltanski."

Jac doesn't know what to say. There's no protest she can
make, no retort she can come up with. Her theory was right.
There's only one explanation for such a consistent difference
in measurements. And what stings about that – quite aside
from how it throws all the project's results into doubt – is that
the UVD is what made her career. Now, she's starting to think
its invention will be the very thing that sees her legacy go up
in smoke.

16

Alix, it seems, is as well-known at the Borlaug as Jac must
be. Everyone they pass has a warm smile for her and she
greets them all by name. A few of them shoot curious looks in
Miri's direction, though if any recognise her as Jac and Alix's
daughter, they do not say.

The Personal Assistant leads them through a labyrinth of
halls and corridors. Opening up a perfectly unremarkable
side door, he waves them through into the greenhouse and
onto a low veranda that overlooks the plants of the botanical
nursery. The air within is muggy, clamping thickly over Miri's
mouth and nose; it's warm enough to make her feel a little
uncomfortable beneath her heavy jumper. Alix who, up until
now, has been ineffectually fanning herself with her hand,
gives up all pretence of elegance and shrugs off her blouse to
tie it about her waist, swiping at the sweat on the back of her
neck with a balled-up handkerchief. The motion clouds the
air with wild rose and poppy. Alix is wearing a loose-fitting
camisole, dusky pink like her blouse, and there are dark
patches of sweat beneath her armpits. After a moment – more
for the camaraderie of it than anything else – Miri joins her,
setting down the plastic tub before pulling her jumper over her
head. As she does, there's a crackle of static and a few flyaway
strands of hair rise up from her plait. She smooths them back
down with her palm and then drapes the jumper over her
shoulders. When she retrieves the tub from the ground, the

rat squeaks a loud protest from within. She snaps off the lid to check that it's still alright in the heat and the rat launches itself at her, coiling its tail around her wrist. With a conciliatory scratch behind the ears, Miri gently coaxes it back into the tub.

"I'd keep a tight hold of it if I were you," says the Personal Assistant. "There'll be hell to pay if that thing gets free and interferes with any of the experiments."

Miri thinks begrudgingly that she knows better than to let a rat loose in a greenhouse, thank you very much, but says nothing.

The Personal Assistant directs them to the cast-iron railing at the edge of the veranda which, he says, is the best place from which to survey the workings of the greenhouse. As Miri and Alix stare around in wonder, he explains what they're looking at, but Miri finds herself tuning in and out. Far above them stretches the vast, curving roof of the old St Pancras train shed, the panels of sheet glass green at the edges with condensation and mildew. Down below run row after endless row of isolated glass cubicles, each one containing its own unique, tightly controlled climate. A thousand mini-ecosystems, filled with all the complexity and particularity of a long-deforested jungle.

A greenish glow emanates from the cubicles, and a wild explosion of plants and small trees can be seen trapped within, leaves and branches crushed against the glass. As her eyes snap from case to case, Miri sees more plants than she can name and several that look thrillingly unfamiliar. There's a bell jar that holds a collection of agaves in eye-popping neons; a curling vine that looks a little like a tomato apart from the fact that the fruits dangling between the leaves have the hard, pleated appearance of walnuts; a tray of freshly harvested baby aubergines, their purple skins shining with iridescence.

The Personal Assistant, evidently well accustomed to giving this kind of tour, adopts a conversational patter and points out the various plant specimens he thinks worthy of their attention. "And over here," he says, "we have a special strain of pitcher plants. They're still under development, but the progress is promising. Soon they'll be planted across the city – an excellent way to control the neon hawker population."

Alix, clearly thinking of the sagittaria in her water garden and her damaged nets, gives a low *ah* of interest and squints out to get a better look. Miri follows her gaze. The Personal Assistant is pointing towards a clump of fleshy yellow-green tubes that sprout from a low crown that stands just proud of the soil lining the base of a wide planter. They are trumpet-like, the top cavity pointing upwards and the rim rolling away to create a lip.

"How do they work exactly?" asks Alix.

The Personal Assistant is all too happy to explain. "There are secretions on the lip that attract the insect. Most pitcher plants secrete nectar but that doesn't work for the neon hawkers – it's one of the things our team are still working on. The upper part of the pitcher is waxy and treacherous. An insect responds to the lure and lands, loses its footing and falls into the digestive fluids at the bottom of the pitcher. The walls are also lined with downward-pointing hairs that make escape practically impossible."

Miri is reminded of the curling red leaf and the aphid. "Like the filterweed," she says.

The Personal Assistant frowns at her. "Filterweed isn't carnivorous."

She wants to protest, to tell him about what she saw in the holding cell at the Eye, that there must be a new mutation, but she stops herself. She doubts he'll believe her and trying to convince him is simply not worth the effort. "Right. Sure. Guess I'm thinking of something else," she says at last.

"Must be," he replies and then quickly presses on, turning to point out the large corpse flowers, adding that they are fortunately distant enough not to be subjected to the distinctive rotting stench they emit.

Looming over everything else in the very middle of the greenhouse is a tall octagonal structure. This, the Personal Assistant tells them, is where the real work of Project Salix is conducted. A narrow spiral staircase leads down from the veranda into the maze of glass cubicles below. Following his lead, they set off down the steps and make for the octagon. Inside, everything is silent except for the ordered swoosh and beep of a hundred priceless machines. The stacks spread out before them, wild with willow trees at various stages of life. Some stand tall in soil containers, others grow up and out from experimental pods and floating pots. Smaller saplings grow in hydroponic tanks or on agar plates under the bright lights of incubating houses; others still are kept in suspended animation under bell jars and in airtight vacuum cabinets. Within the tub she carries, Miri can feel the white rat is squirming more than ever in the heat, but she keeps a tight grip on the plastic.

Towering high above everything else in the greenhouse is what the Personal Assistant describes as the founding tree, the first willow bred for Project Salix. Its thick trunk, grey-brown and deeply fissured, culminates in a knotted crown that then branches out into taller, thinner limbs which stretch up towards the glass roof. From these hang hundreds of thin, whip-like stems, each one bristling with leaves. These are long and tapered, a very light green on one side and, on the other, silvery pale.

The tree, he tells them, is the first willow that was successfully engineered to be radiation hardy. For the project to work, the tree's native DNA repair machinery had to be replaced with that of a radiation-resistant bacterium, *Deinococcus radiodurans*, to protect the trees from mutations caused by nuclear fallout. It was that groundbreaking transformation, he explains, that means the trees can now survive the ARZ.

"I suppose you're both familiar with the term 'ARZ'?"

Alix catches herself mid-nod and turns to Miri with a questioning look. Miri shrugs.

"How about the Kvanefjeld disaster?"

Miri shrugs again. There is something about that name that sounds familiar, but if she ever did know what it means, she has long since forgotten.

"It was the accident that turned the Arctic into a nuclear wasteland," says Alix patiently, glancing over to the Personal Assistant as though to tell him to step in if she misses anything out. "It all started in the Barents Sea. That's where the Russians established a series of floating nuclear power stations. Despite the warnings of past calamities, it was claimed the stations were perfectly safe, precisely engineered to prevent the kind of disasters that had given nuclear energy a bad name... this was long before my time, of course, but I believe there were protests when the stations were first set up?"

"Several," confirms the Personal Assistant. "Not that it made any difference."

"No, I suppose it wouldn't have. Well, as I understand it, several years passed after that without incident. The stations were seen as a success, and their example was used to establish more nuclear plants all over the world – including one in the Kvanefjeld. Which is where, Miri?"

"How am I supposed to know?"

"It's in Greenland," says the Personal Assistant, stepping in. "Not all that far from the site of an old uranium mine."

"Sounds like a stupid place for a nuclear station."

Alix half-smiles, half-frowns. "You're on the side of the history books there."

"So what happened?" Miri asks, interested in spite of herself.

"There was a tsunami. One of the most powerful ever recorded, on a scale never before seen in the Arctic. The floating stations had wave defences, I think, but nothing that could withstand anything on that scale. One by one, the plants were dislocated from their anchor bases. They drifted..." As she speaks, Alix raises her hands flat before her, then skates them through the air until they collide. Her hands explode apart to show the violence of the impact. "Every time the vessels smashed into one another or the shoreline," she continues, "it triggered a catastrophic nuclear explosion. Some drifted for hundreds of miles before they crashed."

"And one such station was the Akademik Lomonosov," interjects the Personal Assistant. "It was cast out from Kola Bay and made it all the way across to Greenland, where it crashed into the shore just below the Kvanefjeld. They say the impact of the explosion was like an earthquake and it triggered another, much larger explosion in the power plant there."

Alix nods, sombre. "Around one hundred people died immediately. Many, many more were directly affected and suffered greatly." There is a brief pause, a moment to consider the upheaval, the brutal loss of life. Then, with a wave of her hand to dismiss the ghosts of disasters past, Alix goes on. "From that day to this, the entire Arctic continent has been in an exclusion zone, considered too dangerous for any human to enter and survive. It became the ARZ – the Arctic Remedial Zone – when it passed into neutral international governance nearly twenty years ago. The only things that can survive there are your mother's radiation-hard trees and the robots that tend to them."

Miri doesn't know what to say. She throws her head back to peer at the branching tree that rises above. "So if this tree was uprooted and moved to the ARZ–"

"It would be just fine. This is the very first willow sapling that the team successfully transformed, the very first tree to express the bacterial genes that make it radiation resistant."

"That's right," says the Personal Assistant, smiling broadly. "And terrible though the Kvanefjeld disaster was, you might say it all worked out for the best. Greenland was a good site for us anyway: the world's largest plantable tundra; average annual temperatures of fifteen degrees; moist, loam-rich soil... and because it's in the ARZ, it's entirely uninhabited. That means it qualifies as the world's most stable location in the

Global North Peace Index. We have eleven billion trees out there now, and all of them thriving."

"*This* one certainly seems to be doing very well," says Alix, returning his smile.

The willow in front of them stands at almost fifty-seven feet tall. It is, the Personal Assistant says, affectionately referred to throughout the Borlaug as *Salix boltanskiae* and will live out the rest of its days in the greenhouse.

Miri considers this briefly, adjusting her hold on the tub as her palms grow slick against the plastic. Then an idea comes to her. With a silent apology, she drops the tub heavily onto the floor. The lid flies off and the rat – startled and disoriented – lets out an agitated squeak and scurries away across the greenhouse floor, pink tail whipping along behind and the ear on its back reddening as the creature passes through a shaft of the sunlight filtering through the glass panels above.

For a moment, the Personal Assistant stares in open-mouthed dismay. Then he lurches into action, scrambling forward as he catches sight of a flash of white darting between the gnarled roots of the willows that stand rank about them. Alix is close behind him. It is all the distraction that Miri needs. Swiping a scalpel from a nearby workbench, she approaches the founding tree, the *Salix boltanskiae*, ducks between the hanging leaves and slashes a rough circle into the bark. Halting the blade before the line is complete, she carves the flat diamond of a serpent's head to close the circle: a crude ouroboros. Miri tilts her head and admires her handiwork with satisfaction. The symbol will be emblazoned on Jac's precious tree for as long as it stands; a riposte to every breeder who dared believe that Project Salix gave them the right to bring another life into this burning world.

Picking her way carefully back across the twisting roots of the tree, she drops the scalpel back on the workbench and then joins the chase. She spots the rat climbing up the trunk of a young sapling, its long pink tail stretched out behind it for balance. The Personal Assistant is closing in on it but Miri is faster, darting in front of him and lunging for the rat. Her fingers close on fur and cartilage with a crunch and she carefully prises the rat away from the sapling. Although the rat struggles to get away, twisting and turning in her hands, she doesn't loosen her grip for a second. She holds it tight to her chest, repeatedly running a thumb across its skull with slow, deliberate firmness until the rat soothes and falls still. Only then does she look up to see the bewildered way Alix and the Personal Assistant are staring at her.

"Sorry," she mumbles. "Lost my grip."

Although they don't look like they believe her, they don't say anything and neither of them seem to notice the pale gashes in the bark of the tree that are just visible through the leaves. But it brings the tour to an abrupt end. The Personal Assistant has clearly had enough. Making an excuse about needing to get back to work, he leads them out of the octagon. Just before they pass out of it and into the wider space of the greenhouse, however, they come across a girl in a lab coat whom Alix recognises and greets warmly.

"Lovely to see you. How's the PhD going?"

"Not bad, thank you," returns the Student, self-consciously smoothing her short natural afro from her brow. "Just waiting for a final report from Professor Boltanski," she adds.

Alix gives her a sympathetic look but doesn't miss a beat. "Oh, you know Jac. Always working hard. I'm sure it will be with you soon."

Miri looks from her mother to the Student, expecting to be brought into the conversation, but it's as though she's become invisible. Alix does not introduce her and the girl demonstrates no curiosity about who she is. Impatiently, Miri nudges Alix and jerks her head towards the door, but Alix ignores her.

"What are you working on?" she asks.

"Some embryonic willow matter," says the Student. "It has to be done in one of the laminar flow cabinets," she adds, pointing to a large, glass-fronted metal box into which filtered air is being continually pumped. "It's a perfectly sterile environment."

"Do you mind if we watch?" asks Alix.

Miri lets out a soft groan but Alix pays no attention, eagerly pulling on her glasses. The Personal Assistant is tapping his foot and glancing anxiously at his watch, but the Student beams and says they are more than welcome to, so now they have no choice but to stay. As their small group gathers more closely around the cabinet, Miri notices how the Student's right eye lists to one side and trails a fraction behind the left.

Despite her reluctance to play along, Miri finds the slow, methodical nature of the Student's work utterly transfixing. First, she pulls on a pair of gloves that she sprays meticulously with ethanol. Then she sprays the interior of the cabinet as well, waiting a moment for the alcohol to evaporate. Once the surface is disinfected, she opens a container and tilts it briefly towards them through the glass so that they can see what it holds: an untouched willow sapling. Using a small scalpel, she removes its delicate leaves. One by one, she places them on a large glass plate inside the cabinet. These are then transferred onto individual Petri dishes, which, she explains, are filled with agar gel. She tells them that the process will speed up the development of the saplings, allowing for hasty cloning from the founding tree lines. When she has closed each of the Petri dishes, she stacks them up and moves them carefully from the cabinet to a nearby incubator.

"I'm testing them for cryogenic sensitivity," she says, as though why she would do so is perfectly obvious. "I don't expect them to take more than two weeks of freezing. Then they'll die."

"Two weeks," says Alix with a tight, wistful smile. "Wish Jac and I still had that much time."

The Student's face falls. Seeing this, Alix knocks her on the arm affectionately. "Oh, don't mind me. Only joking. Now, tell me, once you've measured this—"

As Alix continues with her inquiry, the Student turns and –
accidentally or otherwise – looks Miri straight in the eyes. Miri
holds her stare. A vague line of understanding passes between
them. *Breeders*.

17

Clutching a glass of wine, Jac hovers around the edge of the crowd. Usually she would be in the centre of things but today she's avoiding someone. She wishes Alix could have come with her, but she is back at home, bedridden with morning sickness. While the illness blind-sided them at first – no one at the hospital thought to warn them – really they should have expected that Alix's body would punish her for the pregnancy, just like everyone else is hell-bent on doing. Jac left her reluctantly that morning. "I can miss it..." she said, hesitating at the door. But Alix insisted she go.

The memorial service for the Laureate, hosted by the Royal Society, is being held in a hall of Burlington House. Jac is one of the select few fortunate enough to be invited to this private ceremony. She's not surprised; everyone knew she was his favourite student. Jac met him during her PhD, working in his lab on the trial of the project they all believed would save the world. They stayed in touch after Jac graduated, the Laureate often writing her letters of recommendation that secured Jac a series of enviable positions in labs all across the city.

The hall is magnificent. Intricately carved white stone pillars are recessed at regular intervals between vast panels of gleaming red marble, and the ornate wood-panelled ceiling is covered in gold leaf. Just as Jac tilts her head upwards to get a better look, she is approached by the one person she's been hoping wouldn't spot her.

"Hello, Jac," comes a voice at her shoulder.

Her eyes snap back down to take in the familiar face of the Engineer. She hasn't changed a bit, not since the two first met as students in the Laureate's lab. Jac, as a mathematical biologist, worked on the quantitative aspects of the five-year pilot, whereas the Engineer specialised in biophotonics and dealt with optical microscopy. Their early collaborations proved highly fruitful and an intense romantic relationship soon followed. It didn't last. Their temperaments were too similar and their views too disparate. Although their on-again, off-again romance had been turbulent, they managed to stay friends when it was finally done. For a while anyway, until Jac's meteoric success drove them apart. Now the Engineer looks as radiant and powerful as ever, even if her clothes – frayed and bobbling – tell a different story.

"It's been a while," says Jac.

"Were you avoiding me?"

"No," Jac replies, a little too quickly. "Of course not."

"Funny. I got the distinct impression that you were."

"You always did have an overactive imagination."

The two share a warm, private smile and exchange the requisite pleasantries. Though things are awkward between them at first, Jac soon finds herself relaxing in the Engineer's easy company. When they are called to dinner, she even turns a blind eye when the Engineer swaps her name-card to take up the seat next to Jac's.

Side by side, and aided by the free-flowing wine, the two continue an increasingly animated exchange. Despite the solemnity of the occasion, they are both in high spirits, stifling loud laughter together as the president of the Royal Society drones on about the Laureate's myriad achievements: the numerous groundbreaking discoveries; the noble institutes in his honour; the forty-year marriage; the commendable lack of children. There are about sixty guests in total – the cream of London's scientific community – gathered in clutches around circular tables. Not one of them looks like they are enjoying the speech. As soon as the president reclaims his seat, an audible sigh of relief passes through the room. The guests, looking forward to the five-course dinner ahead, finally relax, sipping Highgate Cru and swapping stories about the late scientist as the white-gloved waiters bring out the entrées on sterling silver platters.

"When did you last hear from him?" asks the Engineer.

"Only a few weeks ago," Jac confesses. "He wanted me to finish the UVD paper. But I ignored him, because it meant–"

"Having to contact me?" the Engineer finishes.

"I didn't want the first time that we spoke in years to be about the UVD," she says defensively.

But this is not the only reason why Jac didn't get in touch. In truth, she simply felt too awkward about the fact the Laureate contacted her and not the Engineer, even though he knew the UVD was mostly the Engineer's work. It was she who had come up with the idea for an electro-optical device to measure growth rings after watching Jac use ultraviolet light to visualise DNA pieces in agarose gels, and it was she who, extrapolating from this, had been able to create what was effectively an ultraviolet scanner for wood. The UVD was revolutionary. Somehow, though, Jac was afforded most of the credit.

Shortly after that, Project Salix passed its pilot test and was given the green light for a full run. The Borlaug won the licence to carry out the research in Greenland and the Laureate was expected to head it up – although now that position was vacant, of course. He'd been keen for them to publish their plans for the UVD so it could be patented for use on the project. That explains why he got in touch with Jac but not why he hadn't contacted the Engineer as well. With a pang of guilt, Jac thinks maybe he forgot the critical role the Engineer played.

Seeming to read her thoughts, the Engineer places a consoling hand on her arm. "You were always his favourite,

Jac. You're both Londoners. He never thought much of me and my Leicester roots. Besides, it doesn't matter. Take the plans for the UVD and publish it yourself. I don't want anything to do with the project anymore."

"I can't. It's not right. You came up with it."

"Don't be precious. If you publish, it'll crush the competition to head up the project."

"What?"

"Come on. Everyone knows you're already the top candidate for the job. And with this publication–"

"Ssh," Jac hisses, looking around to make sure they aren't being overheard.

"Just take the plans and publish it," the Engineer whispers back, waving over a waiter who's passing by with a silver ice-bucket. "Now shut up about work and drink."

And they do. They carry on drinking and talking until late into the night. As the wine and conversation flows, Jac feels confident the two of them will part as newly reinstated friends. Then, in an unguarded moment, Jac opens her wallet and takes out a photograph – Alix's twenty-week scan – which she slides across the table towards the Engineer with a sheepish grin.

Leaning over to inspect it and then straightening up fast, the Engineer's expression clouds at once. "Why?" she asks. "Because you have a death wish?"

"Quite the opposite," says Jac, hastily pulling the photograph back towards her. Her hands are shaking. She grips them tightly together and wills the tremor to stop.

The Engineer lifts her glass to her lips and takes a long slug of wine. Then, with a frown: "You never told me you wanted a baby."

"It never came up."

The Engineer is disbelieving. "The issue of reproduction *definitely* came up." After a brief pause, she presses her point: "What happened, Jac? What changed?"

Jac glances away. How can she possibly answer the Engineer without hurting her? For the truth is simple: what happened was that Jac had changed her mind. It was meeting Alix that did it, it was falling in love: like switching on a light she didn't even know was there. It illuminated everything, made her see how much she needed for her and Alix to have a child, to create a life that would embody and entomb their love. When Alix, more ambivalent at first, had asked what would happen if the world ended, Jac had responded with a new and startling clarity: *So what if it does?* Yes, she would devote her life's work to preventing it, but they couldn't let the threat of annihilation suffocate them forever. To do so was unconscionable: the very antithesis of their love, which strained away from their ailing planet and out towards the stars. Jac wanted to catch something of that feeling and give it form. She wanted proof of their love – to hold its revelation in her hands.

Love before Alix had never felt like that, had never simultaneously sharpened and neutralised the threat of death. All their past fears persisted still, but now they had the antidote, too: new life. A child, the genetic product of both her and Alix. An artificial sperm had been crafted from Jac's DNA and used to fertilise one of Alix's eggs. Because neither of them had a Y chromosome, neither would their offspring. She would be assigned female at birth, just like them. They already have a name for her: Miriam Ford-Boltanski. Their little Miri, their love made flesh. For whoever dies first – whoever is Offset – she will remain. She will outlive them both.

How can Jac explain any of this to the Engineer? How can she tell her ex-girlfriend that it never even occurred to her to think of their love as eternal? That her love for Alix was more than the stuff of bodies and minds: it was more, even, than the life and death of the world? But the silence between them conveys the Engineer's deep need for an answer and Jac cannot deny that an answer is owed, that the burden is on her to try and explain. Finally, choosing to speak in a language they both understand, she says, "I wanted to make the world a better place."

As soon as the words are out of her mouth, she hears how feeble they sound, how insulting. For a moment, the Engineer is very still. Then, with no explanation needed, she rises unsteadily to her feet and announces that she's leaving. Jac tries to persuade her to stay but it's no use. When she's gone, Jac remains where she is for a long time after that, looking at the scan of her baby on the table, replaying the conversation in her head over and over again.

Late the next morning, Jac wakes up in the Warren with a splitting headache. Getting a glass of water, she enters the study – her morning ritual – to check her inbox. Amongst the usual work communications there is an email from the Engineer, sent only an hour before. Jac opens it quickly, but finds it empty. Confused, she sits back in her chair, wondering at the meaning of this, before she notices an attachment. It's the Engineer's half of the UVD plans.

Jac hastily replies with copious thanks and a hopeful "Let's keep in touch?" but she never hears anything back. Although the Engineer has closed a door on their friendship, she has opened another for Jac's career.

Immediately after her publication of the paper on the UVD, Jac is offered the Borlaug directorship. She takes it and never looks back.

18

Once they leave the muggy closeness of the greenhouse, Miri quickly pulls her jumper back on but Alix leaves her blouse knotted around her waist. The Personal Assistant, his original geniality now all but eroded away into impatience, escorts them back to the lobby and bids them a brusque farewell. Alix asks Miri if she'll be alright to wait by herself for a few minutes while she runs to the bathroom. Miri raises an eyebrow. After two years fending for herself a few minutes alone hardly troubles her, but she does not say this to Alix, merely nodding and promising to wait. It is only then that Miri realises she left the tub lying in the greenhouse where she dropped it. Reluctant to return, she lets the rat nestle in the crook of her arm as she crosses the lobby to step through the Borlaug's revolving glass door. As she leaves the building, she catches sight of the slogan engraved above the door, the letters gilded: *Breed fewer. Breed better.*

It is mid-afternoon but, apart from the heat, there's little to distinguish it from any other time of the day. When Miri looks skyward, the hazy smog is so thick overhead that she can barely even discern the position of the sun. Saving the occasional employee darting in and out of the Borlaug's sprawling complex of buildings, the plaza is quiet. Not far off is a broad block of grey stone, a recess cut out of the near side to create a low bench. A solitary figure with short bleach-blond hair sits on top of the block, feet jiggling against the flat of the bench. In this refined setting, he looks distinctly out of place. Even across the square, she can see that he is whippet thin; his sallow skin pitted, his eyes bloodshot. He rolls his neck so that his head makes a weaving motion and it is so instantly familiar that Miri doesn't understand how she missed it before: the boy is someone she knows. They met nearly two years ago when she was staying in a shelter out by the mud flats of St James's. She woke one night to find him forcefully trying to tug the boots from her feet and instinctively kicked the rubber soles of her size sevens hard into his chest, sending him flying across the room. He smacked into the wall and then crumpled to the floor in a broken heap. She hurried over, muttering a string of curses as she turned him over to check if he was alright. He was badly winded and it looked like he was going to have a nasty bruise on his chest. She helped him sit up and waited for him to get his breath back before telling him how sorry she was. As soon as she did, he let out a loud bark of laughter, his head weaving uncontrollably.

"I try to steal your shoes and *you* apologise to *me*?"

The Thief became one of her few friends after that, the sort of friend you never get as far as sharing a surname with. Miri is quite certain that he has no idea who her parents are and she was careful never to tell him, a lie of omission made easier by the fact that he always had little interest in following the news feeds. Although they can go for long intervals without seeing or even thinking of one another, Miri is always glad to run into the Thief. They'd spent a few memorable evenings together; at least one smashing in all the ground-floor windows of a row of townhouses and several more in the company of a bottle of stolen liquor. Even now, when she is struggling to reconcile his presence with the austere grandeur of the Borlaug, there is a bubble of happy anticipation in her stomach.

She approaches. The bleach in his hair is new, but otherwise he looks much the same as ever. Up close, she can see the yellow grime of stale sweat at the neck of his t-shirt, the cold sores that blister the skin around his chapped lips, the peeling scab across the sunken bridge of his nose. Once again, there's that spasmodic rolling movement that sets his head weaving.

She watches him for a full minute but the Thief doesn't look up. Finally, she clears her throat. Now his head snaps up, his mouth drawing into a scowl, his pupils narrowing to hostile slits beneath his monolids.

"Fuck off."

As the words leave his mouth, something clicks into place and he identifies the face peering down at him. The aggression that clouds his eyes lifts at once. His head once again weaves from side to side.

"Miri?" he says. "I didn't recognise you. You look different."

She self-consciously plucks the sleeve of her steel-blue jumper, unsure of what to say.

"Not in a bad way," he adds. "Just, I dunno. Clean."

"Yeah, well, I used soap and everything. Mind if I sit?"

He shrugs and Miri clambers up on the bench beside him. As she does, the white rat scampers up her arm, its clever claws threading into the weave as it crosses the front of her jumper. Seeing the ear curving out of its back, the Thief gives a shout of alarm.

"What the fuck is that?"

"Just a rat," she says, grabbing the creature with one hand and pulling it off her jumper. One of its claws catches in the wool and yanks out a few loops into a messy snag. Ignoring this, Miri offers the rat to the Thief. "Want to hold it?"

"Not a chance." Though he wrinkles his nose in disgust, he is barely able to tear his eyes away from the rat as it slowly clambers down from Miri's sleeve and settles onto the arm of the bench beside him. "What happened to it?"

"I don't know," says Miri. "Escaped from a lab, I guess."

He glances around the plaza. Another jerky weave of the head. "One of these labs?"

"Probably not," she says. "I found it down by the Gallery. Doubt it could have got that far by itself."

"Bet these labs have things like that though," he says. He arches a knowing brow and takes a canvas pouch from his pocket that he pinches open and tilts towards her. "They do all sorts here."

Miri peers into the gaping mouth of the pouch. It contains a few handfuls of dried, shredded leaf. The smell is unmistakable. Tobacco.

"You got that here?"

He taps the side of his nose. "That's for me to know. Want some?" he asks, head swaying from side to side as he pulls out a paper no longer than his thumb and so thin as to be practically transparent.

"Go on then."

She watches as he sprinkles some of the dried leaf into the paper and pinches the long edges together; shaping, adjusting. The paper twists and curls almost of its own accord, reminding Miri of the filterweed she saw in the holding cell and how the leaf wrapped up around the struggling aphid to make a funnel-like pitcher. Once the paper is rolled tight, he moistens the trailing edge with the tip of his tongue and then presses it down. He inspects his handiwork for a moment, giving it a brisk tap on his knee. Then he snatches it up and swings both hands behind his back before holding out his fists for Miri to inspect; knuckles up, thumbs tucked in. It's impossible to tell which one holds the cigarette.

"Left or right?" he asks Miri, a faint smile playing across his lips.

"Right," she says.

"Eliminating the right," he confirms, letting the hand drop to his side. When Miri taps his left fist, he twists it up and opens his fingers out like the petals of a budding flower. The cigarette lies across his palm. Miri laughs and picks it up, placing one end in her lips as the Thief strikes a match. Ducking towards the flame, she inhales deeply, sucking on the end of the cigarette until the tip glows orange. The smoke billows from her mouth and hangs in the air, darkly visible even against the smog. She takes another puff and passes the cigarette to the Thief.

"Hey!" shouts a voice. "You're not allowed to do that here."

Miri looks up. It's the Student from the Borlaug. She's standing across the plaza, her face thunderous. Miri thinks that if they ignore her she'll probably leave them alone, but the Thief is already playing up to it, cupping his hand to his ear and pretending like he can't make out what she said. It's enough to spur the Student into action and she storms across the plaza. By the time she reaches them, she is breathing heavily.

"I *said* you're not allowed to do that here."

Miri conjures up an innocent expression and makes a show of looking around. "I don't see any signs prohibiting it," she says.

The Student is not impressed. "You can't burn anything out in a public space. It's bad for the environment. I'd expect *you* of all people to know that."

The Thief's head snaps up. "Why?" he asks. "Who's she of all people?"

Before Miri can stop her, the Student tells him her full name. He lets out a low whistle, turning back to give Miri a reappraising look. "Fucking hell. *Boltanski*? Like *Jac* Boltanski?"

There's no use denying it now. Under the watchful eyes of the Student, she gives a short nod. The Thief flicks her arm. "You never fucking told me that. But if you're her daughter, then what..." he trails off, confused. Miri knows why. There's no way he can reconcile the famous, glamorous Jac Boltanski with the scrawny girl he considers his friend. From his view, the worlds they inhabit are entirely separate and distinct, only ever brushing together in the course of an occasional black-market trade. His eyes flit back round the plaza, re-examining the grand facade of the gothic palace and considering it anew. Up until now he has, perhaps, believed that Miri was here for much the same reason as him – some underhand deal with one of the lab workers – but now she can see that he's reassessing it as the world from which she comes. "Fuck," he says again and takes a deep drag on the cigarette.

With a click of frustration, the Student goes to snatch it out of his hand but he pulls it back out of reach. "Alright, alright," he says, head weaving. "I'm putting it out, OK?"

Then, before Miri can stop him, he jabs the smouldering end of the cigarette at the white rat, stubbing out the smoking ash at the base of the ear that rises from its back. The rat squeals and writhes, bucking ferociously and squirming to get away, but the Thief keeps it pinned down until the end of the cigarette stops smouldering. When he lets the rat up, there's an angry red welt on the cartilage where the skin has burnt and blistered. The whole incident takes no more than a few seconds, but it feels like a lifetime to Miri sitting as motionless as if she were back in the holding cell, numb and limp under the influence of the tranquiliser. Whimpering, the rat scrambles over to Miri and cowers, shaking, in a fold of her jumper.

The Student stands open-mouthed in horror. "You *monster*," she hisses.

The Thief shrugs. "You were the one who wanted me to put it out."

At that, the Student turns on her heel and marches back across the plaza. Scooping up the shivering rat, Miri shoots the Thief a reproachful glare and then hurries after her.

"Hey, stop," she shouts. The Student ignores her. It's a few moments before Miri catches her up. "What are you going to do?" she asks, panting.

"Call the pigsuits," says the Student, her face set firmly forward.

"Please don't," says Miri. "I know what he did and how it seems and everything... but it's not worth calling the pigsuits over. Please. He has a record. If they catch him, he'll be thrown in the Eye. And that'll be the end for him."

"Maybe he should have thought about that first," says the Student. Although her tone is officious, she slows her pace a little and doesn't tell Miri to leave her alone.

"Are you honestly telling me you've never gone cat baiting before?" asks Miri.

The Student rolls her eyes; she's heard this from people like Miri a million times before. "That's completely different and you know it."

"Is it?"

"Of course. Everyone does it. Besides, it's a humane way to control a swelling population that would otherwise be left unchecked."

Miri snorts, unconvinced. If the city ever was overrun by felines – the feral ancestors of once domesticated breeds – those days are long gone. The creatures now hunted by London school kids are bred for the purpose; she's seen the stinking catteries out in the southern wastes. Besides, there's nothing remotely humane about the way a captured cat is traditionally skinned and boiled alive.

"You're just as bad as he is," she says hotly. "You think what he did was wrong because of how he lives and what he looks like, but what people like you do is fine because–"

"People like *me*?" interrupts the Student, eyebrows raised. "People like *us*, you mean."

Miri's face reddens and she blunders quickly on. "Please don't call the pigsuits. He didn't mean it." She stops. It's not quite right. She thinks fleetingly of earlier that morning when she hurled the fruit bowl at her mother's head. She *had* meant that, and that was part of what made it so horrifying – the regret for wanting to do the thing was just as shattering as the regret for doing it. But she had also been in a bad way. Out of control. She'd acted out against something unexpected and difficult in the only way she could come up with in the pressure of the moment. Perhaps that was what happened with the Thief, too.

Taking a deep breath, she keeps pace with the Student and tries again to explain. "Do you know how hard it is to plan for the future when you're surviving from one moment to the next?"

The Student stops in her tracks but says nothing.

"I know how it seems. He didn't have to smoke or be rude to you or stub his cigarette out on a harmless animal. Those were his choices and he should suffer the consequences. But you're thinking like someone who's in a position to carefully weigh up the outcomes of their actions. Like someone who can take the next hour, the next day, for granted. It's not like that for him. He probably doesn't know where he's going to sleep tonight or where his next meal is coming from. Half the time he's just working out how to solve that problem, over and over. The rest of the time, he has to wander around, waiting it out, never allowed to stay in one place for long before someone turfs him out or beats him up. There's nowhere he can go where he can safely exist and be himself. Until he becomes someone's problem, he's completely invisible. That can get to a person. Make you do things you can't always control."

With a sudden, urgent feeling of having said too much, Miri lets her eyes drop to the ground and shifts her weight awkwardly from foot to foot. The Student stays quiet for a long minute. Then, at last: "He is still responsible for his actions."

"I know," says Miri. "But I think he deserves some slack."

Eventually, the Student agrees that she won't call the pigsuits. Miri watches her closely as she walks back to the Borlaug, not tearing her eyes away until the girl has disappeared from view. At last, she looks back towards the bench for the Thief – only to find, with a jolt, that he's gone.

19

It's Miri's seventeenth birthday, but she didn't tell the Thief that when she invited him to the rave. He's already half-cut, constantly sipping from a bottle that hangs lightly in his hand, the brown glass grubby with fingerprints.

"What's that?" she asks.

"Here, try it," he says, head weaving as he hands her the bottle. Miri takes a tentative sip. It's stronger than she's expecting; the alcohol burns her tongue, her palate, the back of her throat. She splutters into her hand, eyes watering.

The Thief laughs. "Fucking lightweight."

Determined to measure up, Miri tips back the bottle again and swallows a generous mouthful. This time she's ready for it, bracing herself against the sharpness of the liquor. Only a small shudder escapes her as she hands the bottle back.

"Alright, alright," says the Thief, still grinning. "You've proved your point. Let's go."

The rave is due to take place in an abandoned building at the edge of the Southwark wastes. Miri and the Thief head south until they reach the ruptured dome of the old cathedral that now houses an aquaponic farm; the nave of the building is lined with vast tanks of tilapia alongside grow beds of cabbage, okra and kohlrabi. It is here they turn and cross the river.

Reckless with drink, the Thief tears across the bridge, not caring when it begins to shudder violently beneath his feet. There are gaps in the aluminium walkway where entire sections have been ripped up and the railing on one side has all but corroded away. Trying very hard not to think about the swollen river below, Miri races after the Thief. When she reaches the firm ground of the opposite bank, she lets out a sigh of relief.

"Scared?" asks the Thief.

She snorts. "Of course not."

"Yeah, yeah," he says, head weaving. "Come on. We're nearly there."

The site is not far from the bridge, a vast hall of brick that has half-collapsed into the river. Miri can just see where a tall chimney once rose into the sky, now nothing more than a crumbling stump. It had been a power station once and, after that, an art gallery. But that was some time ago now – the building has been empty for as long as Miri remembers. Longer, even.

Before the city first began installing environmental defences, a fire had broken out in an old timber-framed theatre and quickly spread across the whole of Southwark, turning the entire district into a blackened wasteland. It's only in more recent years that activity has started to return to the place: anti-natalist rallies, teknivals, the occasional bare-knuckle fight. Nothing of which Miri's mothers would approve.

Inside, the building is one cavernous room, the walls braced with rusting steel girders. The concrete floor slopes down to where a crowd is gathered, many of them marked with the sign of the ouroboros, which stares back at Miri from a hundred places, tattooed onto biceps and forearms, painted onto faces, stitched onto the backs of jackets.

The Thief, spotting a group of people he knows, takes Miri by the hand and drags her through the crowd. In a moment, he's lost to her, absorbed in conversation with someone Miri doesn't know. She shuffles anxiously on the spot, unsure of what to do or who to talk to, barely able to hear anyone over the repetitive pulse of the music that reverberates from the surrounding speakers.

As if in response to a cue that Miri has not heard, the crowd goes quiet and turns as one to the far wall, where a spot of white light has appeared high above their heads and spreads into a wide rectangle. It's the light of a projector. An image flashes up of a burning forest and is quickly replaced by another, and then another and another: rotting crops, mudslides, drowned land, whole towns that have been flattened by storms. Miri recognises some of the scenes from the news and others from history lessons. Now, as the music begins to build, she sees yet more images she recognises: black and white shots of the mass graves that are found across the Federated Counties and beyond.

All at once, the music cuts and the flickering images give way to a single loop of film. To Miri, the footage is sickeningly familiar. She makes herself watch, determined not to give herself away by flinching back or running out into the night.

"This is for my daughter," says Jac, her amplified voice booming across the crowd. *"This is for us and all who come after: the children of the Arborocene."*

There's a loud jeer as Jac's words fade out, but it's not over. In the next moment Jac's voice returns, remixed over a heavy bass, her words cycling around and around. *"The children of the Arborocene... the children of the Arborocene..."* New images flash up on the wall, one after the other. Though they originate from across the world, they all show a variant of the same thing: a child, thin-faced with malnutrition and disease, alone and dying.

The music is building to a fever pitch. Miri can almost feel it, the swelling excitement of the crowd, the desperation that anticipates the coming drop. She wills herself to go along with it, trying to tap into that shared delirium in the hope that it will drown out the shame. Miri has always known that, for every well-wisher, for every admirer, there was someone who loathed Jac. She tries to convince herself that she's glad of it, delighted that there are others who can see through her mother's charade. But this is the first time she's seen that hatred presented so starkly, and all she can think is: *They aren't showing the whole story. They aren't being fair.*

In the next moment, she is silently reprimanding herself for falling into Jac's trap. She won't be made a fool of like Alix. Besides, she's learnt a great deal more since she left home. Who else is accountable for the resources that are snatched from starving mouths and diverted to Project Salix? Who else gives breeders the confidence to continue adding to the Earth's burden? Jac is at the centre of it all; the target to aim for, the icon to be torn down.

This is *her* fault, no doubt about it; her arrogance is why any of them are here tonight, why Miri exists at all. Jac had made that much clear in their final row when, provoked by Miri's screamed demand – *Why did you have me?* – she had said: *Because I wanted to make the world a better place!* There'd been no going back from that, from knowing that all she was and all she would ever be was a pawn in Jac's game – a game in which the whole world is now ensnared.

When, at last, the music drops, the relief is absolute. Soon Miri is lost in the rhythm of the night, dancing alone where the crowd is thickest. Jac's words stutter in and out as the DJ cross-fades to the next track. In another moment they are gone, replaced by the clipped tones of a politician.

"Breed fewer," bellow the speakers. *"Breed better."*

A new wave of anger crashes through the crowd. There is a wildness to the dancing now, both driven by fear and unbound by it: a fear of life as much as death, of the days that must yet be endured, and how – soon now – those days will come to an end.

20

Regarding herself in the silvered mirror that hangs in the bathroom of the Borlaug, Alix marvels at her ability to feel anything as mundane as embarrassment on the day before her daughter's Offset. Miri, letting that cursed rat loose in the greenhouse. The curl of the personal assistant's lip as he hustled them both out of the place that she – the director's wife – had every right to be. After all this time, it is still painfully familiar to her: being judged and found wanting. A parent who cannot control her child.

What on earth was Miri thinking? Did the girl have any idea how it looked? Then lying about it in that bold-faced way? *Lost my grip.* Alix hadn't believed it for a moment. The girl wasn't fooling anyone – apart from herself, perhaps. And all for what? To desecrate Jac's work? Alix had glimpsed the sign of the ouroboros scratched into the bark of the willow tree and she cannot quite believe her daughter would risk so much to do something so petty. It troubles her more than anything she's seen of Miri since bringing her home, confirming her worst suspicions. Bringing Miri to the Borlaug was supposed to change her mind. Now, Alix fears, the visit has only served to more deeply entrench Miri in her hostility towards Jac.

Alix sighs. In her more optimistic moments – admittedly few and far between these last two years – Alix has secretly hoped that being away from home would be good for Miri, that she would become more mature; better able to appreciate her mothers and the sacrifices she and Jac made on her behalf. Or if not quite capable of that, then at least more objective in her assessment of them, more aware of the responsibilities that come with turning eighteen.

More fool me, thinks Alix. If anything, the opposite is true. She's loath to imagine what her daughter has endured or who she has spent her time with, but the experience seems to have made her angrier and more petulant than ever.

Alix still isn't sure what sowed that first tendril seed of hatred in Miri's heart, but now its roots have grown deep and strong; a stubborn weed that Alix fears she will never be able to extirpate, even if she were granted all the time in the world.

"What on earth did we do to her, Jac?" Alix mutters into the thin air. "How did we get it so wrong?" Her words echo off the hard tiles and reverberate around the empty bathroom. The strangeness of being in the Borlaug without her wife strikes her fully for the first time. Perhaps she shouldn't have persuaded Jac to stay in Inbhir Nis. Even though Alix knows Jac would want to stop her from trying to change Miri's mind, Alix still longs to see her wife. She aches for the reassuring solidity of holding Jac in her arms and being held in turn, for the ally who has always stood by her and whose strength has made even the darkest days bearable, for the woman she loves. Alone here in the Borlaug, Alix can't help but feel untethered, free-floating. All at sea.

"I *need* you, Jac."

Something tremors in Alix's heart and she thinks wildly that it's a sign, a tug at the ethereal connection between her and Jac, an indication that somehow, deep in her being, Jac has heard her plea and is, perhaps, sending some reply. But then the sensation passes. *Just a palpitation,* she realises. Another gift of the menopause.

Alix has never been prone to superstition. Perhaps she's losing her mind. If she is, she has no time to contemplate it now. With a wry shake of the head, she dismisses the thought.

Then she turns the tap of the sink and bends to splash a little cold water onto her face.

A few moments later, as she crosses the lobby of the Borlaug, she casts a final look over her shoulder at the splendour her wife's work has wrought. She knows she will not return here again. Whatever happens, she is glad to have seen the place one last time. Reluctantly, she turns her gaze forward and goes to find her daughter.

21

The Archivist gives Jac a disparaging look. "You want to do what?"

"I told you. We need to work out how far back the problem goes."

"We've been using *your* UVD ever since the pilot, haven't we?"

"Yes."

"Well then. There's your answer."

"We don't know that for sure. A fault could have been introduced since then."

"How, exactly?"

This catches Jac short. "It will be easier to deduce the cause once we've identified the precise point when the problem began," she says eventually.

"You reckon so, do you?" says the Archivist, corners of his mouth twitching. "Well, you're going to have a hard time checking. We've only got cores from the last few quarters here. Everything else is buried deep in the Gunnbjørn Mountain."

Jac curses silently. Of course, it's the standard procedure; once a case of sample cores has been measured and logged, it gets sent back to the ARZ for secure disposal. And if she wants to identify the root of the problem, she'll need to test cores far older than anything held in the facility. It will be the work of months to recall and test representative selections from the deposited cores. *Although…* An idea hits her. She might not have time to revisit all historical measurements, but there *is* a way she can test the UVD. "I want you to get the sample cores from the pilot," she says.

"What?"

"They're held here, aren't they? All the samples from the pilot are protected by a historical preservation clause – we're obliged to keep them on the mainland. I signed the contract myself. They're here in the annexe. They have to be."

"Ye-es, you're right," he says, brow furrowing. "They're in a separate chamber. But I don't see–"

"All the measurements for the pilot were taken by hand. We can remeasure the samples with the UVD and compare."

"We've only got the cores. The project files aren't kept here."

"That doesn't matter. I have everything else we need. Provided I can get something from my bag first, that is."

His obvious consternation increases. "What?"

"A lab book," she says, and briefly explains about the report charting the growth of the first Project Salix trees across the five long years of the pilot project. He looks like he's about to argue with her, but then he seems to change his mind. "Fine. If you want to dig your grave a bit deeper, that's your concern. But you'll have to leave the book behind when we're done so it can be safely decontaminated and destroyed."

Jac shrugs. There's bound to be another hard copy of the pilot study in the Borlaug library. Even if there isn't, she has no choice. If she has a hope of getting to the bottom of the discrepancies, she needs the lab book.

He switches over to a different channel and radios up to the Facility Manager on a private frequency to explain the situation. The next time Jac hears his voice buzz in her ears, it's to say that the Facility Manager, though reluctant at first, has agreed to send someone down on the understanding that this is being officially authorised by Jac.

While they wait, Jac has the Archivist take her to the side chamber where the cores from the pilot study are kept.

Selecting a crate at random, she helps him to shift it onto a trolley and wheel it back through to the room with the glove box. Then his radio goes. It's the Facility Manager.

"Your book is in the airlock," the Archivist tells Jac. "Much good it'll do you."

Ignoring this last, Jac leaves him to finish setting up and heads over at once. The lights running up the sides of the steel door are green. When Jac hits the button, the door slides up to reveal an airlock that is empty but for her lab book, which has been carefully laid on the floor.

Stooping clumsily, she lifts it up and runs a gloved thumb over the title. *Project Salix: a preliminary study and report.* It has long since been decommissioned. She brought it with her for luck as much as anything else. With some difficulty, she flicks open the cover. Tucked between the first pages is a postcard from the Engineer.

Jac studies the front of the card. In the last few days she's received hundreds of cards like this, all wishing her well for the upcoming Offset. They are all of a type: classical imagery, prosaic biblical sketches, sentimental Oedipal daubs, Tullia Minor driving over her prostrated father. The card from the Engineer, however, sent more than a month ago, makes no explicit reference to the Offset and is much more muted. A simple, etched vine pattern in black and white runs across the front. It looks handmade. In her heavy gloves, Jac cannot pick up the card to turn it over and reread the few words scrawled across the back – but there's no need. The message was terse and formal, with little to indicate what she and the Engineer had once meant to one another. The significance it bears is its lack of a counterpart: she was not amongst the well-wishers who sent congratulations on the occasion of Miri's birth. In fact, this is the first contact she's had from the Engineer in a little over eighteen years. Jac knows what that means. The Engineer's views about reproduction have not changed in the long years since they parted company. She wonders whether Miri will likewise remain true to her anti-natalist principles. When they discussed it privately, Alix always dismissed their daughter's tendency to such extreme views as a phase. Jac was never so sure. If Project Salix comes crashing down, she fears the girl will only be vindicated in her beliefs. And now that is a real risk. If all the measurements are wrong, it could take significantly longer for Project Salix to become effective. Jac's not sure how long yet, but perhaps enough that conditions will deteriorate sufficiently to further dampen progress. They'll have to plant more trees. Presuming, of course, that the current strain will be able to survive with the higher CO_2 concentration – if not, they'll have to develop a new variety and replant. It will be like starting from scratch.

She snaps the lab book shut. She thinks of the Engineer and her eagerness to distance herself from the project. Did she know there was something wrong with the UVD all along? It would certainly explain her reluctance to put her name to the paper. But, try as she might, she can't think of a reason why the Engineer would seek to actively sabotage the project – even if she was angry with Jac, there would have been far easier ways to mete out her revenge. And besides, despite her clashes with the Laureate and the rest of the team, she was never anything but completely sincere in her desire for the project to succeed. Or so Jac thinks. Really, she doesn't know what to believe anymore.

She shuts the steel door of the airlock and carries the book back to the room with the glove box, where the Archivist is waiting.

"Pick out one of the capsules," she tells him. "There'll be a code on the bottom. Read it out to me."

As he does so, she opens the book and turns to the appendix at the back where the manual core measurements from the pilot are listed. It takes her a few moments to find the specific code because it is printed towards the end of the list that covers the cores collected in the fifth and final year of the pilot study. In the column alongside the code are a number of measurements.

Jac scans across to the growth ring measurement. 1.256 millimetres.

"Now I want you to measure the same core. We'll confirm the measurement manually with microcalipers and then check it on the UVD and see if there's still a discrepancy."

"*Of course* there's still a discrepancy," says the Archivist. "The UVD's fucked. You confirmed that. When are you going to accept it?"

"When I have sufficient proof," Jac snaps. "Now take the measurement," she adds, gesturing towards the glove box.

With a few low curses, the Archivist takes the capsule to the glove box and opens it, plucking out the core. It's a small cylinder of plant tissue, not more than two centimetres in length and greyish in appearance. Peering at the core through the screen of the glove box, he measures the thickness of the ring with a pair of microcalipers and reads out the measurement.

"1.056 millimetres."

Jac pulls a face. "Are you sure?"

"Are you questioning my ability to measure a goddamn growth ring? The original measurement must have been recorded incorrectly. A simple transcription error, that's all."

"Then let's try another." She selects a different capsule from the case and checks the code against the table in the book. It is also in the section of cores collected in the final year of the project. Then she hands it to the Archivist. Once again, the measurement he takes with the microcalipers is smaller than that recorded in the appendix, even though this, too, would have first been taken by hand.

There's a pause. "Still think it's a transcription error?" asks Jac.

"Maybe," says the Archivist, though his tone is not so confident as before. "We'll have to check more of them to know for sure."

Jac can hardly argue with this. They work their way methodically through the rest of the cores in the crate. But for every core they try, the measurement the Archivist takes with the microcalipers does not match what has been recorded in the lab book.

"How is this possible?" says Jac, slamming the book shut in exasperation.

"Perhaps there's a fault with these microcalipers?" says the Archivist. All his earlier anger has evaporated. Now he only sounds confused.

"What, a fault that coincidentally replicates the same issue with the UVD? Because the error is *exactly* the same. You can see that, can't you? The measurements aren't just off randomly, they're off by 0.2 millimetres every time. 0.2 millimetres smaller, to be precise."

"I know it's unlikely. I just… can't think of anything else." He seems as stumped by his inability to think of a solution as he is by the error itself.

Conceding the point, Jac finds another set of microcalipers and passes them over. But when he takes the measurement again, he gets the exact same result. He taps the microcalipers irritably against the side of the glove box.

"Perhaps there's a bug in the logging software?" he says. "One that alters the measurements after they've been entered into the database."

"That can't be it," she says. "The pilot project didn't use the same logging software we use now. I don't see how that could explain the same error being replicated across both sets of data."

"There has to be *something*," he says with an increasing air of desperation. "That kind of systematic discrepancy, it only ever means one thing: instrumental malfunction. But if it's not your goddamn UVD and it's not the microcalipers and it's not the logging software… it has to be something else."

"Maybe…"

"Come on, think. There must be something we've missed, some part of the process that we haven't properly considered.

It'll be something simple, just one factor that's been the same ever since the pilot."

His earnestness is, Jac thinks, a mark of the situation's gravity. He's not even pausing to sneer or throw her a few barbed comments as is his habitual manner. She reconsiders the problem, mentally sifting back through everything she has discovered: the unexplained variations, the discrepancies between the recorded measurements and what they have observed from the samples themselves. The Archivist is right: there has to be a way of explaining it all, a single factor that accounts for everything else. Of course, there is one simple explanation that accounts for everything, one way of reconciling the variations and discrepancies, but it's too ridiculous for words. Unless...

All at once, Occam's razor slashes through her doubts. She just hasn't been able to see it before now.

If the problem isn't with the tools she's using, then it can only be with the trees themselves. The trees simply aren't the same size as the recorded measurements say they are. Each of them is exactly 0.2 millimetres smaller than it should be. Of eleven billion trees the Borlaug has planted in Greenland, not one has grown as much as they thought – not one has *ever* grown as much as they thought. It goes right back to the beginning, to the start of the pilot. *How can she not have spotted it before?* She swears under her breath, not quite daring to believe it but knowing that it is the truth, the only explanation that, finally, makes sense of everything.

The trees in Greenland are dying.

22

As they turn out of the plaza, Alix steps out into Euston Road to hail an oncoming rickshaw. Miri stares. The Warren isn't more than a twenty minute walk away. And even if it were further, catching a rickshaw would never have occurred to her; for two years it's been walking or nothing. In that time, she's got to know a few riders personally and seen for herself how hard their work is and how they get treated by their customers.

The rickshaw pulls up beside them and Miri hangs back. "I'd rather walk," she says. Her mother grumbles an indistinct reply and tries to persuade her to get into the cab, fanning her face with her hand.

"Is the heat really that bad?" Miri asks.

"It's not that," Alix replies. "But I'm not as young as you are and not as fit as I once was. We've been on our feet for hours."

"Alright then, why don't we sit down somewhere and take a break?"

After a brief negotiation, Alix agrees. With profuse apologies, they send the rickshaw on its way with an empty cab and set about finding somewhere to get a drink. Although Miri is well acquainted with several bars, none of her regular haunts are nearby and, besides, they're not the sort of places she'd take her mother. After a moment's thought, Alix suggests a pub that she and Jac sometimes go to called the Stammering Cobbler that's not far from where they are now.

Despite the close proximity to the Borlaug, it turns out to be more down to earth than Miri's expecting: a small, dimly lit room with a handful of mismatched chairs and tables. In the centre is an old-fashioned wooden counter, atop which a few round-bellied caskets lie on their sides. Apart from the bartender, there are only a couple of people there. Alix tells Miri to pick a table while she orders, and Miri plumps for one in the corner, taking the chair nearest the wall so she can stare out across the room. She plucks the white rat from where it has nestled in the crook of her arm and lets it race around the table, the fleshy ear on its back quivering as it runs, the burn red and oozing.

A moment later, Alix appears bearing two long drafts of pale gold ale. The glasses are so full that the ale slops over the sides when she sets them down.

"Cheers," she says, tapping her glass lightly against Miri's.

For a moment, it's violently strange to be sitting across from her mother in a pub. Everything about it, from Alix's disarrayed appearance – her hair wild from the humidity, her camisole half-drenched with sweat and clinging to her skin – to the choice of refreshment seems wrong. Her mother doesn't drink pints. As she recalls, both Alix and Jac prefer gin to beer. Not that she had many occasions to observe her mothers in such a public setting as a restaurant or bar. Growing up, the three of them rarely dined out together. Jac's fans made it impossible, never fearing to approach them, to disturb their meal, intent on wringing Jac's hand and gushing copious thanks to her for "saving the world". Jac would always reply with the same feeble joke that made Miri squirm in her seat: "Don't thank me, thank the trees!" Now that Jac isn't here, at least they will be spared the embarrassment. Miri and Alix are anonymous, entirely unremarkable. Suddenly her perspective shifts, lurching around to consider what they must look like to the bartender, to the other customers sat hunched over their pint glasses: two women sharing a drink, perhaps related, perhaps not. Well, two women and a half-mutant rat.

Then, all at once, it is the most ordinary thing in the world to be there with Alix. She picks up her glass and drinks.

The ale is surprisingly good, crisp and refreshing. On her practically empty stomach, just a few mouthfuls are enough to make Miri's head spin, but she keeps sipping away, determinedly keeping pace with her mother, who has already put away a quarter of what's in her glass.

"What happened to the rat?" asks Alix with a sudden frown of consternation as her eyes fall on the red welt at the base of the ear on its back.

"Nothing," says Miri.

"It looks like a burn mark."

"It will heal."

Alix sucks air through her teeth. "I wouldn't be so sure about that. Burns are prime sites for infection. It's much harder for the skin to perform a protective barrier. You'd be surprised how many people we had come into the hospital who had contracted sepsis after scalding themselves with boiling water."

Miri hasn't heard that before. She thoughtfully chews at a piece of dry skin on her bottom lip and looks again at the rat. The burn is bad – a blistered, watery bulge – but she can't bear to think about it, can't bear to think about *any* of it now. Eager to move the conversation along, Miri lunges for the nearest topic that presents itself, one that she has been carefully avoiding all day.

"Do you miss working at the hospital?"

"All the time," says Alix heavily. "I mean, there are parts of it I'm happy to do without. I don't miss the long hours. I don't miss being bone-tired all the time. But it feels like I haven't done a single useful thing since I left."

"It must have been hard, though. Dealing with some of the cases that came in."

"Sure," says Alix. "There were some people who came in that we couldn't do anything for, that we didn't even begin to have the resources to help. And those days were hard. Really hard. But for every patient we saved, it was worth it."

Miri nods. Even on Alix's worst day in the hospital, Miri never once saw her break down.

"Of course," she adds, "it's the difficult cases that tend to stay with you. There was one we had... a seven year-old girl from Dorset. Marburg virus. Ever heard of it?"

"No."

"It's a nasty one. Awful." She shakes her head. "First case we'd seen. Comes from North Africa, originally. Highly infectious. Carried by certain species of African bat. Bats aren't usually migratory of course, but these days..." she trails off.

"The girl had this virus?" Miri prompts.

Alix blinks. "Yes. I had the story from her dad. She caught a bat and ate it. Well, you could see they were both half-starved to death. You know what it's like in the Counties. Unluckily for her, the bat was Marburg positive. At first, she suffered high fever, acute vomiting, painful rashes. Her family applied for a visa to bring her to London... I think they were denied at first, maybe a few times after that as well. By the time they were finally permitted to bring her to Ormond Street, she was passing colon tissue in her diarrhoea. We had to put her straight into isolation on the ICU. In the first few hours, she developed oedema of the hands and feet, haemorrhaging from the mucus membranes, haemorrhaging from everywhere. You should've seen the state of her injection sites, she wouldn't stop bleeding when we tried to put in a line."

Alix pauses to take a deep drink from her glass. "Of course, we had to do everything through a plastic screen. It wasn't so much that it made the work harder, it was more that it kept her isolated and cut off. I've never seen anyone more alone. I couldn't properly explain to her what I was doing or why. I couldn't even stroke her face or show her a smile because I was covered in protective overalls from head to toe."

She lowers her gaze to the table, takes another slow drink. "Then she started having convulsions that we couldn't stop. Her dad just stood there on the other side of the plastic with us and watched while we ran around the hospital bed, trying not to say out loud how long we thought she had left, because he'd hear us. The poor man. He couldn't even touch his dying little girl."

Miri wants to tell her to stop but can't seem to engage her tongue.

"There was nothing we could do. No treatment or medication we could give her because no one had thought to develop that kind of medication while we still had the chance. Marburg isn't supposed to affect the children up here, it's only the little girls down in Africa who are supposed to bleed and swell and convulse to death. We couldn't even give her anything decent for the pain because of the clotting... All the while she was begging for water; she was so thirsty the only thing she could say was 'I need a drink, I need a drink.' I had to try and tell her that I could only administer liquids through a line, but when I got anywhere near her bleeding arms with the IV she started crying..." she shudders and falters in her telling.

"Like I say," Alix continues, raising her eyes again to Miri, "it's the difficult cases that stay with you. That was one of the worst. All the same, I wish I'd never left."

"Then why did you?"

For a moment Alix holds Miri's gaze with her own, then she drops her eyes to her lap. "I had to. When you left... it destroyed me, Miri. I managed to hold it together for a couple of months, but I – it got pretty bad. Soon, I was as much a danger to the patients as I was to myself. Everyone agreed it would be best if I retired early. They were probably right. I mean, of course they were. I've come a long way since then, but there are still rough days. It's like I've been picking up the pieces ever since."

23

Alix groans with the pain of another contraction. Her hair is plastered to her forehead with sweat. "I can't do this," she gasps.

"You can," says Jac, clutching her hand. "Just breathe."

"It's too much, I can't, I can't–"

It's the day their countdown begins. Jac is sitting in the cab of an armoured rickshaw with a heavily pregnant Alix. They are outside the maternity wing of the university hospital, an elegant construction of white tiles and tinted glass floodlit from below. Beyond the high roof, the sky is dark; the distant stars just discernible through a thin layer of smog. A strong gust of wind rattles the cab, briefly drowning out the clamour of angry shouts that echo around the hospital complex.

"Traitors!" the crowd jeers. "Murderers!"

Jac leans over to peer through the small, high window of reinforced glass set in the front of the cab. Through the wire grille, she can make out the rickshaw rider ahead – dressed in a heavy uniform complete with helmet and stab vest and standing up on the pedals, ready to take off at any moment. Beyond is an angry mob, fists raised, faces contorted into animal snarls. They've been kettled into a side alley by a cordon of hospital guards standing with linked arms to form a tight human chain. The Activists are growing more daring and savage in their attempts to break through. It doesn't look like the cordon will hold for long.

One of the Activists clashes angrily with a hospital guard, gesticulating wildly with a placard. It shows the female reproductive organs, crudely drawn, with a large red line slashing through it like a knife. Beneath it in a barely legible cursive reads the common slogan: "Say no to life." Jac puts out a hand to the side of the rickshaw cab, desperately glad of the thick reinforced steel walls.

"I can feel a pressure *there*, Jac. I think she's coming now..."

"Hold it in! You can't have her here, Alix. Just... hold it in."

Their plan was to wait in the cab until the pigsuits arrived to disperse the crowd, but Alix is running out of time and it seems like the cordon might give way at any minute. They radio this through to the hospital and an alternative plan is quickly agreed.

Within minutes, a porter wearing a bright-red Kevlar vest appears on the hospital steps – an extra body to shield Alix if the cordon breaks – and hurries down to the rickshaw.

"Someone's coming!" Jac shouts, and then, in what she hopes is a more soothing voice: "Just breathe."

Reaching the rickshaw, the porter opens the door. "Ready to have a baby?" they boom, taking Alix by the shoulders and half-supporting, half-dragging her from the passenger seat.

"Just get her to safety!" Jac shouts. "She says the baby's coming now!"

Impervious to Jac's panic, the porter strikes up a conversational patter. If they're attempting to drown out the screams of the Activists, their words are about as effective as bows and arrows against lightning. Closer now, the faces beyond the cordon are red and crazed with anger. Jac catches sight of the ouroboros.

"What's your birth plan?" the porter asks quickly. "How are you feeling? What are you hoping for; blonde like you or brunette like the wife? Not that it matters!"

"Eighteen years and you'll pay!" screams the crowd.

"You're OK," the porter says again, more urgently this time, as though insisting on the point will make it true. "Whereabouts do you live? Come far?"

Alix puffs and pants as the porter steers her up the steps, still dressed in her pyjamas and clutching a heavily saturated towel between her legs. This baby is certainly in a hurry, taking Jac and Alix unawares in the middle of the night and three weeks early.

For half an hour, Jac had sat with Alix in the living room and timed her contractions. "They're coming every minute now," Jac had said in dismay. "They're not supposed to come this fast yet." It was then that Jac put in a frantic call to the hospital. The woman on the other end informed her that they needed to come in *now* and Jac had rushed to call the cab, knowing it was all her fault, blaming herself for everything.

Now at the steps to the hospital, Jac hurries to catch up with Alix and the porter. She throws a protective arm around her wife's shoulders and wrests her from the porter's hold.

"I've got her, thanks."

The porter shrugs and lets Alix go, moving on ahead to open the doors.

Suddenly racked by another contraction, Alix falters on the steps. At exactly that moment, the cordon breaks. The crowd surges forward, a lone man streaking out ahead of the pack.

"Reproduction kills!" he yells, fiddling to unscrew something in his grip.

Instinctively, Jac steps forward, shielding Alix with her body. Just in time. The man uncaps the bottle and lobs it at her, dousing her in a thick, sticky liquid. "Blood on your hands, Earth traitor!"

The porter takes two swift paces and grabs Alix, pulling her up the remaining steps and whisking her through the door. Jac tears up the steps behind them, gaining the safety of the foyer with only seconds to spare. The doors zip shut. As they do, a platoon of pigsuits arrive, fibre-cartridge shotguns cocked. The Activists scatter at once.

When Jac finally turns her back on the chaos and seeks out her wife, she finds that Alix has disappeared. A set of double doors to her left are marked "MATERNITY". Trainers squeaking on the pristine floors, Jac makes to barge through them, only to be stopped by a firm hand on her shoulder.

"You have to wait here," says the porter, pointing towards a line of plastic chairs. "You can't come in."

Jac stares at them in disbelief. "What do you mean, I can't come in? We were promised..."

The porter is firm. "The head doctor won't allow it."

"There's been some sort of mistake," says Jac, shaking her head and making to push past them towards the doors and through to Alix. The porter's hand – still on her shoulder – presses down painfully, halting her progress.

"You can't come in," they say again.

"But we were given special permission!" Jac is shouting now, helpless in her anger. She shrugs the porter's hand off her shoulder but doesn't move to pass them.

"The head doctor's insistent: one rule for all."

Jac glares but the porter's face is set and their word is final. Looking past them, she stares longingly at the double doors. Her hands ball into fists as angry tears begin to form in the corners of her eyes. She should've known this would happen; Alix had told her it would. There hadn't been any special permission, of course, but she had been convinced an exception would be made for her. It usually was, given her standing. But not now. Now she must suffer the same fear and indignity as every other non-birthing parent: to sit alone and wait.

The porter, taking her more gently by the arm, guides her into one of the plastic chairs. Perhaps sensing that Jac isn't going to make another run for the door – which is, in any case, locked – they disappear for a moment and return clutching a mop. Jac looks at it questioningly and then, following the porter's eyes, sees that she has trailed a line of dark, heavy liquid across the reception floor. Remembering the incident outside, she looks down at her soaked clothes in surprise.

"It's only molasses," the porter explains, dragging the mop across the floor. "Stains worse than real blood though."

Jac nods, not trusting herself to speak or to ask the questions hammering in her throat. *Is Alix alright? Is the baby? What's happening? Will someone come and tell me what's going on?* It's impossible to know. No one speaks about what happens on maternity wards. No one complains. It is shameful enough, having a child in the first place, and there's nothing like guilt to hold the tongue. She turns her eyes back to the double doors, wishing she could see through them, wishing she could be with her wife.

For the first time, she notices a large print tacked to the left of the doors, all soft tones and pastel colours. It catches her eye because she recognises the scene it depicts. The Assyrian King Sennacherib cowers outside a temple at the feet of his son, who stands over him with raised sword, animated with a righteous fury, long robes buffeted by the Iraqi desert wind. Jac looks upon the all-too-familiar scene for a long time; long after the porter has finished cleaning the floor and disappeared, leaving her alone in the reception, sticky and cold.

Her attention snaps when the double doors suddenly open, revealing a harassed-looking doctor dressed head-to-foot in green scrubs. "I'm so sorry!" she says, voice full of regret. "The porter didn't know who you were. Please, come through – she's about to arrive…"

Hours later, looking out of the tall Warren windows and cradling a tiny, red-faced Miri in her arms, Jac swears to do all she can to protect her family and make the world safe for them: the woman she loves more than life and the precious little girl they have created together. And why not? Jac has never yet come across a problem she could not solve, a task she could not complete. She does not know yet that one day, sooner than is fair, she will learn what it means to come up short. To be found wanting. To fail.

24

Her voice gruff over the microphone, Jac explains her theory in a few short words to the Archivist. The trees are dying, and someone's interfering with the records to hide the fact, to hide that the project is failing. That the project *has* failed. The Archivist looks entirely taken aback, the energy sapping away from him. Had he not seen the evidence with his own eyes, she knows he wouldn't believe her.

"But... the Global Average..." he stammers. "I checked this week. Global CO_2 levels are only 500 ppm. If the trees were dying, it would be higher."

"I know, I checked yesterday. But perhaps the carbon levels are no more to be believed than the measurements listed for the sample cores. We have the evidence, right in front of us. Someone *must* be interfering. I could be wrong... I *hope* I am... but if not, then the trees in the ARZ won't live long enough to prevent the onset of the overheating event." She falls silent, thinking of the wasted years she could have spent trying to come up with another solution. It's too late now. Much too late.

The Archivist considers what she has just said. "Who would do something like that? Who would want to interfere with the project's results?"

"I don't know," she admits. "Someone who wants everyone to think that it's still working."

"If you're right—"

"I *am* right."

"*If* you're right, then what?"

"We'll all die." She lets the words float in the air for a breath. Then they take physical form and hang heavy around her neck, a noose she's tied for the world. "And it will happen sooner rather than later. Maybe only a few years from now. We'll burn up in the heat and suffocate on the carbon." Even if the project *had* worked, not everyone was saved anyway. She thinks of the disease, famine and war that has plagued the Federated Counties for years and all the lives that have been lost already. At least now it's fair. Everyone – the whole species – is going to be Offset.

As soon as she thinks this, Jac's heart convulses painfully. *Miri.* Getting used to the prospect of her own premature death is one thing, but Miri's? Whatever her problems with the girl, she never meant for this. Miri isn't supposed to die. She and Alix would never have brought her into the world if they hadn't believed there'd still be one around for her to grow old in.

It took her months to convince Alix that having a child would be alright, that the project would make all the difference, that she was doing everything she could to make the planet safe for her. Years later, Alix joked that it really had worked out for the best, that Jac would never have got the Borlaug directorship if it hadn't been for their little Miri acting as incontrovertible proof of Jac's confidence in the project. Jac had laughed at that – Alix knew as well as she did that she'd taken the directorship *because* of Miri, not the other way around.

It seems so distant to her now. All the years Jac has spent breaking her back on Project Salix are as good as useless and every Offset is rendered null. The world is going to end and there's nothing she can do about it.

"My daughter," she croaks to the Archivist. "I've failed her."

For once, he has no retort for her. His only expression behind the visor is wordless despair. For all his dislike of Jac, he never once doubted the project. Now that faith is crashing down around him.

It is, perhaps, his silent horror that stops her spinning out and instead spurs her to action. With so little time left, she needs to make sure that every second counts. There is only one thing that she can do now that could possibly help: she has to confirm that the carbon dioxide levels are much higher than everyone believes. If she can get that evidence, then she can tell the world. She owes it to her staff and, yes, even to the Archivist; to everyone who had entrusted the future to her. Above all else, she owes it to Miri. But there is only one place she can get the proof she needs.

Greenland.

For many years, the Global Monitoring Division measured global carbon dioxide levels at the Mauna Loa Observatory on the Island of Hawaii. But, as global temperatures rose, the island and its neighbours became ravaged by dengue fever, and extreme drought was followed by periods of catastrophic flooding. Then the devastation of widespread poverty, brought about by the near total collapse of the Hawaiian tourist industry as a consequence of the Bogotá Accord placing a global ban on air travel, broke down what was left of the place. Eventually, the entire archipelago declared itself officially isolated. The Mauna Loa Observatory was rendered defunct.

The global carbon dioxide monitoring station was relocated. Numerous regions were suggested and then rejected for any number of reasons that made them unsuitable: increased air pollution, unstable and untrustworthy local governments, the risk of looting and destruction of expensive technical equipment, and so on. Finally, the Global Monitoring Division hit upon the Gunnbjørn Mountain in Greenland. As the highest spot north of the Arctic circle, it was free of risk of human interference due to the exclusion zone that had been put in place after the Kvanefjeld disaster. It was also in a newly snow-free, windy and clement spot and was, as such, determined to be the safest place where accurate global carbon dioxide levels could be recorded.

Now the station sits high above the Project Salix trees and, as with all elements of the industrious work conducted in Greenland, it is operated remotely. The Borlaug charges a healthy monthly sum for the use of its on-site infrastructure and relations between the two London-based institutes are kept necessarily smooth.

In a flash, Jac sees what must be done. She needs proof that the global carbon levels are far higher than they should be – proof that they cannot trust the numbers on which their parables of planetary restoration are founded. Getting it will mean putting her life on the line. But her life's been on the line since the day Miri was born.

To get her proof, she must climb the Gunnbjørn Mountain and record the level of carbon dioxide at the station using an analogue method. *Easier said than done*, she thinks, folding her arms across her chest. Quite apart from the problem of actually getting there, she doesn't have any of the right tools to take the measurement. *Although…* she shifts her weight from foot to foot as the idea forms. There must be test kits somewhere in the facility that would be quick and simple to use.

What else would she need? Jac shifts her weight again, rocking gently from side to side. She'll have to bring back tangible evidence, something from Greenland that can be used to independently verify the levels of carbon dioxide. A soil sample should do the trick. Because of the radioactive isotopes present in Greenland and in Greenland only, a sample can be unequivocally assigned to that spot. To that end, she'll need to take a hermetically sealed, radiation-shielded canister to bring the soil back – for which one of the spare capsules should serve adequately.

If she's right and returns safely with the soil, she'll need to lean on her pool of contacts to arrange a conference and announce the findings, offering the sample for independent analysis, but that can be dealt with later. Once the results are confirmed, there's no saying what will happen next. Maybe there'll be an expedition to Greenland. Perhaps they'll be able to unmask whoever it is who has been doctoring the records.

As plans go, Jac knows it leaves much to be desired but she has little alternative. There is, however, one insurmountable issue. Getting to Greenland.

At last, she falls still and then, with an effort, she turns to the Archivist and, reluctantly, explains her idea. Although she braces herself for an excoriating reply, to her surprise, it never comes. He stares blankly at her for a moment as if unable to believe his ears and then glances down at the floor.

"What about the NAX?"

As soon as he says it, Jac wonders why she hasn't thought of it before. The pneumatic cargo pipe runs beneath the sea all the way from Alba to Greenland. If she stows away on a departing pod, she can be there within three hours. Then she can ride the cable car up to the station, take the measurement and wait for a pod back. She will only be on radioactive soil for a matter of hours.

As if reading her mind, the Archivist makes a feeble protest. "That level of exposure… you won't survive."

"I might not," says Jac. "But these suits are the best protection available and if I'm not in Greenland for long, maybe it won't be too bad. At the very least, I'll be able to get back before the effects set in. Then I can spread the word. Whatever comes after that… it doesn't matter. If I'm right, we'll all be dead before long anyway."

"You're mad," he mutters just loud enough for his mic to pick up his words. Then he steels himself and looks her squarely in the eye. "What do you need me to do?"

25

With her glasses perched on the end of her nose, Alix is peering at a beer-stained menu. "If I don't get something to eat soon, I'll fade away."

Miri looks at her mother. Alix appears to be in good health and is evidently well-nourished. It has only been a few hours since breakfast; she is nowhere close to fading away. But Alix is not accustomed to going without. Miri remembers well what it was like when she first left home, how her hunger almost consumed her. Eventually, her stomach adjusted to the more restricted diet, but for a couple of weeks there was a deep ache in her belly that was all she could think about.

When she finally got used to it, there were a miraculous few days when she marvelled at how little she could consume and still survive. She wondered if that was how the human body was designed to really live, on the spare and intermittent diet of the forager. It instilled in her a secret pride for her new, hard-won stoicism. But that didn't last long.

Her body quickly began to show the toll malnourishment was taking: her hair thinned, sores appeared on her face and chest, her stomach became painful and bloated. She started spending most of her time just trying to get warm, even when everyone else was complaining about the sweltering heat. Although it's what her body needs most, eating now seems to cause as many problems as not, making her nauseous or turning her guts to liquid or leaving her doubled over in intense pain.

She knows she's sick and needs help but mostly she just tries not to think about it. That's easy enough when you're on your own with no one paying attention to what you put into your mouth. Now she has to contend with Alix's needs as well. After what her mother has confessed about her reasons for leaving the hospital, she's not inclined to argue.

Seeing her hesitation, Alix reaches across the table and squeezes her arm. "You need to eat, Miri. Don't look at me like that. I've had patients like you before. You've been hungry for so long that you can't see the coping strategies you've invented are part of the problem. Tell me eating something this morning didn't make you feel better."

Miri is about to tell her no, actually, it didn't, but then she stops. Since the initial wave of nausea subsided, she *has* been feeling better than usual. She isn't shivering with cold anymore, and her usual aches and pains haven't been bothering her quite so much. And her head is certainly a lot clearer now; it has been ever since she woke up.

"Alright," she says at last.

Calmer after her resistance that morning, she lets Alix order for her. When the bowl of soup arrives, Miri obediently picks it up and raises it to her lips. The soup, little more than a thin broth, is warm and palatable, laced through with a rich seam of salt and oil. It contains a few chewy grains of some pulse or other – unidentifiable after being freeze-dried and rehydrated – and Miri has to pause every so often to mash these between her teeth. She drinks until the bowl is empty and then wipes the oil from her lips with the back of her hand. Alix smiles at her from across her own half-eaten dish of fried lacewing rice.

When Alix sets off down the street that leads back to the Warren, Miri hangs back. Her appointment is fast approaching. The Celt is expecting her. Realising that Miri is not with her, Alix stops and turns, her eyes questioning.

"Are you alright?"

Miri nods then moistens her dry lips with her tongue. "I need to go to Soho."

A look of consternation crosses Alix's face. Miri's not surprised. Soho has a reputation as a rough area. Growing up, she was warned never to venture into the tenements there alone – advice that she obediently followed until she left home. She's not sure if her mother has ever set foot in the place. But that doesn't stop her from asking if she wants to come with her. She has an idea that Alix might find the trip worthwhile.

"Come with you?" repeats Alix blankly. "To Soho?"

"Unless you have other plans?"

A look of pain crosses Alix's face. It occurs to Miri that her mothers will have long since planned how to spend their last day together – that Alix is only here now because Jac thoughtlessly absented herself. As usual.

Miri wonders what they were planning. Perhaps they were going to have dinner and spend the evening looking at old photographs before the memories they preserved were cracked through with grief. Perhaps they were going to act out the ancient parting ritual of sharing salt and honey. Certainly something in the privacy of their own home, not striding out into Soho.

Miri is about to rescind her offer when Alix unexpectedly says, "OK. I'll come."

It takes them the best part of an hour to cross the city. By then, the air has begun to cool, enough that Alix has pulled her crumpled blouse back on over her camisole. Miri can tell that she is starting to get nervous.

"Are they... these people we're going to meet. Are they anti-natalists?"

"What? No. Well, some of them must be, I suppose. But not all."

"Oh. I thought–"

"What, that I was taking you to some sort of rally?"

Alix gives her a sheepish look. "Well, I don't know. They'd probably eat me alive, wouldn't they?"

Miri stifles a grin.

"But that's what you've been doing these last two years, isn't it?" Alix continues. "Agitating for the anti-natalist cause?"

"Not exactly, no."

"So, you really meant it when you said you were on your own? You haven't been indoctrinated into some sort of cult?"

Miri gives a wan smile. "No, Mum. No cults. I've got some anti-natalist friends, but…"

"But what?"

"I'm not really interested in doing what they do. Campaigning and everything."

"What *have* you been doing, then?"

Miri shrugs. She doesn't know how to explain that being alone was the entire point, the only thing she really wanted, the only thing that seemed honest.

As they cross the abandoned wastes of Oxford Street, Alix hums lightly to herself and keeps smoothing her hair with her hands, like she's trying to make herself less conspicuous. Miri knows, of course, that it won't be lack of neatness that causes Alix to stand out, but the expensive cut of her blouse and skirt. It doesn't matter how crumpled they have become, there's no mistaking the quality. She doesn't mention this, however, but takes her mother by the arm and steers her firmly down Wardour Street, where they hook a right onto D'Arblay and then take the next left. Berwick Street.

On either side of the narrow road, squalid towers of apartment blocks loom above them. No two buildings match in dimension, style or material; tall brick structures stand next to brutalist concrete facades and squat shelters cobbled together from corrugated iron and plasterboard. The reflective whitewash on every surface has been allowed to fade and peel away. In most places it is completely invisible beneath a thick layer of soot. Hard metal studs have been fixed to the pavement and every alcove and windowsill in sight sports wire spikes or shards of broken glass that cut upwards. The purpose is to make it impossible for anyone to loiter or sit idly out in the street – or at least, this is the excuse. The real point is to make sure that the inhabitants of the Soho tenements keep to their homes, for that is where they can be more easily controlled.

The people who live here are not London-born. That much is evident from the tattered flags and pennants that hang sadly from the grimy windows. Some have come from as far afield as Alba, but most are from various parts of the Federated Counties.

"Look, Miri," says Alix, pointing with surprise at one limp flag, a black-gold split cut through by a diagonal white band pitted with black markings. "Is that–"

"The flag of Norfolk," finishes Miri. "There are people from Cambridgeshire here, too."

Alix stares open-mouthed. "It can't be. The fens were lost to flooding decades back, long before you were born. I remember watching the news coverage of the relief efforts… after the banks of the Wash broke. There was no one to rescue. Only bodies to bury."

"Some people must have survived."

"It's not possible."

Miri shrugs. She's heard otherwise. She's heard that there are even a few inhabited islands, but she's not going to push the point. The people she has met claiming to be from the fens are much the same as others she's met from across the Federated Counties: hungry and desperately trying to carve out a living.

Everyone in the Soho tenements has come here to work. They make up the best part of the contingent of skilled foreign workers on which London heavily relies. Because it is nearly impossible to get a visa that covers family members, the majority of them have come alone. Their existence is precarious. They are paid at half-rates and most of that goes on rent and the associated costs. What little they have left, they often try to send back to their families, though it's getting harder and harder to send money safely across the Counties. Most are on visas that mean they will be denied re-entry if they ever stray beyond the city's limits. Although all are encouraged to apply for permanent residency – an application for which there is, of course, an exorbitant fee – it is rarely ever granted. The people who live here are trapped, completely and utterly. Unable to leave but not welcome to stay.

Miri doesn't know how much of this Alix is aware of. Her expression certainly grows more grim as they follow Berwick Street south and Miri spots her shooting nervous glances at the numerous pigsuits they pass. There are far more here in Soho than she will be used to seeing at home or in the areas around St Pancras. Here, a pigsuit stands at nearly every street corner. Not only are they in better condition than many Miri has seen, but their central casings have also been blacked out, making it impossible to see through to the empty pit within.

As one turns to follow their progress down the road, Miri has the unerring feeling of being watched. For the first time, she finds herself wondering if there are real human eyes staring out at them behind the tinted acrylic. A shiver runs down the length of her spine.

There aren't many locals out in the street, but the few they pass seem to take a keen interest in Alix. Miri notices more than one thin face pressed up against a window, pointing out Alix's pink blouse and wild hair, eyes following her as she passes. Miri isn't entirely sure whether it's because they recognise her as the wife of the famous Jac Boltanski or because she so obviously looks like she doesn't belong here. Miri's not overly worried though – either way, Alix will be perfectly safe, particularly if they stay together. Her only concern is that her mother will realise the attention she is attracting and panic. But so far, she seems to be holding herself together.

They turn onto Peter Street, which quickly becomes a dead end, culminating in an old three-storey building; the bricks are black with soot, the glass in the windows warped and discoloured. At road level, there is a wide steel shutter, blue paint all but eaten away by rust. There are no pigsuits here and the street is completely deserted. Even so, Miri is careful to scan around and make doubly sure they are alone. Then, with a sudden thrill of realisation that she is closer than ever to the Celt, she stoops down, grabs the handle and heaves the shutter open.

26

The Archivist has been subdued ever since their discovery. Jac isn't foolish enough to believe that his feelings towards her have changed, but she's grateful at least that he has decided to set them to one side while they deal with the matter at hand. He's as troubled as she is by the project's failure and, like it or not, they're in this together. With his assistance, Jac puts together a list of all the things she'll need for her expedition. A torch. An empty capsule and a trowel. A test kit to check the atmospheric carbon. And, just for good measure, a core extractor and a pair of microcalipers.

"Alright," says Jac to the Archivist. "Help me out. Where are we going to get hold of all of this? The microcalipers are easy enough," she adds, brandishing the last pair they used to measure growth rings.

"There are empty capsules here in the annexe as well," says the Archivist, glancing back over the list. "Everything else we should be able to find in the main part of the facility. Do you want me to go?"

Jac shakes her head. "There isn't time. We would have to scrub down first."

The Archivist nods. The NAX command centre is buried deep within the nuclear annexe – as only befitting given the radioactive nature of the cargo shipped over from Greenland. If they're to go through with this plan, they'll both have to keep their hazmat suits on. Not to mention the fact that it will be her only protection from the radiation once she gets to Greenland.

After a moment, the Archivist suggests radioing up to the Facility Manager. "She's already sent a lab book through the airlock. Let's see what else she can do. Should I tell her about the plan?"

"No," says Jac at once. Although she wields the authority of the Director, there is no escaping the fact that riding the NAX will count as a gross breach of regulations. She hardly expects to be allowed to go ahead with her plan if she is found out.

At her instruction, the Archivist radios the Facility Manager on a frequency they can both use and tells her what they need. When he finishes, there is a brief silence on the other end of the line. Then she asks why the items are required.

"I've been told that information is restricted," says the Archivist.

Another silence. "I see. Is the Director there?"

"Speaking," says Jac into her mic.

"Professor Boltanski–"

"I need those items," says Jac, not allowing her to finish. "Consider this my official authorisation."

"But what are they–"

"It's better that you don't know. Please, I need you to trust me on this."

"Doesn't your train leave in less than an hour?"

"I'm afraid it will be leaving without me," says Jac.

A loud sigh makes the line crackle. "Very well. I'll have those things sent down now."

"No," says Jac.

"No?"

"No, don't have them sent down. Bring them yourself," she says. Now she thinks of it, the fewer people involved, the better. "And I caution you to be discreet."

"I don't see why I should–"

"Do this for me and I'll see that my report to the Board of Oversight about the incident that happened here on your watch is favourable. If they do threaten suspension, I'll vouch for you." She glances at the Archivist as she speaks, who doesn't so much as raise a brow at the baldness of the bribe, perhaps more out of respect for their temporary truce than anything else. Jac doesn't care. It works. After a moment, the Facility Manager agrees to do exactly as she asks.

Jac thinks fleetingly of her bag on the other side of the airlock. Her golden wedding ring is tucked away in the inside pocket. It will be safe there, she knows, uncomfortable as she feels without it. *I'll just have to make sure I come back for it.* Though what state she'll be in, she doesn't like to think. No human has set foot inside the entire ARZ since the Kvanefjeld disaster. As much as Jac would like to believe she won't be in Greenland long enough to receive a fatal dose of radiation, she knows better than to hope. If there is any silver lining, it is simply knowing that it will be days before the exposure kills her. Presuming nothing else goes wrong, she'll have time enough to come home, to share her evidence of the project's failure, to say goodbye to her wife and child.

The thing she most wants to do now is call Alix, but Jac's phone is in her bag along with her wedding ring. Even if she asked the Facility Manager to send it through with the rest of the items, Jac wouldn't be able to use it while encased in her hazmat suit. For one thing, it would be difficult to hear anything Alix said without the phone being connected to her in-suit radio. For another, even if she placed the call and screamed a message at the top of her lungs, the sound would get no further than the visor of her hood.

Something inside Jac caves at the thought of not being able to speak to Alix. She needs to apologise, to say sorry for failing to make the world safe for their daughter like she promised, for not coming home when she said she would, for leaving in the first place when the Offset is so soon. What if she doesn't make it back in time for the ceremony? No, it's no good worrying about that now. It's bad enough that she's six hundred miles away when she should be at home, when she should be at Alix's side. For years she's lived with the knowledge that she and her wife would have to part forever when Miri turned eighteen. This is not the way she planned to say goodbye, not the way she planned to face her death.

Her only consolation is that if there's anyone who can understand what she's doing and why, it's Alix. She's never once questioned Jac's commitment to her work or the importance of it. How could she? In some ways, her work at Great Ormond Street had been just the same – consuming and absolutely critical. In the course of her time there, Alix had done a thousand times over what Jac is trying to do on the macroscale: save lives. It's a great honour to take on that work, but a burden too. Alix alone knows exactly how that crushing weight feels. Jac's not going to let her down now. She's not going to give up, no matter how much she wishes she could.

27

The building at the end of Peter Street is more spacious than it first appears. Once a multi-storey car park, it has stood empty for long years, ever since the Bogotá Accord placed a global ban on the private ownership of motorised vehicles. Now, though, it operates as a ReproViolence Clinic for the residents of the Soho tenements and anyone else who cannot afford the fees of a fully licensed hospital. It is run by a small contingent of volunteers who are always overstretched and have to scramble to get hold of even the most basic medical supplies.

After Miri secures the steel shutter behind them, she leads Alix through to one of the clinic's makeshift wards. In each parking bay marked out on the concrete floor is a patient. Mostly, they lie on thin foam mattresses, but there are not quite enough of these to go around, so some beds have instead been made up out of old cushions and scrap fabric stuffed with polystyrene packing chips. Around one or two of the bays are rigid dividers of corrugated cardboard, concertinaed out like a standing screen. It's all that can be done to afford the patient within a little privacy while intimate medical procedures are conducted. Sometimes, though, the dividers are set up to protect the other patients from the sight of a dead body. With so few resources, deaths are common and it's not always possible for the volunteers to collect the corpses right away.

Although the volunteers do what they can to keep the place clean and disinfected, the thick odour of faeces and vomit is unmistakable beneath the acrid top notes of bleach. It is a cloying stench of decay that pools beneath the tongue, then suppurates and trickles down the throat. Above everything rises an unceasing chorus of groans, coughs and splutters that is only amplified by the echoes of the hard, concrete surfaces.

Briefly, Miri's mind wanders upwards to the floor above, where there's a second, quieter ward. It is there that the Celt is waiting for her. Miri is struck by a sudden urge to go and find her – now, immediately – but she resists. The Celt is not expecting her until seven.

No matter. There is plenty to do in the meantime.

As they cross the clinic's lower ward, Alix glances around eagerly. There's a spark in her eyes that Miri doesn't think she's seen once since she came back. It doesn't take them long to hunt down the on-duty volunteer, an ex-medic with acid-bright hair.

When Miri introduces Alix, taking care to mention her professional credentials, the Medic's face lights up.

"If you have some time spare, we could really use the help," xe says, holding up a list of patients who require urgent attention. Alix doesn't need to be asked twice. Lifting her dangling glasses onto her nose, she takes the list and examines it methodically.

"I've got time," she says.

With a grin, the Medic points out places where she can clean her hands and find supplies. Then xe turns xyr attention to the white rat sitting astride Miri's shoulder. "You can't have that in here."

"I'll make sure it doesn't get loose. It's well behaved."

"I don't care. We might not be state of the art, but there's absolutely no way I'm allowing a rat to stay on the premises. It's not hygienic."

"What am I going to do with it then?"

The Medic shrugs. "Your call. Put it outside?"

"You want me to abandon it?"

"What I *want* is for you to have thought about this before deciding to bring a *rat* into our *clinic*, Miri. It can't stay. If you won't get rid of it, I'm going to have to ask you to leave."

"That's not fair. And I have an appointment–"

"I don't have time for this. Lose the rat. I don't care how. Snap its neck, take it home, whatever. And make sure you wash your hands when you come back."

"A clinic is really no place for a rat, Miri," Alix adds quietly.

"Too right," says the Medic. "And I don't think the Celt will be pleased when she finds out you brought one in here either."

That settles it. Now Miri has no choice but to track back through the lower ward. She peers through a gap in the rusted shutter to check that the coast is clear and then heaves it up, stepping out into the silence of Peter Street. There isn't enough time before she's due to meet the Celt to take the rat back to the Warren. In her head, she runs through a catalogue of all the places she has stayed in the last two years that might be safe enough to leave the rat. None of them are close enough.

She scans the street, half-expecting to find something she will be able to use as a cage to keep the rat contained until they're done at the clinic, but of course the street is completely empty. She should have gone back for the tub she dropped in the greenhouse when she had the chance. Now there is really only one option.

At least she's alone. She is all too aware of how foolish her reluctance to release the rat would appear to anyone else, how ridiculous it is to have formed such an attachment to a dumb beast in the space of twenty-four hours. She tells herself that it needs her, that it will be safer with her, but the angry burn mark on its back seems to say otherwise. It was probably managing perfectly fine before she came along. It is, after all, a rat, and rats survive. Of all the creatures, it is the one that has adapted most thoroughly to the perils of a ravaged environment. The brick-lined street might not look like the place to set loose a wild animal, but it is ideal for a rat. Whatever has been done to it, the survival instinct will not have been shorn from its DNA, however trusting it may seem.

Swallowing hard, Miri gently lifts the rat from her shoulder and holds it cupped in both hands. Then she places a rough kiss between its two ears – the end of her nose just brushing the helix of the human ear on its back – and stoops to set it down on the pavement. She straightens. On the cracked flagstone, the rat sits back on its haunches and squeaks loudly, its whiskers twitching.

"Go on," she says, shooing it with her hand.

The rat doesn't move.

She nudges it with her boot and it scampers to the side and then stops again, its red eyes peering up at her as if in reproach.

"*Go,*" she says again, giving it another nudge. This time the rat scrambles up onto the toe, anchoring its tail around her heel. Groaning, Miri stoops to pick it up and carries it further down the street to put it down again. She starts back towards the rusting shutter, but she hasn't gone far when she hears the click of claws on stone. She turns. The rat is hurrying after her, the spliced ear trembling with the movement.

"Fuck's sake," she mutters, brushing an angry tear from her eye. She tries the procedure again, this time taking the rat all the way to the end of the street, but once more the rat chases after her.

She tries a third time, dropping the rat at the street corner and then running back the way she came. As soon as she hears the familiar click, click, click, she stops and spins around.

Grits her teeth.

Aims a hard kick at the rat.

The toe of her boot connects with its side and sends the creature sprawling. Stunned, it sits up, cocking its head to stare at Miri. Then it gives a violent shudder and looks away. For a moment, it stays where it is on the pavement, licking at its paws to cuff its face clean. Then, at last, it turns tail and runs.

Miri watches it go. As it veers course and crosses the street, she notices for the first time the dense patch of filterweed growing from a crack in the base of the wall. The stems are short and thick, heavy with the red leaves that trail down to the pavement. The rat is heading straight for it. As she watches, they seem to shiver and incline further towards the ground.

A shout of warning dies on Miri's lips. She is frozen in place; unable to move, unable to look away. The rat advances towards the writhing plant.

Time is jagged, it happens fast and slow. The rat scurries across a leaf that lies stretched out on the pavement. As soon as the rat's claws touch the plant, a few fronds of the filterweed list towards it, lowering with artful menace. The rat does not seem to notice. With a final flash of its long tail, it disappears into the mass of hungry, trembling leaves.

28

The clinic is better equipped than Alix feared it would be, though that isn't saying much. There is no running water on site, but Alix is pleased to see that someone has rigged up a decent tippy tap. It looks as good to her as any she's used before, back when she accompanied some of the aid teams on missions to the neighbouring Counties. A heavy plastic canister of water hangs from a simple H-frame. There is a hole to the top of one side with a simple spout attached, and a length of cord has been tied around the base of the spout. The cord hangs down all the way to the floor, where the other end is tied to a short length of wood that looks like a slat from an old bed. Keen to test out the mechanism, Alix places her foot on the piece of wood and gently draws it towards her, causing the plastic canister to tip forwards. When it reaches the right angle, clear water streams from the spout and falls into a large pail on the ground. Alix wonders what happens to the used water, whether it is carried off to the drains, or whether it is boiled, treated and reused.

Fortunately, there is plenty of soap available. Alix takes off her watch and wedding ring – always a wrench – then slides back the foot lever to briefly tilt the canister and moisten her hands with water. Filling one palm with liquid soap, she works it into a lather and begins to cycle methodically through the old routine. Palm to palm, fingers interlaced one way then the other, backs of fingers to opposing palms, thumbs. When she was a student – a lifetime ago now – she and the others had been made to practise handwashing with an oil that could only be seen under a UV light. Under an instructor's watchful gaze, they would apply the oil, execute the handwashing protocol and then hold their hands under the light to see where the residual oil had not been properly washed off. Alix still remembers the mortification of that first time, of washing her hands meticulously – or so she had thought – and then seeing the glowing stains along the outsides of her palms, the base of her wrists, the insides of her fingers. A few simple adaptations had been sufficient to account for the worst of these, though she soon found that the marks around the cuticles and nailbeds were not so easily dealt with. It had taken a while for Alix to get the hang of it, but in the end she'd perfected the protocol. Now she does it without thinking.

Perhaps it is the habitual familiarity of the procedure or perhaps it is the evocative scent of disinfectant, but as she works through the steps Alix feels a calm conviction taking hold of her. It's something she hasn't felt since leaving Great Ormond Street.

I know what I'm doing, she thinks. For the first time, she feels keenly that she is in the right place. She wasn't sure about accompanying Miri here, but now she's glad she did. She can help these people, she's sure of it. And perhaps they can help her.

Miri is beginning to waver. The girl doesn't know it yet, but Alix can see it as plain as anything. Somewhere along the way, she's started to suspect that the violence of Miri's protestations mask the fact that she already knows, deep down, what she must do; what nomination she must make. All Miri needs is a final push in the right direction.

I know what I'm doing, Alix thinks again. *I'm in control.* She remembers a time when she was as certain of that as she was that tomorrow would come. Now the sentiment is disconcertingly alien. It is little surprise after the last two years, which have been trial enough to puncture the ego of even the most self-assured narcissist. It has become part of the story she tells herself, how all the confidence was knocked – kicked, beaten, pummelled – out of her after her daughter ran away. Now she wonders if that was ever true or whether she simply wanted it to be, whether it was just an excuse to give up. For here it is still, a residue of the self-belief she once took for granted. Alix nurses it tenderly, determined not to let the last of it slip away.

I know what I'm doing. She repeats the words silently until they become a mantra that matches the rhythmic movements of her hands. *I know what I'm doing.*

She won't let herself forget it again. Not now. She might not have saved the whole planet, but at least she knows how to save a life.

She is nearly done. Pulling once more on the foot lever, Alix rinses away the lather and dries her hands. Then she steps out into the lower ward and goes to attend her first patient.

29

With the Archivist at her side, Jac goes to collect the items the Facility Manager has placed in the airlock. Everything she requested is there, all stored neatly in a small silver rucksack. The Facility Manager has thoughtfully tied long tabs of elastic to each of the zips, which makes them much easier to operate while wearing the bulky gloves of her hazmat suit.

"Everything there?" the Archivist asks, his voice tinny and distant on her radio.

"Yes," she says, yanking the bag out of the airlock and shutting the door. Kneeling, she adds the few things they were able to source from within the nuclear annexe itself, placing the empty capsule into the main pocket of the bag and sliding the pair of microcalipers into the front pouch. Then she tugs the zips shut and swings the whole thing onto her shoulders. She turns to the Archivist.

"Ready?"

"Ready."

The NAX command centre is sited deep within the nuclear annexe. For the first time, Jac is truly glad of the Archivist's assistance, for she's sure she would get lost in the maze of corridors without him.

Before long, they reach the gaping mouth of a vertical mine shaft, where steel girders descend eighty metres down into the hewn rock. The cargo lift – a narrow platform caged by a metal grille – is ready and waiting for them at the top of the shaft.

Passing through the access gate, Jac steps tentatively onto the platform, not quite daring to look down. The Archivist, stopping only to retrieve a key that hangs from a nearby hook, follows close behind.

"You know how to work the lift?" asks Jac.

"Fully licensed operative," he replies, closing the access gate and stepping up to the control panel. There is a long cord attached to the key and he loops this over the wrist of his hazmat suit before inserting the key into a slot at the bottom of the panel.

"Dead-man's switch," he says, in response to Jac's questioning look. "If I get jolted out of the lift, my body weight will rip out the key and everything will stop. The external controls will reactivate and you can take it from there. Not that you'll need to, of course."

Jac nods. It is strange to think that even this small eventuality has been accounted for and protected against. No expense was spared on the project's infrastructure, not one fail-safe overlooked. And all for what? Perhaps this was always the problem, perhaps they spent so much energy on the small details that they lost sight of the whole: the wood for the trees. And now, for all their care, the project is failing.

The Archivist turns the key and hits a green button. The platform slowly descends, groaning threateningly as it carries them down the mine shaft. As they progress ever further downwards, Jac notices a disconcerting tightness in her left ear, as though it's been plugged with wadded cotton. Seeing how the Archivist has begun to hinge his jaw open and shut behind his visor, she guesses that he, too, is experiencing the same painful shift in pressure. But neither of them speak of it. Jac waits for the discomfort to slowly abate, and the Archivist eventually falls still.

Finally they reach the bottom of the shaft. The Archivist expertly brings the platform to a stop and waits for Jac to get out before turning back the key and reverting the override. From there, it is a short walk to the command centre.

NAX runs are only made a couple of times every quarter – once to bring new crates of cores from Greenland and once to send the older crates back. The next run isn't scheduled for a few weeks yet, so when Jac and the Archivist reach the command centre, it is empty.

The motion-sensor lights flicker on automatically when they enter, revealing a room that is wider than it is long with a vast island-bank of computers standing in the centre. These boast a dizzying array of silver switches, buttons and blinking LEDs. Above them, a wide display screen stares blankly down. The far wall is made entirely of thick sheet glass. It overlooks the loading bay of the NAX, currently empty save for the rows of trolleys onto which the crates are stacked when they arrive from Greenland.

Though Jac has spent little time in the command centre, she knows how it operates in almost forensic detail. Being one of the most significant elements of the project, Jac has studied and discussed the repurposed section of the NAX a thousand times: in meetings, at the Borlaug, in interviews and conferences. There hasn't been much call for that sort of thing in recent years, but the knowledge is fresh in her mind as ever. The first thing she does is switch on the display screen, firing up a map of the pipeline, a complicated network of neon lines. Most of the routes it shows are no longer operational. When the Borlaug took over the defunct system, it could only afford to repurpose the Greenland-Inbhir Nis pipeline, but there was a time when it had been possible to travel almost anywhere in the world using the NAX.

The map is annotated with data from the signallers and controllers that are built into the cargo pipe itself. Jac scans through the information but everything is as expected; there's nothing to point to any faults in the pipeline or any operational errors. At least whoever's interfering with the Borlaug's digital records doesn't seem to have breached the NAX's automated systems. Effortlessly, Jac manipulates the controls to call one of the pressurised cargo pods into the loading bay.

In a moment, one of the pods glides into view on a levitating chassis of structural aluminium that houses the pod's propulsion system and magnets. Despite its large size – nearly nine metres long and three wide – it is a thing of sleek beauty. Shaped like a bullet, its black carbon fibre aeroshell, lightweight and strong, has been polished to a high gloss. The letters "NAX" are picked out in electric blue at the tail.

At the press of a button, the pod's hatch door slides open. Jac turns to the Archivist, painfully aware of how much she has already asked of him today. She's known all along, of course, that there's no way for her to get to Greenland without someone else to stay in the command centre and remotely operate the pod, but she has not yet mentioned it to the Archivist.

"Feeling up to running this thing?"

Slowly, he nods. "If you show me what to do."

"It's simple enough," says Jac. She walks him through a list of instructions.

At every step, he repeats the instruction back to her over the radio, making it clear that he's understood. Jac finds herself trusting him in a way she never expected would be possible. For all his deep-seated dislike of her, it is clear to her now that he takes the project as seriously as she does. And she knows the NAX. If he follows her instructions exactly – and based on everything she knows of the Archivist, he will – then it will go off without a hitch.

Taking a deep breath, she grips the strap of her rucksack and heads down to the loading bay. The pod is even more impressive from up close. She tries to think what makes it so appealing to the eye and then she has it. It looks new. Even in the high-tech areas of the Borlaug, she is used to working with equipment that bears the hallmarks of age: missing or broken parts, cracks, grime, rust. By contrast, after decades of use, there isn't so much as a scratch on the NAX pod.

As she clambers through the hatch, she turns back to look across the loading bay and up through the window of the command centre. The Archivist is staring down at her from the central bank of computers, his hand hovering over the door release. She's still in range of his radio.

"I have another favour to ask."

"What?"

"I need someone to call my wife. Her number will be on file. Tell her... tell her where I've gone. And my daughter..." she trails off. There are a thousand things she wants to say to Miri, that she wants the girl to know, though right now she's struggling to clearly express a single one of them even to herself. "Alix will know what to tell her," she says at last. "She always does."

"I'll see what I can do."

"Thank you," she says, surprised to find she really means it. "For everything." Then she steps through into the pod.

Unfortunately, the Borlaug never recommissioned any of the old passenger pods. If they had, she would have summoned one of those instead, and enjoyed the journey in the comfort of a cushioned chair. As it is, the inside of the pod is stripped bare, its hollow belly devoid of any distinguishing features save for a shallow recess in the floor that allows for sample crates to be held securely in place. Setting down her rucksack, Jac lies down flat, careful not to damage her hazmat suit. She radios through to the Archivist.

"Good to go."

"Copy that. Good luck, Jac."

She braces herself and the hatch lowers shut, throwing her into blackness. There's a crackle of interference in her earpiece that she registers with disquiet. In just a few minutes, her radio will be out of range for good – she'll be completely alone.

The pod rockets forward, casting out towards the sea.

30

When she returns to the clinic, Miri doesn't tell anyone what happened to the rat. Alix is already hard at work tending to patients and everyone else has enough to deal with, from the overstretched staff to the sick patients silently awaiting aid.

As she crosses the lower ward, she passes the Medic who is rushing in the opposite direction with a cardboard kidney dish. Noticing the absence of the rat, xe gives an approving nod as xe passes.

"Don't forget to wash your hands," xe shouts over xyr shoulder.

Miri does so, methodically soaping between her fingers and all the way up to the elbow, suppressing something big and black that is threatening to engulf her.

Moving quickly to dispel it, she goes to help Alix. She is sitting with a young woman who has straight black hair and a haunted expression. She stares listlessly up at the ceiling and barely speaks when Alix asks her a few routine questions. Glancing at the notes, Alix tells the woman that she needs to check her bandages and then carefully pulls back the sheets. Beneath them, the woman is half-naked, a thick strip of white gauze bound around her abdomen.

In a low voice, Alix tells Miri what supplies she needs and Miri scrambles over to where they are kept, returning a few moments later with her arms full. Snapping on a pair of latex gloves, Alix unwraps the gauze with deft gentle movements and then casts an appraising eye over the wounds beneath.

There is a long, savage gash along the woman's belly, thick and scarring to purple. It has been sewn together with black stitches but there is a greenish tinge around the edge of the wound and it's starting to give off a dank smell. Infection.

Alix does what she can to clean the wound and then carefully redresscs it. She sends Miri to get painkillers and any available antibiotics. Although there are plenty of the first, she can find none of the second. When she tells Alix, she merely gives a knowing tut.

"Maybe just as well," Alix says. "There are very few strains that are still effective on the London population. It's just like with the Marburg – not enough was done to develop critical medications while we still had the chance. It wasn't seen as profitable. Now we all reap the benefits."

She gives the woman a dose of painkillers and then makes a detailed record of the wound. Without any medication to fight the infection, the woman will need to be checked frequently.

Once they have done all they can, they move on. Only when they are safely out of earshot does Alix explain to Miri what was written in the woman's notes – that she told her boyfriend she missed her period and he, fearing she was pregnant and desperate to avoid the Offset at all costs, tried to cut out her womb.

The next person they attend is also female, but at least twice the age of the girl with the rotting gash in her belly. This woman is sitting up, propped against the wall, and her little boy sits in her lap. Although she chats animatedly to her son, singing nursery rhymes and stroking his soft, dark hair, she is obviously not in a good way. Her face is badly bruised; her lip is split on one side and one eye is swollen shut. She holds her right arm awkwardly across her chest. It's obvious from the strange angle of the wrist that she's broken a bone.

"I tripped," she croaks when Alix asks what happened. "Fell down the stairs."

Her little boy shakes his head. The motion is slight but definite. No one sees but Miri.

Alix raises an eyebrow but says nothing until she's finished conducting her examination. There are bruises on the woman's throat, too, ones that Miri fancies line up exactly with the fingers of a gripping hand. When Alix points this out to the woman, she starts to shake violently but continues to insist that she only fell down the stairs. Adopting a soothing tone, Alix calms her down and then busies herself seeing to her injuries, setting the broken bone as best she can with a splint and then smearing a thick, yellow ointment across the swollen eye. When she's done, she rips off a scrap of paper and writes down the address of a refuge, which the woman takes and hastily stuffs into her pocket.

"Do you think she'll take your advice?" asks Miri as they head over to the next patient.

"No," says Alix. "Probably not."

Miri nods. The woman's situation is hardly unique and she's heard several variations of it before. From the look of the woman's injuries, her husband tried to kill her and Miri is certain she knows why. If one parent dies before the Offset, then the survivor is pardoned for their crime of procreation. There are all too many families where this exemption acts as an incentive for murder. In heterosexual couples, that parent is nearly always the father. Sometimes it is the children who are beaten into submission instead of their mothers. Sometimes it's both. The victims vary but the motivation is always the same: survival at the expense of all else.

Somewhere between the fourth and fifth patient they attend, they are interrupted by panicked shouts and the heavy stomp of boots racing on concrete. Miri's head snaps up, searching for the source of the noise. A bearded man is sprinting through the lower ward, a small bundle cradled in his arms. With a squeeze to Alix's shoulder to tell her she'll be back in a moment, Miri heads over to find out what's going on. By the time she reaches the man, he is already pleading with the Medic.

"You must save her," he says, thrusting forward the bundle. It is a baby, so small that it must be a newborn. It doesn't so much as squirm within its swaddling of rags. When Miri leans forward to get a better look, she sees that the infant's lips are blue. She knows at once that it is dead.

The Medic knows it, too, but the man is still screaming at xem in his desperation, begging xem to do something. Somehow, xe manages to prise the bundle away from him. As soon as xe does, the man collapses to the floor, sitting down in a low squat and rocking back and forth on his heels, his hands clasping his head.

Exchanging a look with the Medic, Miri squats down beside the man, doing her best to adopt the calm, friendly tone she's seen Alix use on the other patients, distracting him while the Medic deals with the corpse. As she talks to him, he becomes less and less agitated.

"It's not mine," he says at last. "I would never... please, you have to believe me–"

"It's alright," says Miri. "What happened?"

"I– I was out looking for scrap. Something to sell, you know? There's not much to be had in these parts, but in the wealthier districts... well. Anyway, I found this skip. It was tucked away down a side street and all covered in rust, hadn't moved in years. Didn't look like there was much to be had out of it either, but I went to see all the same and... there she was." His voice breaks. "Half-buried beneath a rotting wooden beam. Don't know how long she was there for. I dug her out and... this was the only place I could think to bring her."

"You did the right thing."

He nods, settling again after the second wave of shock. "I did, didn't I?" Then he frowns and glances nervously around the ward. "Where is she?" he asks, meaning the baby. "I won't have to take her, will I?"

Miri has to fight down the sudden and overwhelming urge to tell him the baby is already dead. In the grand scheme of things, is he any better in his reluctance to take responsibility for his actions than the breeders that brought the baby into the world and then left it to die?

"No," she says flatly. "You're done here. You can leave."

She watches him go with a stab of loathing for not taking the responsibility that fate had handed him.

When she returns to Alix, she finds her mother tending to a teenager just a few years younger than herself. He is laid out on his front with the sheets pulled down to the waist, his bare back gleaming with a criss-cross pattern of red cuts. Every time Alix touches a disinfectant-doused cotton swab to one of the cuts, he winces and cries out.

Miri checks his notes. She sees that he stumbled in three days ago after his mother whipped him to within an inch of his life. Clearly she had tried to beat into him what the right decision would be when it was time for the Offset.

"I can't believe it," says Alix when the Medic next passes by. "We never saw half as many of these kinds of cases in Ormond Street." She gestures out towards the ward, to the patients curled and broken in their bays.

"Of course not," xe says. "It's government-run. And you know what the official view is on ReproViolence. It doesn't exist, remember?"

Alix nods sadly.

It is a commonly held belief that the Offset is a matter of balance. The parent creates life and, in so doing, renders their own in forfeit. The omnipotence of the parent-creator wanes until finally, as the child enters adulthood, it deserts them entirely, taking a new form and a new master: the child-destroyer. The old make way for the young. Life is met with death, creation with destruction, age with youth. The selfishness of procreation is pitted against the altruism of self-sacrifice and, in that way, a precarious balance is maintained. So it goes.

Miri knows that there are other, more rational reasons why the Offset – originally introduced as a public health initiative – is allowed to continue as a cultural practice: critically, it provides a much-needed check against the human want to procreate when the planet is suffering from overpopulation. In that way, it's not so different from any other adaptive social behaviour.

When there was still an African savannah, the wildebeest adapted to grazing in large herds because it reduced the risk of any individual wildebeest being attacked and eaten by a predator. Even though this reduced the quality of the grazing site, the behaviour was advantageous in helping the species survive. So too with the Offset; reducing the strain the human species places on the environment is more advantageous for survival than unlimited reproduction.

Despite knowing these things rationally, the Offset is still deeply ingrained, occupying a place in her mind beyond conscious thought. It is a truth, a fact. Children are born and parents die. That is the price. That is how it has been for longer than anyone can remember and that is how it will always be.

At least, that is what she has believed for most of her life. Since she started coming to the clinic, she's had ample opportunity to see that this is not always the case.

At some point in between patients, the Medic draws Miri aside, beckoning her over to where the supplies are kept – which is about as private as it gets on the lower ward.

"Everything OK?" Miri asks.

"Yeah," xe says. "I actually just wanted to check in with you while I had ten seconds. How are you getting on? Last time I saw you, you were in a real state."

Xe is, Miri thinks, putting it lightly. Miri came into the clinic a couple of months ago with pneumonia. Although the ReproViolence Clinic specialises in treating injuries related to the Offset, Miri begged the Celt and the Medic to take her in so that she wouldn't have to go to Ormond Street and face her mother – not knowing, of course, that Alix was already retired. It wasn't the first time she'd been ill, but it was the most serious. It was the only time that Miri had caved in and sought medical attention. By all accounts, she nearly died. *Would* have died, if it wasn't for the Medic and the rest of the volunteers.

Although she appreciates that xe is taking the time to ask, Miri can't help but feel that xyr concern is needless. She is in better health than she has been for a long time. She tells the Medic as much.

Xe nods. "I figured. Well, whatever you're doing, keep at it. It's working."

She wants to say that she hasn't been doing anything at all, but then she thinks of the healthy meals she's eaten, and the invigorating shower. Of being cared for by her mother. Perhaps she needs Alix more than she has been willing to admit.

Before she can contemplate this any further, Miri realises with a jolt that it's time for her appointment. The Celt is waiting for her upstairs.

As soon as she is sure that Alix is sufficiently occupied, she slips away and heads up the spiralling ramp that leads her to the next storey. Like the floor below, this has been converted into a kind of ward, but one that houses longer-term patients. There are not many of these – with the limited resources available, critical patients mostly either recover or die. Some, though, hold on fast and keep fighting, even though all the odds are stacked against them. They have sustained injuries that will never go away. Brain damage, paralysis, blindness. And there are those, too, suffering from the poison that wells deep within the mind, the traumas that permeate every thought, every sense, every moment of their lives.

These people are kept away from the lower ward, in part because it's easier for the volunteers to manage and in part because it gives them more room to spread out. Each patient has a few bays to themselves and many of them have sought to turn their small patches of concrete into something approximating home, decorating the walls and floors with anything they can get their hands on – paints, foil wrappers, scraps of brightly coloured fabric.

Miri nods at the upper ward's occupants as she passes through, making a beeline for the set of bays at the far end, which belong not to a patient but the woman who founded and runs the clinic. Compared to the others nearby, these bays are meticulously neat, the floor swept clean, the bed made. The only decoration is a large Alban flag stretched across the wall, the white saltire bright in the gloom.

Sitting at the end of the mattress with her back against the wall is the Celt. She has on a hard-wearing flannel shirt and a pair of jeans that have been cropped and stapled together over the two short stumps that project forward from her hips. She is thickset and strong, the muscles and sinews of her powerful arms and shoulders evident beneath her shirt. Every so often, the patients cast furtive looks in her direction according to some unknowable, internal rhythm. Their glances are frequent and nervous, like rabbits gathered around a sleeping fox. But the Celt, seemingly unaware of the effect she has on the patients, keeps her eyes focused, trained on the page of the book she is reading. The whole thing is falling apart: the front cover has been torn off and the glue of the spine has melted so that the pages, dog-eared and yellow with age, sit loosely together, a collection of disordered leaflets. Whatever its contents, they appear completely absorbing.

The Celt doesn't look up even when Miri comes to stand next to her bay, close enough to see the dark speckles of stubble on the dome of her shaven head.

"I wasn't sure you would come, given the circumstances," she says at last, not looking up from her book.

Miri falters, uncertain of what to say. Somehow, she's already on the back foot.

"Not many would seek the company of a mere stranger so soon before their Offset."

"A… a stranger?" Miri stammers, her mouth paper-dry.

For the first time, the Celt looks up. Her eyes are round and wild, the irises so dark as to be almost black. After a long moment, she invites Miri to sit down. Miri does so, perching on the edge of the thin mattress. At first she stretches her legs out across the floor and then, self-conscious of the stark difference between her and the Celt, quickly draws them back into a right angle. She has to sit half-turned in order to keep the Celt in view, and it's an awkward position, but she says nothing.

Miri has only met the woman a handful of times before and she thinks she's still a long way from understanding her. There's something about the Celt that Miri finds deeply unnerving, something that strikes her through every time she is subjected to the woman's powerful gaze. It is as intoxicating as the way she moves when she walks on her strong hands; with more fluid grace than most can manage on their feet. Sometimes she talks to Miri with an intense intimacy, like there's no one else in the whole world but them. But at others, it's like she's not even aware of her existence.

"The colour suits you," says the Celt.

Blushing furiously, Miri looks down and picks at the front of her steel-blue jumper. With all the distraction of the clinic, she had forgotten how different she must look to the last time she saw the Celt. Apart from the neat clothes, Miri wonders how she comes across now and what else the Celt has noticed: the lack of dirt griming the creases and folds of her skin. When she ran into the Thief, she wanted to pretend that nothing had changed. Now, her only hope is that the Celt approves of the alteration.

"Why did you want to see me?"

"It's my Offset, tomorrow…" Miri begins.

"And you were hoping I would tell you who you must nominate? I see from your expression that I'm right." As Miri struggles for a response, the Celt turns back to her book and idly neatens the loose pages. "It's your decision to make, Miri," she says quietly. "No one else's."

"It's not that," says Miri. "I've made my decision. I have. It's just–"

"You want me to reassure you it's the right one?"

Yes, she thinks. "Not exactly," she says. "I just need to… *talk* to someone. There isn't anyone else. I mean, not really." She thinks of all the times she and Alix have spoken about the upcoming Offset without ever truly discussing it. How could she talk to Alix when her mother had already decided what Miri should do?

The Celt nods. "Then talk," she says. "And I will listen."

Miri's leg begins to tingle beneath her weight; she shifts a little in her awkward position and then settles, hands in her lap, eyes downcast. It takes a moment before she has her thoughts in order, but the Celt does not interrupt, nor does she urge her to hasten.

At last, she is ready.

"If Jac dies…" says Miri. Her voice wavers and she has to start again. "If Jac dies, there's a real possibility that Project Salix will fail. At least, that's what everyone keeps telling me. And I thought… you told me before that, if something like that ever happened, it would destabilise… well, everything. Critical resources will stop being diverted to the project and there'll be a chance for real progress."

The Celt inclines her shaven head. "Perhaps," she says. "And perhaps not. There would be unrest, certainly. Violence, even. Many of those who are already worse off will suffer."

"But you said… you said before now that Project Salix is precisely what keeps everyone in their place. That it's why nothing changes."

"I stand by my words. For as long as the people cling to their hope for a better world – a world that has been promised to them by the laboratories while remaining a distant possibility – nothing will change. If Jac Boltanski dies, there is a chance for progress. But I cannot pretend that, if change does come from that destruction, it won't be with an extraordinary cost."

Miri waits for her to continue, to draw some final conclusion, but the Celt has come to the end of her speech.

"So what should I do?" Miri asks. "What would *you* do if you were in my position?"

"I am not in your position," she says, not unkindly. "The burden upon you is great, Miri. I will not add to it further by dictating what you should or should not do. You are free to choose however you think best. That you must remember above all else. Do you understand?"

"No," says Miri stubbornly, disappointment crashing over her. It's as though the walls of a dam have been broken. For the first time, Miri realises how much she has been relying on this, on this moment, on believing that the Celt would finally tell her what she most needs to hear.

"I'm sorry I could not give you what you wanted," says the Celt. "The only reassurance I can offer you is this: however you decide, whatever outcome is brought about, I will think no less of you."

Miri does not mistake the finality of her tone. She is being dismissed, albeit with diplomacy and tenderness. She turns away abruptly, her disappointment compounded by a sudden stab of shame. How childish the Celt must think her.

"I'm sorry, I shouldn't have come," Miri says.

For a moment, the Celt is still. "I'm glad that you did. You cannot know… you cannot know how it pleases me to see you. I wish there was more I could do…" the Celt gives a soft sigh. "Come and see me again when you have made your decision. I… I don't want it to break you."

Not knowing what else to say, Miri gets to her feet and begins the slow walk back along the upper ward, feeling the Celt's eyes upon her but not daring to look around. Only when she reaches the lower ward does she allow herself to give silent voice to her resentment. She trusted the Celt above all others and now what does she have to show for it? Nothing. The shame of it stings beyond belief; an indignity worsened by knowing how easy it would have been for the Celt to help, to make things clear, to tell her what to do. But the woman refused. *You are free to choose however you think best.* If that's what counts for freedom, then Miri wants no part of it.

Rounding a corner, she finds Alix tending a new patient. Her mother looks up at her with a smile and Miri feels something within her shift; a fragment of her dashed hopes beginning to settle and quietly rebuild.

"There you are," says Alix warmly.

"There you are," repeats Miri, grabbing a fresh pair of surgical gloves and hastening forward to help her mother.

31

Deep below the North Sea, Jac is experiencing first-hand what it means to be sealed into a narrow, windowless capsule and shunted through a thousand miles of pipeline. Driven by linear induction motors and axial compressors, the NAX pods are capable of reaching tremendous speeds and right now, the acceleration force is crushing.

This is her fault, of course. If she'd thought to tell the Archivist how to control the acceleration of the pod at the start of the journey, the pressure might be more bearable. But she didn't and now she's reaping the consequences, pinned down to the floor and overwhelmed by a nausea that does not improve when she considers what would happen if she vomited inside her hazmat suit. She tries to distract herself, thinking of cool waters, clear skies. A drink of sweet cordial over crushed ice. The images do not come easy in the all-consuming dark.

Jac's only real comfort is the knowledge that her ordeal will be over soon. In the space of a few hours, she will have crossed an entire ocean; travelled from one continent to another in less time than it would usually take her to get from London to Inbhir Nis. It won't be long before she can leave her lightless prison. For the time being, the promise of this is enough.

She tries not to think of the strangeness of it, of how, saving the occasional trip to Alba, this is the first time she has been outside of the Federated Counties. Before, the prospect would have excited her. Now, it only makes her nausea worse, knowing she is further from home than she ever imagined she would be.

The first turn nearly blinds her. Without any warning, the cargo pod hurtles around a bend and she is thrown against the side, pinned there briefly in a gravity-defying contortion and then released, falling back to the floor. Her head hits the metal with an almighty crack and then something warm trickles down her lip; blood from where she caught her tongue between her teeth. She lets out a thin groan and thinks wildly of the damage that might have been done to her hazmat suit: did the visor shatter? Were the connections of her air supply knocked loose? Even as her breathing becomes ragged and frantic with desperation, a cooler part of her mind kicks in. Her air supply must be alright, or she'd be suffocating to death already. As to the rest of the damage, there is nothing she can do about it now. Even if she could move beneath the crushing G-force, she wouldn't be able to tell the extent of it from touch alone, not through the thick gloves. All she can do is stay still and hope, concentrating on her breathing until it slows and steadies.

When the next bend comes, she is ready for it, and the next and the next. Or, rather, she accepts the inevitability of being once more smashed into the side of the cargo pod. She keeps her eyes screwed tight and her jaw clenched. She focuses her entire conscious mind on breathing, on that one single act that reassures her she is still safe – no matter how battered and bruised – and that her air supply is still working.

Then, when she feels she cannot have got more than halfway, there's a change in the pod's movement. She senses it at once, though she can't tell what it means. Only when the crushing weight begins to ease does she realise what's happening. The pod is slowing down.

For a space, she is not entirely sure she can believe it, convinced it must be some trick of perception, some expression of the enormous strain under which she has placed her body. But soon there's no denying it. At last, everything falls still.

The pod has stopped.

Jac's mind wanders inexorably to the sea above the cargo pipe. Suddenly, the walls of her pod seem laughably fragile beneath the hammering pressure of all that water. If only she could laugh. But she's never been more frightened.

What is it? she thinks, her eyes still screwed shut. *What's happened? Why have we stopped?* All at once, an image emerges unbidden out of the swirl and prickle of colours behind her eyelids. There's a flash of bright white, followed by neat lines of black type. A document. Something she remembers finding its way onto her desk in London. Something she signed. In another moment, she has it.

The Energy Diversion Measure.

Fuck.

For years now, the Borlaug's Inbhir Nis facility – including the NAX – has had a chokehold on the Alban power-grid, receiving priority supply. About six months ago, following a series of local outages, she was finally pressed to sign a measure loosening that chokehold as a show of good faith. Now, whenever there's a major drop in the electrical output of the Alban grid, energy is diverted as a priority to local services, hospitals chief among them.

On these occasions, energy usage within the facility itself has to be prioritised accordingly, most of it being channelled into ensuring the continued safe storage of nuclear materials. But the NAX... that can be temporarily suspended with minimal risk. If any samples were in the pipe, they could simply be held in place. Travelling in their hermetically sealed cases, they would incur little damage and could be held indefinitely. Once energy levels returned to an agreed baseline, the NAX would start up again. No harm done.

Or so she thought when she signed the measure.

So, she's stuck. And with no way of knowing how long the NAX may be suspended. With increasing alarm, she thinks of her suit's air system. It was enough, she hoped, to get to

Greenland and back. Now there's no telling. The outage might last for hours. Or it might last for days. When the oxygen starts to run out–

Don't think about it, she tells herself firmly. *Don't panic before you have to. In fact, don't do anything. Don't talk. Don't move. Don't do anything that will increase oxygen consumption.*

She lies there in the dark – in what will likely be her coffin – and hopes. Time slips by in quick seconds, drains out in agonisingly slow minutes – she has no idea, no reliable way of measuring its passage.

Please, she thinks. *Not like this. I can't miss my Offset.* No one has ever missed an Offset. She remembers well when the final trading bloc fell and how the Governor of London marched up the steps of the Gallery to his own Offset regardless. The pigsuits stood in lines outside his family home to protect the child against the Activists begging for her to change her mind: "Pick your other father!" they screamed. "Leave our Governor alone!"

But it was the Governor's duty to climb those steps. Not just to the people of London – blinded though they were by their craving for the continued security of his leadership – and not just to the world, either; it was his duty to his child, to whom he was bound in covenant before all others.

Jac's life is Miri's alone to take away. In putting herself in mortal danger now, she has risked something unthinkable. The greatest taboo.

If she dies here, her body will likely never be recovered. When the NAX finally makes it to Greenland, the contents of the pods will be processed and securely disposed of – she'll probably end up buried deep in the Gunnbjørn Mountain along with the rest of the radioactive cores. What will happen when her disappearance is noticed? What will it mean for the Archivist, the last person to have seen her alive? What suspicion will fall on him? For all her animosity towards him, the idea of him being burdened with that is intolerable. And as for Miri–

No, she says silently to herself. Enough. She can't let herself keep thinking about it.

She doesn't know how long it's been before she begins to feel a creeping light-headedness that might be exhaustion and might be something far worse. A desire to fight comes with the clawing at the edges of her consciousness and she forces herself – really, this time, *really* forces herself – to concentrate, frantically summoning a hundred images to mind. The Energy Diversion Measure, the pages of her report that meticulously charted every discrepancy she found, long streams of numbers, figures... the Archivist, his face behind the visor... Alix, the freckles that dapple her cheeks and nose, her strawberry-blonde hair, her wild rose and poppy perfume... Miri, Miri as a baby, red-faced in her arms, Miri as a petulant teenager, slamming the door to the Warren... *Miri...*

When the pod begins to ease forward, Jac gives a cry of relief. Soon she can't move again beneath the accelerating force, but it doesn't matter, not now. She isn't going to die. Not there, lying still, crushed at the bottom of the sea.

32

When Miri awakes the following morning – the day of her birthday, the day she turns eighteen, the day Jac Boltanski will die – it is with the unfamiliar feeling of health. Her mind is perfectly clear, the constant discomfort of her bloated stomach has eased off, and the hundred aches and pains which normally plague her do not bother her in quite the way they once did. When she looks in the mirror, she even fancies that the sores on her face are beginning to heal, though that may well be pure fantasy on her part.

It was late by the time she and Alix made it back from the clinic the previous night. Miri, keen to avoid being drawn into answering questions about where she disappeared to at the end of the day, allowed Alix to insist on getting a rickshaw, even if only for the sake of making the journey shorter.

As it turned out, she had to do very little to conceal the things that were troubling her. Alix, tired but evidently energised by her spell of volunteering, kept up an animated but somewhat one-sided flurry of observational remarks all the way back to the Warren. It was only when they finally entered the house that her wide smile had slipped and contracted. Miri understood why at once. Jac was supposed to be there, but the house was dark and empty.

Miri couldn't say she was sorry that her mother had been detained. Dealing with the Offset would be easier without having to see her first. But she was sorry for Alix. Whatever

Jac's faults, Miri had never doubted her love for Alix. It was absolute and above question. Or so Miri had thought. Now she wasn't so sure. What could be so important that it would be worth spending her final hours apart from the woman she loved?

Alix's first response on discovering Jac's absence was to check the phone for messages. There had been a landline at the Warren for as long as Miri remembered. For the first sixteen years of her life, she had thought it was normal, assumed that every house had one. Then she had abruptly discovered that, for most people, reality was quite different.

"Well?" Miri prompted, watching as her mother stood in the hall, phone cord winding round her thumb, the receiver pressed to one ear.

"There's a message," she said. She listened for several long minutes, her expression serious but inscrutable. At long last, she put the phone down and jabbed at the combination of buttons on the dial pad that would delete the message. "Wrong number," she said.

Miri didn't believe that for a second. Alix bade her goodnight then and there, marching up the stairs to the master bedroom without so much as a backward glance.

Now, the morning of her eighteenth birthday, Miri leaves her old room and goes in search of her mother. The light is off in the hall outside and the house seems to be quiet. Miri crosses to the top of the stairs and stops, arrested by the sudden ring of the telephone below. She waits, expecting Alix to come bustling out any moment to answer the call, but the phone just rings on and on.

Frowning, Miri slopes down to the kitchen. Alix is there, sipping coffee from a shallow china cup. Her eyes are half-shut and the corners of her mouth are drawn down, her lower lip protruding slightly as she holds her jaw slack. When she sees Miri, she hastily composes her expression, flattening it into something more agreeable.

"Happy birthday. Did you sleep well?"

Miri shrugs and heads straight for the coffee pot. Everything is just where she remembers; the fine china cups, the sterling teaspoons in the drawer. The coffee is tepid but strong. She drains her cup in one and then pours out another. Only then does she notice the loaf cake on the counter, the top dusted with sugar. She freezes. Then she turns back to her mother, taking in for the first time the places that have been set with elaborate care: the rose-patterned plates, the delicate cake forks, the cloth napkins folded into neat triangles.

"It's a big day," says Alix, voice barely above a whisper. "Why don't you bring over the cake? There's a knife in the drawer."

"I'm... I'm not hungry."

Alix gives her a look. "I think we both know that's not true. We've spoken about this—"

"It's just too early," says Miri quickly. "I'll have something later." Even as the words leave her mouth, she knows the excuse is a feeble one. She waits for her mother's rebuke and is surprised when none is forthcoming.

"Bring it over for me then," says Alix. "I'd like a piece."

Struggling to find a reason why not, Miri does as she asks, rummaging in the drawer for the silver knife and then bringing it over with the plate. Then she retreats to the safety of the countertop where she left her cup.

"Why don't you come sit with me while you finish your coffee?"

"Please, Mum—"

"I don't think it's so much to ask, is it?" says Alix, cutting her off. "Really, Miri, it won't hurt you to sit down for five minutes."

Miri falters. She doesn't want to argue with Alix, not today. Hesitantly, she carries her cup to the table and takes a seat across from her mother.

Alix gives a wan smile. "That wasn't so hard, was it?" Then she picks up the knife. "Now, how are you planning to get to the Gallery?" she asks, sinking the blade into the cake. "Do you want me to come with you? I could call a rickshaw."

"I'll walk."

"Suit yourself. Here," says Alix, sliding a thick-cut slice onto one of the rose-patterned plates.

Miri stares at it. "I said I didn't want any."

"Don't be ridiculous," says Alix. "It's your birthday. It's only right you should have a little something to celebrate." She gouges a forkful from her own slice and takes a bite. "You're not going to make me eat this alone, are you?" Then, catching the look on her daughter's face: "Come on, Miri, don't be so stubborn. You always loved pound cake when you were little. It was your favourite."

Was it? thinks Miri. She looks at the cake; the soft yellow sponge, the rich brown crust. It looks blandly ordinary and stirs in her no recollection, no residual fondness. And yet Alix is so certain.

"Come on, try a bit."

Miri shakes her head, wishing she could find the words to make Alix stop. Finally, she pushes the cake away. "I don't feel like it, sorry."

All at once, her mother's face goes blank. For a moment, everything is still. Then Alix casts her fork down with a ringing clatter. "If that's how you want it…" Getting abruptly to her feet, she reaches for the plates of uneaten cake and scrapes them unceremoniously into the bin.

"Mum!" shouts Miri, as dismayed by the waste as she is by her mother's sudden distemper.

"You didn't want it," replies Alix coolly, dropping the plates into the sink. Then her lips tremble and curve downwards as her anger gives way. "I don't know what I did to deserve this," she says more quietly.

"Please, Mum. I don't want to fight. I don't want to upset you."

"Don't you?" she snaps. "Why are you still *here*, Miri? Just go. Go make your nomination. I don't care anymore." She stumbles from the room, tears cascading down her face.

Miri starts after her and then falls back. Without realising what she's doing, she brings her hands level with her chest and starts to lace them together, finger over thumb.

33

Jac is uncertain of what time it is when her pod finally makes it to Greenland. When the hatch opens, she stays lying where she is for several long minutes. At last, she feels strong enough to get up and she pulls herself to her feet, straightening one vertebra at a time, going extra slow to make sure that she's not overwhelmed by a sudden rush of blood to the head. Picking up the silver rucksack, she steps out of the hatch, relieved to at last escape the confines of the cargo pod.

The dosimeter on the front of her suit beeps once, signalling an effective dose approximate to a full-body X-ray. The shrill sound is muffled through the protective shell of her hazmat suit. Jac shakes her head and moves on.

Sited at ground level, the Greenland loading bay is the exact replica of the one in Inbhir Nis, save for the bank of robotic arms that hang dormant, waiting until the next batch of core samples are ready to be despatched. She walks the length of the bay until she comes to a heavy door of marine steel with a hand wheel set in the middle. Taking a firm grip, she heaves it to the left, cranking the wheel round and round until the door clunks open.

Her first impression is one of rich darkness.

This far north there's only a little light in the day: the sun only just makes it up past the horizon before sinking down again. For all the time that it hovers below the horizon, the light takes on an astonishing blue that is neither the indigo of night nor the cerulean of day, but somewhere between the two: a deep cobalt tinged with aqua. If she thought the skies at Inbhir Nis were remarkably clear, it's nothing compared to here. With no light pollution and little in the way of industry, there's nothing to choke up the atmosphere and today there are no clouds either.

Above her in the dark loom the shadows of broad gantries and cranes. Nearby are the warehouses where the sample cores are held, racked high in their crates. Wide asphalt tracks branch and loop across the ground, providing easy access for the AGVs on their heavy-duty wheels.

Although she's seen this all before in drone footage, Jac's itching to go and look round, to linger in this place that is at once so familiar and so alien. The site has always been managed remotely. Even its initial construction was done robotically. No human has walked where she now walks. No human has seen with their own eyes what she now sees. The knowledge of that – of being the first – makes her reel. But she must focus, not let herself get distracted. There is a task at hand.

Fumbling with her bag, she digs around for the torch that the Facility Manager found for her. It's a headlamp. With a little fiddling – tricky as ever in the bulky gloves – she adjusts the straps so that she can fit the thing over her hood. Once it is securely in place, she jabs at the button on its underside and trains the beam across the landscape.

A tree-lined slope rises steeply up from the dock. In the light of her lamp, she recognises the distinctive shape of the Project Salix trees, the long, hanging stems of silver-pale leaves swaying gently in the wind. Willows are not native to Greenland, but Project Salix trees have been engineered specifically for its radioactive soil. Once, Greenland would have been far too cold, but the shift in climate has proved perfect for the willows. Greenland has become ever-temperate. The expansion of the Gulf Stream out towards the North Pole keeps the island constantly protected by warm waters and means that no snow or ice forms even in the darkest winters, and hasn't done so for hundreds of years.

The trees are managed by a variety of robots, each one with a specific function. Even in this small part of the landscape, there are several hard at work, their anti-collision LEDs and work lights glowing gold amongst the dark trees. Jac can't help but draw a tight smile as she watches them go about their work. A few drones hover among the treetops, monitoring the trees for anthracnose, scab and black canker. She spots a surgeon-rover – a pair of metallic arms that terminate in massive, vice-like claws – moving with mechanical precision from tree to tree, gripping a branch with one claw and reaching out for the other with the next. It stops every so often, pruning a defective shoot here, applying a targeted fungicide there. In this way it can cover a vast amount of terrain without ever touching the ground. A cutter briefly roves into view and then vanishes into the depths of the forest, its strimmer whirring furiously to clear the understory.

In the distance, a sower trundles over the hillside, off to plant more seedlings. She doesn't spot any of the spring-footed borers, though, that cut the sample cores from the trees. Doubtless these are all consigned to a separate quadrant somewhere out of sight, maybe even on the other side of the island, days away. Jac doesn't know; she hasn't had cause to check the timetables in months.

Rising high above the tops of the trees are the pylons of the cable car that runs all the way from the loading bay to the top of the mountain. The car is mostly used to carry crates of harvested cores down to the dock, though it occasionally comes in handy when shipments of spare parts and heavy machinery from Inbhir Nis need to be transported up from the loading bay, or to transport the materials required to maintain the global monitoring station at the top.

Moving stiffly in her hazmat suit, Jac heads for the base terminal of the cable car and climbs into one of the waiting cabriolets. It is, essentially, an open-topped carriage attached to a steel cable. Less at home here than she was in the command centre of the NAX, she looks around uncertainly for the means of operation. She spots something that looks like a control panel and approaches it nervously, sure that she's going to find a dead-man's switch similar to the one the Archivist used to run the cargo lift down the mine shaft, but it turns out just to be a maintenance hatch. Taking her time, she examines the cabriolet thoroughly. Except for the buttons that control the doors, there doesn't seem to be anything she can push or twist or turn. Nothing to set the thing in motion. *What if only the robot workers can set the cabriolet going?* she wonders. After all, the site was never intended for human operatives.

Cursing herself for not having thought to check the schematics before she left, Jac steps back out again to take a better look at the terminal. There's a sheltered area where several cabriolets are nested together. She can see the housing where the bull wheel turns the cable and, set into the ground, a large electric motor. Suddenly, she understands: the cabriolets aren't motorised individually, all the components move at once.

Now she knows what she's looking for, it doesn't take her long to spot the tall lever concealed behind the nest of cabriolets. She yanks on it hard. To her relief, as soon as she does, the entire cable car creaks into action, the motor puttering into life, the bull wheel turning in its housing to run the circulating cables. At least now she need not fall at the first hurdle. One by one, the cabriolets move forward, swinging into the sky as the cable pulls them up.

Several of the cabriolets pass her by before she works up the confidence to climb in. Wearing her bulky and precious hazmat suit, boarding a moving cart by the light of a headlamp is no mean feat, even if it is going very slowly. But she manages it all the same, gaining the security of the cabriolet just as it lifts from the ground. Gripping the side tight in her gloved hands, she looks out as the cable car bears her up the mountain, quickly picking up speed as the terminal falls away so that the wind whips across her suit.

Suddenly, the cabriolet crests a peak and the rest of the rolling mountains come into view, each one bristling with orderly rows of Project Salix trees. The sight of them crushes the breath from Jac's lungs. The view is a world apart from the drone footage. She's never dared dream that she would get to see in person the physical manifestation of her life's work and here it is; as far as the eye can see, her trees stand proud and tall. She wishes that Alix and Miri were there with her to see it too, that she had some means of capturing it and bringing it back for them. The trees are tall and graceful, their drooping branches thick with bristling silver leaves. As they stretch out beneath her, it is almost impossible to believe they are dying.

When the top terminal comes into view, a black shadow on a rocky outcrop, Jac readies herself to disembark. The cabriolet slows as it pulls into the terminal. She opens the doors and steps out onto the platform, only this time she misjudges it, planting her front foot at an awkward angle that throws her off balance. Half-in, half-out of the cabriolet, she fights to stay standing while it continues its slow progress through the terminal, dragging her back foot along with it. At the last moment, she manages to snatch her foot forward. Already listing at a precarious angle in her unwieldy suit, this motion is enough to send her sprawling to the ground. She lands heavily on her front and the impact sends her headlamp flying through the air. It clatters down on the platform a few feet away, its beam angled up at the bull wheel.

While Jac recovers herself, the cabriolet gracefully completes its circuit of the terminal and then begins the descent, quickly disappearing into the dark.

The dosimeter beeps for a second time.

With a groan, Jac gets to her feet and stumbles over to pick up the head torch. By the light of its beam, she carefully checks her suit. To her relief, there doesn't seem to be any sign of abrasion or damage, and the breathing system is uncompromised. Snapping the headlamp back into place above her visor, she looks around. The sky is darker now, the stars no longer visible behind a tranche of thick cloud. The terminal stands just above the treeline and a flat, even path has been drilled out of the rock to allow for easy transport of crates and machinery to and from the cable car.

The meteorological station – a tall, upright mast held in place by a number of tensioned guy ropes – stands but a few feet away, drawing from the same powerlines that feed the cable car. It resembles nothing so much as an oversized weathervane, with a number of modular components hanging from the mast. These are attached to a supercomputer and allow for the measurement of air temperature, atmospheric pressure, humidity, wind speed and so on. One of the instruments nestled amongst the rest has been specifically dedicated to measure the level of carbon dioxide in the atmosphere; a figure that Jac checks regularly from her office in St Pancras and has, for some time now, been sitting at 500 ppm, hailed by all as a respectable improvement. But now the Project Salix trees are beginning to fail, she knows the figure must be wrong and that the records from the meteorological station must have been tampered with just like those relating to the core sample measurements.

Jac has been half-expecting to see some evident signs of interference on the mast but, as far as she can tell, everything is as it should be. This doesn't offer any particular reassurance – she's still struggling to work out at what point the data gets intercepted and altered – but that's something to think about later. For now, she just needs proof that the carbon reading is wrong. To that end, she once more swings the rucksack down from her shoulder and unpacks it, setting out the test kit, empty capsule and trowel in a neat line on the ground. Once she's measured the carbon, she'll take a soil sample to bring back to Inbhir Nis as evidence.

The test kit consists of a sampling syringe, a length of rubber tubing and a colorimetric detection vial. Picking up the syringe, she selects a patch of air at random. It doesn't matter what sample she takes, everywhere here will give the same result. The result that's *supposed* to be transmitted to the Borlaug servers. She pulls the plunger back along the plastic casing. Now she has the sample. Then she pushes the rubber tubing onto the nozzle of the syringe and attaches the other end to the detection vial, a thin shaft of glass filled with a chemical reagent. When she slowly depresses the plunger, the air is passed through the tubing and into the glass vial where it reacts with the chemicals. From the change in colouring and the carefully calibrated scale within, she can determine the level of carbon dioxide in the sample.

She holds the glass vial up to her visor, squinting at the minute scale in the light of her headlamp. Then she frowns.

Her reading is 480 ppm.

That can't be right, she thinks. She's been expecting to find the carbon dioxide level to be significantly higher than that transmitted by the meteorological station. What she's found is the opposite: the carbon dioxide level is not only dropping, but dropping by a much greater amount than anyone had cause to believe.

Jac isn't sure she does believe it. Perhaps the colorimetric detection vial is faulty. Thankfully, she had the foresight to bring a backup. Taking up the trowel, she kneels and makes three incisive cuts into the ground, then she lifts up a plug of earth to deposit in the capsule. As she does, she thinks over the carbon reading. It doesn't make sense. She's seen for herself that the trees are failing. She has measured their very cores herself and observed with her own eyes that they're smaller than they should be. If their growth is stunted, they simply can't be sequestering as much carbon dioxide as they should. The carbon level *has* to be higher.

Unless... Unless she's wrong about the trees.

Jac takes the increment borer and microcalipers from the rucksack and heads down the slope to the nearest tree. Assembling the increment borer is easy enough, even hampered as she is by the constraints of her hazmat suit. When she is done, the device looks like nothing so much as a large capital "T", a rigid blue handle serving as the cross stroke, a black auger as the stem.

Satisfied that it is correctly assembled, she holds the borer at roughly chest height and places the tip of the auger against the bark of the tree, guiding it with her hand for the first couple of centimetres until the drill has enough purchase. Then she grips the handle with both hands and begins to turn it in a slow, clockwise motion. Once she reaches what she judges to be the centre of the tree, she slides the silver extractor tray into the auger and then gives the handle a quarter of a turn anti-clockwise. When she slides the extractor tray back out, it holds a cylindrical core of wood, perfectly intact, and identical to those that she handled in Inbhir Nis. Leaving the increment borer stuck into the trunk, she holds the core carefully level in its extractor tray and takes up the microcalipers, trying hard to remember what size the core was projected to be by this point of the project. After a moment, she has it.

Holding her head still to keep the light steady, she carefully pincers the core with the microcalipers and takes the measurement. Then she lets out a frustrated roar. The core is 0.2 millimetres too small. *Again.* She was right, the trees *are* failing. Her carbon reading *must* be wrong.

Jac feels her knees go from under her and she keels forward onto her hands as the true enormity of the situation hits her. She is no closer to understanding the problem than she was several hours ago back at Inbhir Nis. And she has risked so much since then, travelling hundreds of miles, exposing herself to fatal levels of radiation, and all for nothing. She should have stayed put. She should have got that train and made it home to hold her wife in her arms one last time. Now it's too late. She wasted that time for nothing.

She stays in that awkward position, completely frozen. A single tear peels down the side of her face, smearing off onto the visor of her facepiece and leaving a cloudy stain.

Then something lands on the back of her hand, white against the silver glove.

At first, she thinks it's just dust or maybe something in her eyes. But the speck doesn't move. Instead it slowly melts away, only to be immediately replaced by another, and then another and another. It takes her a while to realise what she's seeing. Something that no living soul has ever seen. Something impossible.

Snow.

For the third and final time, her dosimeter emits a shrill beep that rings through the Arctic sky and in her ears long after the sound has died away.

34

Miri is in the drawing room of the Warren. It's another sweltering summer and she tugs at the front of the scratchy black dress that Alix picked out for her, wondering how long it will be before she's allowed to escape to her room and change. The only child present, she skirts warily around the groups of sombre-clad adults and goes to linger beside the long table that groans beneath platters of glazed soy skins, tempeh parcels and crumbling spirulina cakes.

For the most part, the adults ignore her too, though every so often one will catch her eye, come over and mutter something about how much they admired her grandmother and how Miri must miss her terribly. The appropriate response to this, Miri has discovered, is to say thank you and look downcast. This certainly seems to meet with more approval than what she did first, which was to shrug her shoulders as though she didn't really mind one way or another.

The truth is, Miri barely knew her grandmother. Even though she lived only a few miles away, she rarely ever came to the house. And up until now, it hadn't occurred to Miri to question why.

There is a sudden commotion as several of the guests beat a hasty retreat from where Jac is holding court in the centre of the room, taking long drafts from her gin glass and growing increasingly combative.

Curious, Miri picks up a bio-cassava farl from the table and gravitates towards her.

"…she didn't speak to me for ten years after that!" Jac is saying as Miri approaches. Of those gathered, some nod in sympathy and understanding, others twist away in embarrassment, surreptitiously nudging their partners to signal that it's time to leave.

"My parents were the same," says a woman Miri doesn't know. "After my own Offset–"

"My mother wasn't like other parents," says Jac, cutting her off. "She was completely wrapped up in herself. Didn't give a damn about *anyone* but herself."

"You can hardly accuse her of selfishness, Jac," says one man reproachfully. "Her charitable work–"

"Was a smokescreen at best! A way of making herself feel important and less guilty. She didn't *care* about any of those charities. She was only ever killing time."

This elicits a few moans in the crowd. One couple peels away, making a beeline to the door with an apologetic glance in Alix's direction.

The old man, animated now, continues to challenge Jac. "Did her intentions really matter in the grand scheme of things? Can any of us, hand on heart, say we think of the plight of others every single minute of the day?"

"I can," insists Jac. "I *do*. And my work is serious, not some fucking *hobby* for the wealthy and bored. I'm actually trying to make the world a better place. If you can't see the difference in that, you're a fool!"

Affronted, the man turns on Jac. "You children are all the same. You never do forgive your parents, even when you become parents yourselves."

Jac gives a bitter laugh. "And people like *you* always think you're better than people like *me*," she says. "But remember, when you die – which I doubt is that far off – there will be no one around to remember you. No one will ever even say your name."

It is then that Alix comes rushing over. "Jac, please," she hisses, sweeping Miri away from the circle. Looking over her shoulder, Miri sees Jac's unsteady gaze follow her and Alix from the room. Her expression is one of surprise, as though she wasn't expecting to see Miri there at all.

The next morning, Miri wakes to find Jac sitting at the end of her bed. She's in a poor state, her eyes bloodshot and her face almost grey in the dim light. Nevertheless, she is dressed for work.

"I'm sorry," says Jac, seeing Miri is awake. "You shouldn't have seen me like that last night. I got carried away and said some things I didn't mean."

Miri pushes herself up on her pillow. "So you *don't* hate Grandma?"

"Of course not," says Jac. "But she... she was wrong about a lot of things, Miri. And she wasn't a very good mother."

"What did she do?"

Jac shakes her head. "It's too complicated to explain. Maybe when you're older. But we didn't have a good relationship. Not like you and me."

At this last, Miri feels something squirm in the bottom of her stomach. Jac, catching sight of her troubled face, prods her playfully.

"Come on, Miri, I'm trying to make you feel better, not worse." She glances at her watch. "Listen, we can talk about this more later if you want. But I've got to get to work." Her tone makes it clear that the matter is closed and Miri knows better than to argue.

Jac pushes herself to her feet and starts away from the bed. She has only taken a few steps when Miri calls after her. "I don't want to die," she blurts out, the words bursting from her lips before she can stop herself.

Jac turns back to her sharply. "What did you say?"

"I don't want to die," Miri mumbles, eyes firmly on the bedspread as she tries to gather her thoughts, to find a way to explain the hollow ache in her chest. Before she can say anything, Jac interrupts her thoughts.

"Why do you think I'm working all the time, Miri? It's to keep you and Mum safe. To make the world better. You don't need to worry about a thing."

Miri looks up at her mother, who's already hovering at the door, itching to leave.

"But we all die one day, don't we?"

"It's so far away, Miri. There's no point thinking about it now."

When Miri says nothing, Jac takes it as a sign that she's free to go. The door closes behind her with a final click. Miri lies still in the bed and closes her eyes. It is a long time before she can bring herself to open them again.

35

Snow. Jac can hardly believe it. In the entire course of her investigation, it never once occurred to her to question the records of atmospheric temperature. If it's cold enough for snow, then she knows that these, too, must have been tampered with. It stings a little that, even after her careful preparation, she's managed to get all the way to Greenland without any analogue means of checking the temperature. Well, no matter. A soil sample will serve as evidence enough of the lowered carbon level.

Her head starts to spin as she clumsily scoops earth into the capsule. She kids herself that it is merely giddiness borne of relief. She has convinced herself that the project was doomed, and now she's discovered the opposite. The trees' growth is stunted because the world is healing. The temperatures have dropped such that the project's estimates will have to be completely revised.

However, something continues to trouble her about the discovery. She draws a blank every time she tries to come up with a theory as to who might be interfering with the project records and why. Attempting to conceal the project's failure is one thing; there are certainly board members who would happily do so simply to save face, although truthfully Jac doesn't think any of them have the expertise to do it. But trying to hide the fact that the world is recovering... that's surely news to be celebrated rather than suppressed.

Behind these concerns lingers an unpleasant idea that she cannot quite bring herself to acknowledge; that perhaps the world is healing *in spite of* her efforts with Project Salix and not on account of them. It shouldn't matter, one way or another, but it leaves a foul taste in her mouth. She's given everything to Project Salix, sacrificed her marriage and her motherhood on its altar. And all for what?

Perhaps the world would have got along just fine without her, perhaps all this would have happened regardless of whether she made it her life's work or not. For the longest time, she's feared the project would fail. She told herself that was only to be expected with so many relying on her, with the fate of the world – and her daughter's future – at stake. Now she's not so sure.

Maybe she was never as scared of letting Miri down as she was of proving her right. Call it duty, call it ambition; whatever it was, she let it drive a wedge between her and Miri, something for which she cannot forgive herself. At least success would have meant it was worthwhile. But if her work is and always was irrelevant–

It's getting increasingly hard to concentrate. She's starting to feel weak, and doesn't doubt that the vomiting and diarrhoea will begin soon. The nausea is already intense and being compounded by a splitting headache. Really, she's in no fit state for another journey on the NAX. But she has no choice. She has to get back for the Offset.

She assures herself that at least Miri will have nominated her instead of Alix. Even if Miri had a last-minute change of heart, Jac knows that the news of her having exposed herself to a fatal dose of radiation would've quelled any misgivings on Miri's part absolutely. Yet the Archivist's phone call to that effect was only ever a fail-safe. While there are so many things Jac does not know or understand about her daughter, that Miri does not love her is one thing of which she is certain.

For once, this knowledge brings her some comfort. Bitter as it is to be so hated by her own child, it is just as well. After all, she's already dying. It might take a few weeks, but there's no doubt that the radiation dose she has received is fatal. Besides, Alix is much better equipped to look after Miri than she is. It is Alix who their daughter will need most in the years ahead. And she has always been prepared for this, always known that on this day, the day Miri turns eighteen, she would be called upon to lay down her life for her daughter. Well, her life has been laid down already – though in service of what, Jac is no longer certain.

Steeling herself, Jac pushes herself to her feet and then has to stop when the world swims around her and the edges of her vision blur to grey. After a moment, the dizziness passes. With an effort, she lifts her bag – heavy with the weight of the sealed capsule – and begins to stagger down the mountain.

36

Miri goes alone to the Gallery. She is not due before noon, and it's some hours before then, but she wants to get it out of the way.

The walk over is a blur and all too soon she spies the tall, ancient building slide irrevocably into view. She runs up the steps of cracked white stone that look out onto Trafalgar Square and walks right past where the Offset ceremony will be held.

At the Gallery entrance, she spots a patch of filterweed at the base of one of the pillars and flinches as the image of a white rat crosses her mind. Then, taking a deep breath, she pushes through the doors.

She finds herself in a foyer that is sparsely furnished. A bored-looking receptionist sits behind a curving beechwood counter. It has a series of plastic trays running along the front, the kind designed for flyers and leaflets, only the trays are empty. The receptionist doesn't look up when Miri enters, his gaze instead fixed on the far wall. Miri turns and sees that he is staring at a small circular clock that hangs on a nail roughly halfway between floor and ceiling. It is more than an hour slow.

Miri clears her throat as she approaches the counter but the receptionist ignores her. Only when she comes to stand right in front of him and says "Excuse me" in a loud voice, does he take his eyes from the clock.

"I'm here to make a nomination," she says in response to his blank stare. Without saying a word, he takes a scrap of paper, scrawls out a number and hands it to Miri.

"Wait over there until your number is called." His eyes snap back to the clock.

Feeling distinctly wrong-footed, Miri retreats from the counter. There is a wide upholstered bench in the middle of the foyer and she perches awkwardly on one edge of it, picking a spot that means she can keep an eye on the counter.

For ten minutes she sits in perfect silence, nervously lacing together finger and thumb. No one comes in. No one goes out. The receptionist does not move from the counter. Then, as if prompted by an alarm, he jerks into action, shouting a number and staring around the near-empty foyer.

Given that there is no one else present besides her, this behaviour seems so odd that it makes Miri think the number the receptionist is repeatedly shouting must belong to someone else, someone either invisible or absent. But when she checks her scrap of paper, she sees that the number is, indeed, her own. She gets up and crosses back over the foyer, handing the scrap of paper to the receptionist, who scrutinises it as if never having seen it before.

"This seems in order." Taking a new scrap of paper, he scribbles out a new number that he hands to Miri and then points to a set of doors beside the counter. "You may go through."

Perplexed as she is, Miri pushes through to find herself in another waiting room. The best part of it is taken up with several rows of plastic bucket-like chairs, all empty. Along the left-hand side is a series of cubicles. Most of them are concealed from view by a heavy grey curtain drawn across the front, but one has its curtains pushed back, revealing an empty desk behind a pane of glass.

Clutching her new number tightly, she sits down in the nearest chair and waits.

There is no clock on the wall here and, in that windowless room, no way of discerning the time. For all Miri knows, the world has come to a perfect standstill. She has no way of knowing whether she has passed five minutes or five hours. With nothing to do but sit, it certainly *feels* like the latter.

Finger, thumb, finger, thumb.

Every so often, she hears promising sounds from behind one of the curtains: the shuffle of papers, the dull scrape of chair legs on carpet, the whisper of a hushed inquiry. Every time she thinks something is about to happen – that one of the curtains will be pulled dramatically aside or someone will come in and tell her what to do next – the sounds die away to silence and she is left waiting with no further idea as to what is going on.

The sudden rasp of the PA startles Miri so much that she nearly falls out of her chair. Coming to her senses, she realises that it is her number being called over the microphone along with the instruction to present herself to Desk Three.

Hoping she's identified the right one, Miri hurries over and twitches aside the curtain. A woman sits beyond the glass; an administrator who is heavily wrinkled, her skin drooping from her cheeks and jaw, and wearing the same bored expression as the receptionist. She looks like she might have been sitting there for all of time.

"Is this Desk Three?"

The administrator raises a weary brow. "Number?"

Miri slides the piece of paper into the tray beneath the glass. The woman draws it out with a single finger. After staring at it for a long moment, she screws it into a ball and tosses it over her shoulder.

"There's a scanner to your right. Please place your thumb upon the device so that we can identify you."

It takes four goes before the thing works, a little red light flashing angrily each time it fails to identify Miri. At last, it shines green.

"Miriam Ford-Boltanski," says the woman, peering at the read-out on her side of the desk.

"Yes."

"What can I do for you?"

Because the administrator speaks in a flat monotone, it's a moment before Miri realises she's been asked a question. As soon as she does, she tersely explains that she's here to make her nomination. The woman listens impassively and then stoops to retrieve something from a drawer.

"You need to complete this form," she says, sliding the sheet of paper beneath the glass.

It is unutterably simple, bearing only a short statement with a few choice blanks and a place beneath for a signature and date.

I, the undersigned _____, do hereby nominate _____ to be Offset on the occasion of my eighteenth birthday (__/__/____).
I verify that I have come to this decision of my own accord and that all information I have provided is correct and lawful.

"Is that it?" Miri asks. "Is that all it takes?"

The woman gives her a blank look and slides a pen beneath the glass. "Take your time," she drawls, turning her attention back to the document she had been working on before Miri arrived.

Miri fills out the easy parts first. She puts in her name and birthday, then signs the bottom and adds the date. Then there is only one blank left.

It is a long while before she finally commits a name to the page. It's not the name she has, for the best part of eighteen years, imagined writing, but it is, she realises now, the only name that can possibly fill that gap, the only name that is fair, however wrong it feels. She slides the form back through the glass and marvels that her hands don't so much as shake.

The woman looks it over and then sighs. Taking her own pen, she crosses out part of Miri's name where she's written it in the first gap. Then she passes the form back over.

"Name needs to match the one you'll be legally identified by from the date of the Offset. Given the parent you are nominating, please confirm that this will be your name by initialling my correction."

Miri looks down at her name. "Ford" is crossed out, brutally cut through with a single stroke. She feels her heart tremor, but there's no going back. Not now. Gripping the pen once more, she quickly scrawls her initials and pushes the form away.

37

A cold front cuts eastward and the sweltering humidity drains from the city. The day becomes clement, the first of the year when it's bearable to be outside. Bodies fan out amongst the parched sedges of the Barbican rain gardens, welcoming the ragged breeze that catches at loose hair and grazes skin. Bicycles zip up and down the whitewashed streets, picnic baskets groan with the weight of clinking bottles and fragrant soy fruits. The birth of another magnificent winter. And who can say how many more there'll be before the temperatures soar and the planet burns? All the more reason to seize upon it, drink it in.

Perhaps it is for this reason that only a small crowd has assembled in Trafalgar Square. Or perhaps it is because word has got around that Professor Jac Boltanski has not, after all, been chosen. Only the hardiest of the anti-natalists have turned up, and even they cannot seem to muster the will, their specially prepared placards lying abandoned and trampled on the ground.

The sense of missed opportunity is compounded by the paraphernalia in evidence on the platform: nothing more than a rough concrete wall and a row of sandbags. Today's Offset is by firing squad. Quick, clean. There will be no show, no excitement. Those who have gathered in the Square can't help but feel they've been cheated of a spectacle. The air of disappointment hangs over them like a cloud of gnats.

When a rickshaw pulls up at the intersection with Charing

Cross Road, only the pigsuits seem to notice. They have turned out in full force, their visors gleaming in the sun to obscure the shadow-hollows within. Moving to some wordless command, a unit peels away discreetly from the crowd and makes for the cab. Bracing herself, Alix steps out to greet them.

She is wearing a simple beige trouser suit, one she picked years ago for precisely this occasion. With some approbation, she notes that her jacket got creased on the journey over and thinks fleetingly that she should have worn something else after all. That seems to be the way things are going today, her plans crumbling beneath the weight of reality.

It's not fair, not when Alix has been planning this day in painstaking detail ever since Miri was born. It has brought her some comfort over the years, knowing what it will be like, knowing exactly what she will do and when. Only, when it came to it, everything she'd planned felt absurd and insubstantial, like some sort of futile performance, and all for the sake of what she couldn't say. In the end, she had done little but sit at the kitchen table, wondering how to kill the time.

Finally, when she couldn't take it anymore, she called the rickshaw and went outside to wait, stopping only to look herself up and down in the hall mirror. She slicked down a stray hair and stepped through the door without a second glance. Now she's here. Early.

The heels of her brown brogues clack on the pavement as she lets herself be whisked towards the steps of the Gallery. With iron grip, the pigsuits steer her onwards. Upwards. Only then does a ripple of attention pass through the crowd. Arms stretch, heads turn.

Breaking free of her guard, Alix reaches the wall in a few swift steps and claims her position. With a jerk of the chin, she gestures at the nearest pigsuit who obeys her command, stepping forward to tape a mark on the front of her jacket. Alix takes the moment to scan the crowd beyond the platform, searching the faces, half-hoping to catch a final look at her wife or daughter. But she knows, deep down, that neither of them are there. The faces blur.

Alix knows she should be proud: a soon-to-be-martyred mother, facing the most honourable of Offsets – albeit one that was planned for her wife. She will die so that others can live. Better, in fact; so that *Miri* can live.

It's what I always wanted, she thinks. To be a mother, even if it means dying for the privilege. For Jac to live. For Miri – and the world – to be saved.

I wanted this. I chose this.

Finally finished with the tape, the pigsuit straightens. A black X now emblazons Alix's chest. She glances at the pigsuit and swallows hard when – for just a second – she thinks she sees a pair of bright eyes glaring out at her from behind the visor. But then the pigsuit moves and she realises it must have been a trick of the light, casting her own reflection back at her. She watches as the pigsuit drops back to join the others waiting at the platform's edge. There are five of them in all, each one clasping a .30 calibre rifle in the empty gauntlets of their hands. They stand motionless, looking for Alix's sign, the unspoken symbol of assent.

She thinks fleetingly of her wife, but even Jac's absence means nothing now. They've had eighteen years to say their goodbyes. Now she is alone, truly alone, and she must go on with an open and willing heart.

I chose this, she reminds herself.

Then, less certainly: *Didn't I?*

Unbidden, an image of her daughter bursts into her mind's eye. It is the Miri of that morning, back from the Gallery. Clean and fresh, a runaway no more. But a beaten Miri. A Miri who gave in. Gave *her* in. A Miri who told Alix exactly what she had always hoped to hear and whose every word had nevertheless been like the scrape of a flensing knife.

Now, Alix cannot escape the fact that, in spite of everything

– or, perhaps, because of it – Miri had after all seen fit to mark her for death. It doesn't matter that it's what Alix wanted. Wants. The knowledge of it is dreadful.

Flinching away from the memory, she twists her hands into tight fists at either side, nails biting into the skin of her palms. It hurts, enough that the heartache begins to dissipate beneath the rush of physical pain. The two mix together, like blood in water. *All of this was war,* she thinks. *All of this was war.*

She lets it crash over her then; the anger and despair, the fear, the aching loneliness. And somewhere within that fierce roar she hears it. Silence. Instinctively, she hones in on it. When she does, she's surprised to find a notch, deep within herself, where there is nothing at all, just a gap, a break in the noise. She takes refuge in it at once, pushing all else away. As she does, the emptiness responds to her, expanding and spreading until, at last, it overtakes her.

She becomes hollow, so light she might be made of nothing at all; emptied out and every cell replaced with particles of air. For an absurd moment she feels like a helium balloon limply grasped in a child's hand, ready to slip loose and float away on the breeze.

Is this oblivion? She leans back against the wall, feels the hard certainty of the concrete against her shoulders and back, the curve of her skull. It is all that grounds her now.

At her signal, the pigsuits raise their rifles, not a beat before they carry out the child's wishes. There is no pause for dramatic reflection, no time to console or reprieve–

A salvo of shots and the Offset is made.

ACKNOWLEDGMENTS

From the very beginning, *The Offset* has been a work of collaboration. So many writers are alone – they deal with the second-guessing, the waiting and the angst all by themselves. We are lucky; we have each other. What's more, there's a crowd of other people in our corner who have encouraged us, supported us and fought for us, and we owe our thanks to the following:

John Ash for his editorial insight, dedication and advocacy. Along with his excellent colleagues at PEW, John has been championing us from the very beginning and we could never have hoped for a better agent.

The team at Angry Robot for all their hard work and to Gemma Creffield in particular for her keen editor's eye and her understanding of our more idiosyncratic ways of working.

Angela Saini, David Benatar and Ken MacLeod for their early support of the book.

A certain "literary whore" who took us out for coffee, asked us to rewrite the entire novel and then ghosted us when we did. We'd have hated for this to have been easy.

Our partners, Andrzej Harris and Eamonn Bell. Special thanks to Andrzej, who discussed every aspect of the book with us in its various versions, carefully researched the scientific content and helped us make it coherent. Any errors that remain are entirely ours.

Alan Calder and Olga Travlos (and also with our apologies to Olga for writing something so grim – unfortunately we can't promise that the next one will be any cheerier).

Ann-Marie Harris, not just for the free childcare, but also for reading every single draft.

Hieronim Lev and Orlando Franciszka, for more than either of you will ever know.

Rox Middleton, for being part of Gangu and galvanising us into action.

Kaity Barrett, for her creative help.

For their support and encouragement, further thanks from Emma are due to: Sarah Jones and Christopher Cole, Jolanta and Zbigniew Szewczak, Lindsay Carter and Sarah Cox, Melanie Davies, Claire Thompson, Ben Luisi, Rev'd Ank Rigglesford, and my two favourite teachers Gavin D'Costa and Hazel Stephens.

Similarly, Natasha would like to thank: Alex Calder, Graham Bloomfield, Alex Whatley, Ciarán O'Rourke, Nick Bland and Ellen Pilsworth. Also to the 2018 Clarion West cohort – you are all right – and in particular to Nassos, E.C. and Rachel Prime.

Finally, from both of us to Mark and all the team at Tranquillity Base Hotel and Casino: we couldn't have done this without you.

ABOUT THE AUTHORS

Calder Szewczak is writing duo Natasha C. Calder and Emma Szewczak, who met while studying at Cambridge University. Natasha is a graduate of Clarion West 2018 and her work has previously appeared in The Stinging Fly, Lackington's and Curiosities, amongst others. Emma researches contemporary representations of the Holocaust and lives in Cambridge with her parter and two children.

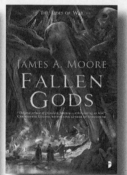
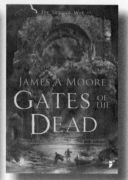

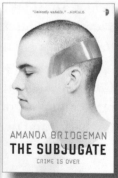

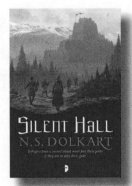
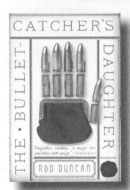

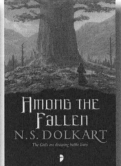

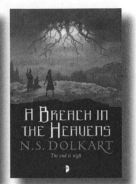

We are Angry Robot

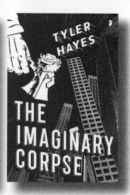

angryrobotbooks.com

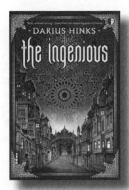

Science Fiction, Fantasy and WTF?!

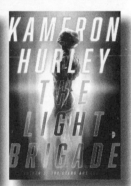

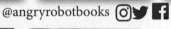

We are Angry Robot

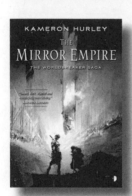

angryrobotbooks.com

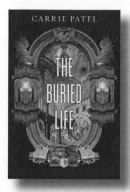

CARRIE PATEL

THE BURIED LIFE

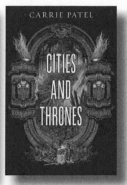

CARRIE PATEL

CITIES AND THRONES

CARRIE PATEL

THE SONG OF THE DEAD

We are Angry Robot

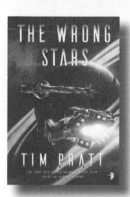

THE WRONG STARS

TIM PRATT

THE DREAMING STARS

TIM PRATT

BOOK III OF THE AXIOM

THE FORBIDDEN STARS

TIM PRATT

angryrobotbooks.com

THE SINGULAR & EXTRAORDINARY TALE OF MIRROR & GOLIATH

BY ISHBELLE BEE

THE CONTRARY TALE OF THE BUTTERFLY GIRL

BY ISHBELLE BEE

UNDER THE PENDULUM SUN

JEANNETTE NG